AMBUSH!

With no warning, something slammed into Holly's back, along his ribs. The sharp report of the bullet came to him as he fell. Too late. His fall sent the dun plunging back on the reins.

Holly's breath came short, deep lancing pain taking hold with each attempt to draw in needed air. He tried to push up on his right arm, but even the barest movement brought spasms of agony. Bright flames went through his side, dulling his mind. The blackness beckoned; he could feel a pool of blood underneath his stomach.

Holly began to close his eyes in relief and acceptance.

But there was something he had to do. Sarah Hubbard. Down at the end of the valley, she had mounted her mare, responding to his signal that all was well—she was riding into a trap. . . .

HIGH LINE RIDER

by William A. Lucky

ZEBRA BOOKS
KENSINGTON PUBLISHING CORP.

For Jim Osgood

ZEBRA BOOKS

are published by

Kensington Publishing Corp.
475 Park Avenue South
New York, NY 10016

Second printing: May 1987

Printed in the United States of America

CHAPTER ONE

He was running again.

He could still see the loaf of bread put out to cool on the window sill. It had been a simple matter to reach out and gently lift it from its perch and hold it while he turned the footsore chestnut mare away from the kitchen window. He threaded his way through the narrow alley in back of the house perched at the edge of town; he did not expect anyone to follow, but still wanted to be headed for the mountains looming dark and heavy in the early evening light.

The crust of the loaf was a rich brown and still hot to his touch. He looped the reins over the saddle horn to examine his treasure. With his left hand he carefully tore the heel away, cradling the steaming body in his curled right fist. The soft, heated inner flesh was exposed, and a curl of escaping heat wound around his face, enticing him with its sweet aroma. The mare settled into a tired shuffling walk, her rider unaware of the shift in gait. He took deep teasing breaths of the grainy flesh. A twist of hunger pained his belly, reminding him how long he had gone this time without food. But here in his hand was a reward, unexpected and perfect.

With the broken loaf carefully balanced, he put a large piece of the golden heel into his mouth; the hard crust melted into drops of rich salty sweetness, the soft pulp warm on his tongue. He chewed slowly, determined to keep the flavor as long as possible. The mare walked on, following the muddied track across the sloping plains. Her rider closed his eyes and breathed deeply again, enveloped in the simple and amazing pleasure of eating a piece of bread.

The mare stumbled beneath him, then lurched forward into an awkward run; the whine of a bullet close to his head came just after the animal went down. The sharp report of another gun came to him, then a rapid fire of bullets blazed around him, none finding their target. He turned in the saddle to see a group of riders coming at a wild run, waving pistols and yelling in high excitement. The loaf dropped from his right fist, the fingers unable to take hold. He actually reined in the mare to stop and pick up the muddied bread, but another shot winging past his ear brought him back to the moment. The chestnut responded to the heels drumming on her sides and galloped heavily away from the pursuers, carrying them all to the foothills.

In the dimming purple light, the rider could make out a faded trail to his left, barely a dent in the winter-packed grass. The riders behind him were a blur, their outline just visible against the blue-black sky. He kneed the mare onto the left-hand track, which reached into the mountains sooner and offered him a better chance to hide. The chestnut stumbled frequently, a reminder that she could not continue the fast pace much longer. Behind him he could still hear faint yelling and an occasional shot kept him pushing the tired horse, squeezing with his legs and asking for more with his hands. He cursed his lack of spurs, traded for a set of shoes for the mare two months back.

Ragged sobs were all he could hear now as the chestnut mare labored for each stride, her sides expanding in desperation to gulp in needed air. Heavy shapes of rock wall came in on each side to form a funnel, keeping the horse and rider galloping straight ahead. Slowly he became aware that the pursuit had faded to nothing, and the mare stopped uncertainly in answer to his pull on the bit. Her body shook beneath her rider as he stepped off the trembling animal and moved to stand by her head. Running his hand along the soaked neck, down the bony skull, he found a thick foam at her nose and mouth. He stroked and patted the shivering animal until, with a groaning sigh, she sank to the cold ground and lay on her side.

His pursuers had given up their chase. No more shots searched for him in the dark. His stolen supper lay buried in the mud; only a few flakes caught in his torn, denim jumper sleeve remained to taunt him with the memory of that first bite. And his horse lay dying at his feet. The lean man hunkered down next to the head of the still-sobbing mare. Intermingled with the white foam surrounding her muzzle he could see a darker, thicker liquid. Hot anger came up in his throat. He had destroyed this mare. He looked longingly at the rifle jammed into its scabbard, useless to him now without shells.

With unsteady hands, the rider started to strip his gear from the horse, but could not free the cinch from underneath the flattened body. He opened the tattered saddle roll tied to the back of the cantle, searched, and found his knife. He returned to the bony head, leaned down, and gently lifted the living skull. With shaking hands the man drew the sharpened blade across the mare's throat, tearing a gaping hole in the slick neck. Heavy fluid pumped quickly from the wound in rhythm with the labored breathing. A quiet sigh came from the mare, and the rider laid the head back gently to the earth. He rested on his heels, watching the blood pool at his feet, and shivered deeply, shoulders tight against the evening cold and the ghost of the dead mare.

The horseman was taller than he first appeared; just an inch over six feet. Always on the edge of hunger, his wide sloping shoulders, narrow hips, and loose-jointed walk made him appear smaller, less powerful, than he really was. His thick dark hair, already streaked with gray, was long and

7

matted, tied back with a bit of leather. His face was long and gaunt, almost wolfish in its thinness, with wide cheekbones and a high bridged nose. The eyes were a curious pale hazel, almost amber; clear, large, rimmed with a green that mirrored a violent temper.

He allowed little expression to show, from years of schooling. A smile was a rare thing, and usually at his own rowdy thoughts. A white scar started above his right eye, and went through the dark brow at an angle before slicing to his torn ear. There was no extra flesh on his spare frame, only ropy muscles that pulled and slid as he moved, exposing the bones too close to the surface. His hands were long and bony, the right one heavily scarred, the fingers thick and misshapen. He was watchful, alert, always careful even when alone. Survival was a hard-fought battle for him, and the battle showed in his every move.

It was easier now to shift the thin body and pull the cinch loose, freeing his saddle. He stood for a moment looking down at the shrinking corpse, then gradually became aware of his surroundings. It was a poor place, trapped up in a high-walled canyon, nothing to keep him warm, no food, no horse. And unsafe to backtrack, to venture out onto the plains again. He sat for a short time next to the carcass, head bowed, hands still. Then he stood up and shrugged, removed the finely braided hackamore from the bloody head, and picked up his battered hull. He walked away quickly from the dead horse, awkward with his high boots and horseman's stride. He headed up further into the canyon; anything was better than sitting the rest of the night with a corpse.

Hunger came back to him. In the rising moonlight the rider looked back on the faded outline of his mare. He dropped his gear and pulled out the knife again, walking back to the body. He cut into the hide by the thin hind-quarters and skinned back a section, exposing stringy haunch muscles. With quick, deft strokes of his left hand he pulled out long lines of flesh. Not a delicacy, not even a good

8

meal, but something to chew on, to keep him going.

He wrapped the greasy strips in the canvas roll, picked up the gear again, and continued on in the shadowy light. Walking kept him from sitting and stiffening like the dead beast behind him, but it offered no relief from the cold spring winds. His mind played tricks with him; shadows became saddled horses just out of reach, ridden by screaming blank-faced riders. The rock walls came closer, turning to prison walls. His steps were short, uncertain, unbalanced. An unseen rock tipped him and he went to the ground; he put out his right hand to stop the fall, but the blunted and twisted fingers refused to hold and doubled back to drop him on the rock-strewn path. He heard the distinct sound as his pants leg tore, could feel the warm trickle of blood.

The tall horseman smiled grimly to himself in the flickering darkness. He'd run often enough in his past. But this time was different, this time he had run out—of every-thing. No horse. No shells for his rifle; no handgun at all; not even his own boots. This pair he'd lifted from a back-alley junk pile and he could feel every damn rock through their worn soles. The faded denim jumper offered little to protect him from the seeking winds, and his black hat had so many holes the wind almost whistled through. He'd been running for near to fifteen years now. It was a long time to run.

His mind skipped over the past. The small Kansas town had been celebrating, Lee had surrendered, and the war was over. But his family had little to celebrate. His father had come home to a darkened house. The small boy slept in the lean-to off the kitchen where he could hear his mother's harsh breathing through the thin walls. He had listened to the sound every night, waiting for a change that would release her. The boy wanted only to remember good times, hours spent reading, the encouragement to go on, try something harder. And before the war, when his father would take him out to fish or hunt, and they'd spend more

9

time talking than hunting. Even the hard times, plowing with the tired mule and blunt-edged plow; picking up the splintered rocks when his father had to dig the new well. But most of all he treasured the memories of warmth, of thin arms wrapped around him, the clean herbal smell when he was held close and loved.

The war changed all that. His father leaving changed their lives, left them frightened, hungry, finally bringing on the illness that was killing her. Just after Lee's surrender his father returned. The Kansas border patrols were looking for a bearded man, a raider heavily armed, wild eyes hidden under shaggy dark hair. A clean-shaven man traveling with his son would not come under their scrutiny. The father had planned to return the boy after he was done using him, but the sound of his wife's thick breath, the long hesitation needed to force air through damaged lungs let him know she would not be there if the boy returned.

They buried the exhausted woman. Then the father and son traveled fast, past the guards who ignored the clear-faced man and his sullen boy. The man forced contact only when someone was watching. Otherwise he left his cold-eyed son alone. He hadn't known a ten-year-old could hold such righteous disapproval. The boy stared at his father in fascination, remembering his love for this hard-faced man before he'd joined the distant and dividing war. Clear of Kansas, the pair fell to an uneasy truce, built by hunger and the need for shelter. At first they worked an easy scam. The boy was sent to beg at a big, clean house, to tell a story of an invalid father unable to walk. The boy refused to steal, but would accept what kind folk would give him, taken by his clear hazel eyes and good manners. The begging worked for a while, satisfying their immediate needs. But it lacked the danger and excitement his father had grown used to, riding with Quantrill and Bloody Bill.

An old friend rode out of the brush and joined them. They stole two horses and the boy rode his own dun bareback. He still was sent to beg, but for two men now. Then another companion showed up in a small town in the Wyoming territory. And another. The boy spoke less and less, doing what he was told, keeping to himself in silence. The men robbed whatever might hold money or gold: banks, stages, small ranches. The boy held their horses and waited, becoming more and more reserved, doing what he must to survive as the years slowly passed.

A horse was shot out from under the father, and the son stopped to help. The others kept riding. Hidden in the woods, the embittered man watched as his tall, lanky son gave short answers to the posse, sending them in a mad gallop after the robbers. Riding double, they searched for another horse. A corral full of broncs left unguarded looked an easy mark. But the rancher had seen the pair ride up to the fence on the one horse and look over his stock. He was waiting, watching as the man roped out a rugged bay and put their only saddle on the mare. The boy sat on his roan and said nothing, his face expressionless as he watched his father steal again.

They hung his father. And they made the fourteen-year-old boy stand and watch, to teach him a lesson. His face tight, the boy barely twitched as the bay ran out from under its rider, leaving the body twisting and swinging from the tree, to die in slow strangulation. The boy watched, his tears ignored, while his father fought the slow death, finally to give in to the lack of air, all his body systems shutting down in an agonizing and humiliating death.

Shocked by their own brutal act, the ranch crew found it hard to face the tall thin boy. He demanded to be allowed to bury his father's body, and the rancher could not deny him this. And after, he stayed at the shallow mound for a short and solitary moment. A prayer came to mind, words from a peaceful past, said in the sweet voice of his mother. It was the last time he would allow such thoughts to enter his mind.

With nowhere else to go, no family to take him in, the boy stayed to work at the ranch, doing all the simple mindless chores that no one else would do: chopping stove wood, filling the kitchen box, the water tank, cleaning out the stables, even learning to milk the cow. He remained detached, quiet, and remote despite attempts to give him some sort of comfort. His light hazel eyes and thin face showed no emotion. He'd learned that from his father. During the first winter one of the older punchers, battling the picture of the swinging man in his conscience, set his hand to teaching the boy skills with leather and horsehair. Bridles, fancy breast collars, carving on saddle skirting, braided hackamores, fancy quirts, any type of leather and repair work. His hands soon worked fast and easily with the strands of hide to fashion the best equipment. But he rarely spoke to the cowboy, unless to answer a direct question. When spring came, and the warm air had the crew back working the stock, the teacher and his student separated and rarely spoke again. But the boy had gained a skill.

The spring of his fourth year at the ranch, the boy was near to eighteen years and stood almost six feet. No longer a child, he was lean, muscled, and ready to fight. The rancher hired a man that year to work out the rough string, and apprenticed the boy to him, to test the building strength and skills. Again he remained silent, this time infuriating the talkative wrangler. His readily apparent skills with the half-wild horses also insulted the bronc rider. He took on the boy's favored sorrel colt with spurs and quirt, determined to beat the gelding into a cow horse or break his spirit. When he finally dismounted from the bleeding horse a fury assaulted him, fists pounding at his face and body. Helpless, off balance, the man went down under the attack and a bunkhouse companion joined the fight. The two men found themselves tangled with a wild man. The boy fought with all the pent-up fury of the four years, the anger jarred loose by the rough handling of the colt.

One man went down in the corral dust, nose bloody, one eye battered shut. The wrangler picked up a loosened fence rail and laid hard blows on the thin back and shoulders of the attacker. The boy went forward with the unexpected force of the blows, then struggled to his knees and came up to swing again at his opponents. The fence rail connected again, this time across his temple, splitting a thick red line from his eye to his ear, tearing off the top. He dropped to the corral floor unconscious. The onlookers left him there, and took their compadres into the bunkhouse, where water and a bottle of whiskey cleaned their wounds.

The boy pushed himself to his knees, head hanging, blood crusted on the side of his face, his shoulders on fire. The dark was complete, no lights from the main house or the bunkhouse. He crawled to the water trough, pulled himself up by holding on to the pump. Once he had plunged his head in the bitter cold water, he found it possible to stand erect. There was nothing now for him at this ranch, no one who cared for him, to wonder if he was badly hurt. A horse nickered softly from an adjoining corral. It was the boss's good gray gelding, well trained and easy to ride. He saddled the horse, taking his father's old stolen saddle and a blanket hanging from the wall. The only thing belonging to him was a fancy braided hackamore. He had little more than that from his four years on the ranch.

The gray moved out easily in the soft darkness. His bright clean coat had a sheen that glowed in the dark. The rider patted the shining silver neck and the horse swung his head to one side in answer. By morning they were less than ten miles from the ranch. The gray's rider had fallen off just before dawn, his head throbbing from the bloody wound, no longer able to balance in the saddle. The rancher and a few cowboys found him. They stayed on their horses and looked down at the thin body curled protectively, the gray standing over him like a guard. The lines on the rancher's face were deep, drawn tighter by the night ride and the scene

13

before him.

"Guess we got to him too late, growin' up just like his pa. Ought to of hung him too back then, save us the trouble now." The rancher shook his head at the old puncher, crossed his hands on his saddle horn, sighed, and told his foreman to roust the boy. Times were more civilized now. They rode him into the small Wyoming town and left him for the law to handle.

The fifteen months in jail did little to soften his disposition. He fought the confinement bitterly and in silence, until a vicious whipping and a month in a sweat box settled him. He worked out the rest of his sentence, becoming even more remote and reserved.

That had been over six years ago. He had come out of the prison with his battered saddle, the hackamore, and cheap clothes courtesy of the prison system. It was easy for him to pick up a horse; sometimes he traded his skills for a spoiled animal, sometimes he worked off the ownership breaking the rough string. But he never stole another horse. Once, in desperation, he had walked down an outcast mustang stallion. It had taken three weeks and the horse was never fully broke, but it carried him and it was his, free and clear.

Between his leather work and skills with the rough string, he managed the years. Then a hammer-headed paint dropped a foot down a hole while in full gallop and went down, pinning the rider underneath. In the struggle to get up, the horse stood for an agonizing moment with its heavy weight on his right hand, crushing it. The hand ached briefly as he shoved the vivid memory aside. Three broken ribs and the busted hand left him waiting out the winter in another bunkhouse. This time he had no skill to pay his way; the thick bandages tied his fingers tight. The rancher let him stay out the bad weather, but when the doctor removed the wrappings to expose the shrunken and twisted hand, fingers stiff and frozen in a curve, he gave the silent cowboy his time.

And gave him the weedy chestnut mare and a rotting canvas saddle roll, figuring he owed the drifter nothing more than that.

Time and pain straightened out the right hand, leaving the fingers with some mobility, but little of their former skills. It took more time, but he gradually transferred the skills to his left, using his right as a balance. He could still do the work, ride out the rough string or work up a fancy set of reins, but one look at the battered hand, the faded scar and nicked ear, the wary pale eyes, and most honest ranchers turned him away, some without a meal, others kind enough to feed him and let him sleep the night. He worked less and less, found himself riding the grub line too often, spending too many nights cold and hungry.

And now there were only the unknown mountains ahead, behind him a stolen loaf of bread and a town angry enough to send out riders willing to kill. The moon had slipped from its overhead position, effectively blocked out by the high walls. He did not know how far he had walked, or what was ahead, but he did not want to walk back to the mute body of a worn-out chestnut mare.

CHAPTER TWO

He walked on, almost blind in the dark canyon, pushed by a restless hunger. His progress was slow; the walls of the canyon moved in closer and closer as he negotiated the rock-strewn trail. Finally it seemed he had come to the end of the canyon. Ahead, the walls met in a murky blackness, impenetrable. But off to his right a thin stream of moonlight opened a narrow way, offering another escape route from the ghost behind him. His gear did not fit between the walls; he could either leave the meager possessions behind, or stay with them on the dead-ended trail until morning.

It was possible only to move sideways down the funnel. The moonlight stayed ahead of him, illuminating the carved walls on either side. He shuffled quickly, unwilling to chance getting caught in the close confines of the alley. The light became brighter, offering a better look at his surroundings. The walls of the alley had been laboriously chipped and carved to allow passage. He looked closer at the minute carvings that created the narrow passage, then realized that it wasn't the moonlight he had been following, that dawn was near and he had passed the night.

The alley came to an abrupt halt. He stood sideways, trapped in his memories of hot, tight walls, intense heat, violent smells. He backed up, swinging his head, looking for anything that would get him away from these confining walls. He tried turning in the confined space. The graying light showed him a handhold in the austere rock wall, carved at eye level. Lifting his eyes, he could follow a ladder of carved holes winding up the wall above him. They would lead to something, for much work and sweat had gone into their construction.

The toe of his worn boot just fit in a hole; his large bony hands found a secure grip in another hole further up the wall. And another hole came into view. Once in rhythm the climb went easily, but it seemed to go on forever. Then his head came above the gray wall; he pushed his shoulders up, leaving his left hand wedged in a hole. He swung his right arm over the lip of the wall, then freed his left and, shoving with his right foot, shimmied up onto a level plateau. He lay briefly on the flattened area, long enough to know that it too had been chipped and flattened by hand, pieced away with sharp rocks until the top of the wall offered a small, level resting place.

He rolled over and sat up. It was an odd sensation; to be perched way up on an oval. From his viewpoint the entire Colorado plains were open to him. He could make out the shapes of the town off in front of him, a long distance away. Below and near the edge of the plains was a grassy bluff, sloping down to a tree line. He was literally on top of the world. He stood up, spread his legs, and surveyed his domain. It took only a minute to walk around the oval, staying well back from the precarious edge.

A dull white shape flickered under his feet; he sank to his heels and picked up the small piece. A fragment of bone, weather worn and smooth, hidden in a small mound of chipped rocks. He picked up another fragment, this one gray and brittle; it appeared to be an arrow head, painstakingly chipped from a bigger piece. His fingers dug into the pile, scattering the bits, exposing more bone pieces, shards of arrows. There were other similar mounds scattered across

17

the oval.

He sat, facing east out over the plains, feeling like a monarch. The bare tip of the sun pushed up from the horizon, then rose in easy stages to become a yellow circle low in the sky. A restlessness swept over him; all the beauty before him did nothing for his immediate future. Hunger, cold, the long walk—they were the important problems now, and they were not appeased by standing to look out over the hard country he had put behind him. Food was the most immediate concern.

The trip back down was made easier by the daylight, and the knotted cramps in his empty belly helped to hasten the descent. Once at the bottom, he slid along the alley to his gear, still in semi-darkness, shielded from the invading daylight by the high pitched rock walls. With his saddle slung over his shoulder, the dark-faced drifter hesitated only briefly; what he had thought was the end of a box canyon was only a turn in the walls, blackened in the night and now open to him. He had a choice, he could go back to the mare or walk forward.

The foot-weary man stepped around the bend in the walls and out onto a widening of the trail. A few bent and scraggly bushes had caught their roots in breaks in the rock floor, and were struggling to survive, waving limp branches in the brisk winds. They signaled the possibility of fuel to cook the strings of meat, but they themselves were not enough. An hour of painful walking brought him out of the rock walls into a different landscape, one of low scrubby bushes bent and twisted by the winds, rocks settled in clumps, a few stunted pines, spikes of witch grass. It was a bleak landscape that offered little shelter or food, but at least there were bits of wood that might burn. Using his knife, wiped clean of its bloody coating in the sandy soil, he hacked several chunks of wood free, and laid a small fire. Dried pine needles caught from one of his few matches and burst into a quick, bright flame.

18

Within minutes he had the grease-coated strips of flesh hanging over his small fire, the thick fat sparking and popping in the heat. Before the strips were finished, his hunger won and he tore at the warmed flesh in frantic desperation, shredding the meat with strong teeth. It had a rank, gamy taste but it fed him. Once the initial flare of hunger was appeased, he sat back and waited while more strips cooked on the dying fire. He ate sparingly of the remaining meat, willing it to fill him, wanting to leave some for another meal. He thought briefly of going back to take more flesh from the mare, but the recollection of those tight, high canyon walls deterred him. Ahead, the trail seemed to make its way through the rough land in a winding pattern. His rider's mind shuddered at the thought of the long walk ahead, but he had no choice.

All the strips were roasted and rolled in the canvas. He kicked at the dying ashes to spread them across the trail. With his gear once again swinging over his shoulder, he started his walk, watching carefully for the faint markings of the ancient trail that he hoped would take him through the mountains and out to a more friendly town. The sun was fully overhead now, and the trail looked no different than what he had walked on for the past hour. Small rivelets of melting snow ran across the path, but he saw scant evidence of game, few rabbit tracks, the spoor of some small rodents, no sign of deer. Not that he could bring down anything without shells for the rifle. A faint smile crossed his bleak face. A picture came to mind, both vivid and comic: He would have to run down any game he saw, slit its throat like he had done with the mare. A silly picture of worn boot soles flapping, shirt tail waving as he lumbered awkwardly behind a graceful buck, arms windmilling to keep his balance as he stumbled from rock to boulder in the chase. His smile died, the picture faded. He was back to reality.

The hours of unexpected walking soon wore him down. He sought out a hidden place in which he could roll up and sleep. A clump of winter-worn brush, struggling to put forth tiny spring buds, offered some seclusion. He rolled himself into the still-damp saddle blanket, put his head on the saddle skirting, and was asleep almost instantly. He woke just before dark and came quickly to his feet, alert for any trouble. A fire would help through the night, so he searched carefully in the fading light for some wood, dried leaves dug from under a leaning rock, and more pine needles. This time the debris would not light, so he stopped trying, unwilling to waste his few matches.

One of the remaining strips of meat was supper. He chewed slowly on the tough meat and washed it down with cold stream water. He splashed some of the icy runoff on his face, scrubbed his hands with sand to remove the greasy remnants of the meat, and then rolled back into the blanket, covering himself with layers of branches and leaves to add insulation. His sleep was invaded by flashes of nightmares: great skulls covered with moss leering at him, walls pushing down on him, endless miles of rock-strewn trails leading nowhere.

The next day he covered a few more miles. To his dismay, the trail headed up higher into the mountain peaks, not down into some warm spring valley. He kept doggedly at the walking, the unused muscles in his legs complaining with each step. Breakfast had been half of one of the remaining strips; noon, more cold water. He walked on because there was no point in remaining where he was.

A well-worn trail made a narrow track through thick undergrowth. It intrigued him. It had to go somewhere important. Pushing against the tangled bushes and spiny weeds, bumping over more rocks, he followed the path. At times he had to go down on his hands and knees to continue. The thicket opened finally onto a bare patch of ground, behind it rocky mounds stood large on both sides of an inviting opening. The path joined another trail coming in from the right on an angle. He stepped cautiously through

20

the opening to find himself in a small valley, lush with emerging grasses, its sides studded with random groupings of quaking aspen and small fir.

He stayed in the small valley three days. The horsemeat soon showed green spots which he scraped off before he ate. It left him with a queasy feeling in his belly. On the second day, he sliced a pigging string from his saddle, and with a supple small pine fashioned a simple snare. One small hare obligingly stepped into the rawhide circle and became dinner. He simmered the skinned carcass with new ferns and wild onion bulbs, using his battered coffee pot for a kettle. The stew lasted two more days, and then he was unable to catch another rabbit. So it was hunger that once again moved him on.

The ancient trail wound still higher into the mountains, offering a succession of cold nights and bright cool days. Wet melting snow covered the trail; he walked aimlessly through the slush, often lost from the faintly marked trail. Several times he slept through the day, hunger weakened and too cold to move. Dry wood was scarce, and without food to cook, having a fire was a luxury.

Once he watched a hawk come down straight and fast to strike at a small hare; the slayer lost its grip on the upward flight, and the broken body fell back. The man was there before the hawk to retrieve the treasure. The angry bird circled him twice, then flew on to search for its next meal. He quickly stripped the skin, cut up the warm flesh, and stuffed it into his mouth. His stomach cramped at the onslaught of raw meat and he went to his knees to vomit back whole pieces of barely chewed meat. After wiping out his mouth with clean snow, he carefully picked out the larger pieces and washed them. Taking more time, he closed his eyes and chewed slowly on another morsel, washing it down with handfuls of snow. It came back up again in a series of gagging, retching heaves that left him kneeling in the snow, head hanging, face hot, body shaking.

21

Sick to the core, he burrowed up like a dying animal against a boulder which offered scant shelter and tried to sleep. Digging at his back were sharp points, bits of wood still dry in their protected spot. He dug them out and was able to start a cooking fire. The roasted meat stayed gingerly in his raw belly this time, giving him hope and renewed energy. In the morning he picked up the remains of the cooked meat and started out again. It seemed to him that the trail had started through some kind of break in the mountain range, at a high elevation, with a rise of short dense trees interspersed with boulders and rills of rushing water. The far side offered a sloping trail heading down out of the mountains.

The trail became easier; the snow melting and running in shining streams alongside the moss-covered path sounded cheerful now. There were glimpses of small grassy areas hidden by thickening trees, with an occasional deer seen tearing at the greening fodder. A head would come high at the sight of him. He would stand and watch the graceful animal as it leaped away from him, taking high, slow leaps in no hurry, as if it knew enough not to be afraid. The sun now warmed him and there was more dry wood for fires, but without matches or food he had to ignore the abundance. He tried eating the moss, but could not swallow it, spitting it out in disgust. A few slowly unrolling ferns along the creekside gave him some nourishment, but not enough.

He stopped suddenly. Ahead he could hear uncertain sounds. He hunkered down to concentrate, not sure if he were finally going mad and hearing things in the closely packed woods. It was voices, or one voice, high and angry, cursing with a florid imagination and no restraints. He walked slowly toward the source of the sounds and came out of the low pine woods onto a muddy road showing little recent use. A man, middle-aged, bowler hat sitting on a wagon seat, stood with arms wild and waving, cursing and hollering at a team of chunky brown mares. The rear wheels were off the road, imbedded to their hubs in thick dark mire.

The mares were frantic, working the wagon in deeper with their lunges against each other, ears flat in anxiety. The silent man out of the woods watched in shock, too numbed to react.

"Hey, you, mister, come give me a hand with these two wooly-headed strumpets. That near 'un, the one with her eyes closed took it as necessary to shy at a respectable pine tree, a goddamn pine tree, mind you, and pushed the other female off the road. Can't get them together, they fight like saloon gals over a high spender. Give me a hand, will you?" The driver's voice rose higher as he tried to catch the wandering attention of the still-silent traveler out of the woods. His light brown eyes narrowed in speculation as he watched the man put his gear down and step up to the lathered team. One bent hand went to a wet muzzle and gently stroked the flapping lip; the other hand begun to rub a widening circle on the mare's broad forehead. The dark chunky mare settled slowly, her eyes open and calm. He reached for the other; when she flinched and shied from his seeking fingers he wound one hand in the bridle while the other stroked softly. All the while the strange man mumbled quiet sounds.

Finally, the two mares stood quiet; their owner also was stilled, hands at his sides, no longer clenched in threatening fists. The odd-looking man still said nothing to the driver, only stared and waited. Face florid with exertion, the driver pushed back a lock of graying hair and spoke, "Well, I'll be damned, yessir, I'll be damned. Here now, you hold them two, I'll get me a log, see if I can jam it under the rear axle. You get them two ready to pull and we'll be out soon as you can rope a painter."

Once the log was jammed deep into the mud and wedged up against the sinking axle, the man spoke words of encouragement and lifted the reins. The two mares moved forward in unison and dug deep into the thick road mud, the strain showing in their bowed necks rigid with distended muscles. A sucking roar, and the rear end of the wagon slid free of the mud. The driver, still jamming with the log, fell forward toward the hole, but caught his balance at the last moment and jumped to one side, letting the heavy log take his place in the gaping mire.

The mares stood still, their bodies trembling from the exertion. Their owner climbed into the wagon seat, shoved his round hat back on his balding head and waved a generous arm at his savior. "Here now, come sit up here, we'll be in town in no time now that these two ladies are out of their trap. Sit here." He patted the worn board seat of the wagon for emphasis. A big smile covered his open face; he was eager for conversation, wanting to know how this man had worked the miracle with the mares, willing to trade stories on the way to town.

The dark-haired man reached for his gear, looked briefly at the smiling, inviting driver, reins in one hand, whip carried loosely in the other, and walked stiffly to the back of the wagon. He pulled down the tailgate and threw his saddle in back, then hauled himself up on the narrow boards and sat, waiting for the mares to move out. The driver finally realized his passenger had chosen to ride in the back, to ignore the proffered friendship. He cracked the whip hard over the muddy, willing backs, and the wagon lurched forward on the choppy road, carrying its passenger to an unknown destination.

The brown mares slowed their headlong trot to take a sharp corner. The dark-haired man slipped from his tailgate perch, hauling his battered saddle and roll with him. He landed heavily in the muddied street and took a few steps to catch his balance. The driver sitting rigid-backed in the wagon seat did not turn his head or acknowledge in any way his passenger's abrupt leave-taking. He pushed his round hat harder onto his head and touched the mares with the whip to pick up their trot.

There was no one around to watch as the loose-limbed

man straightened slowly, conscious in the warming sun of a deep, abiding stiffness within him. He had landed in a town built to last, evidence of the faith of its early builders. Hidden up in the southern sprawl of the Rocky Mountains, the small town of Guffey Creek was the center for the surrounding ranches. The town street was lined with solid, sturdy buildings devoid of pretense. A mercantile proudly displayed its ownership in red painted letters, "Timmons' General Mercantile, Everything You Need." Next to it a smaller, square building housed the local stockman's bank. No fancy glass in the door, just a wide plank floor, solid wooden teller's desk, and the town's pride—the looming black safe.

The rest of the town was built the same: a doctor's office above the barbershop, a high glass window showing the skill of the bootmaker inside the small, slightly tilted building next to the barber. Set back from a wooden walkway was a comfortable looking building, home of the only eating place in Guffey Creek, Simpson's Cafe. There was only one road in and out of town, and only one saloon, which catered more to the locals than to passing strangers.

A lopsided sign declaring a livery stable within hung at a dangerous slant over a partially open door, beckoning to the travel-weary drifter. The building was simple in design, a companion to the rest of the town, a rough barn of hand-hewn timbers, the corrals sturdy with their six-foot-high railing designed to hold any number of horses. Nothing fancy, but built to last. The lettering was also simple: "Kelleher's Livery, Horses For Hire, Bought, Sold, Traded, George Kelleher, Prop" was its hand-lettered message. Inside, the barn looked cool and empty, offering a welcome to the traveler.

He hesitated, all too aware that he was a stranger entering a small settled world. A flicker of movement down the quiet street caught his eyes; it was a swamper brushing out last night's rubble from the saloon. He was leery of towns; people knew each other too well, and didn't want strangers in their midst. But he knew this was the best he could hope for, and he was hungry and horseless.

He stepped quickly inside the barn and waited. A quick sweep told him a great deal. Gear was piled everywhere; broken bridles hung from random nails; saddles were dumped unceremoniously in dusty heaps; blankets rotted in a corner. The strong invading smell of ammonia almost took his breath away; it had been a while since the barn had been well cleaned. A few horses stood in straight stalls, their active tails marking the beginning of the fly season. At least the stock looked good: fat, shiny coated, and content. But there was dirty urine-soaked straw clogging the aisle; oats leaked from a damaged grain bin; dust was everywhere, in cobwebs hanging from the low ceiling, wherever there was an empty surface. A lot of work here for someone. Enough work to earn a few days of meals and a free bed.

Unexpectedly the shakes hit him. Being inside did that to him, brought back the memories of closing walls, human stench, his own acrid smell. He almost backed out of the stable, fighting hard against the unwanted images. He'd learned, but almost too late, to stay away from the booze; it turned him loose, uncorked his temper, landed him in small dark jails that were infested and close. A hard snort from a stalled horse brought him back to the moment. These walls weren't the ones that held him in; he was here to ask for work; no more stealing, no more whiskey, no more jails.

The shakes started again. His thin shoulders hunched against the tearing images. He was light-headed from hunger and almost drifting. He grabbed a deep breath to clear the tension, and the sharp bite of the urine helped push away the walls. The smell of horses and leather brought him back. A door rattled in the far wall; the office sign nailed to it swung with the effort to open. A fat round man, bent with his age, came bulling through the opening, brushing his hand over a brilliantly balding head, lightly fringed with white wisps.

The man stopped suddenly at the sight of a potential

customer. Bright blue eyes took in the size and quality of the pocketbook in front of him, quick and sure with years of practice. His words came fast and definite, offering no argument. "Nope, no can let you bed here, don't want saddle bums around, keeps off the good payin' folk. 'Sides, you drifters most all want your smoke, a bottle, then I get to worry about fire along with you takin' what don't belong to you. Out." The voice reached through the shakes. Here it was again, the fight to survive.

Softly now, easy, don't push the old man; give him another chance at you, give him something to think about. The tall, bony man spoke quietly, his words hard in coming. "Mr. Kelleher, I don't ask for a handout, purely business." He took another breath, eased his shoulders, put his desperation into the words. "You got busted harness, bridles and such, doing you no good just lying there. I can mend anything, put it right, even build you a fancy headpiece for your private horse. I can work, pay my own way." He looked up at the thick pile of cured grass overhead. The sight and smell encouraged him. "Can work your rough stock, too, put manners on any bronc, make you a lady's horse if you need one." He stopped. To his ears the pleading was too strong. He wasn't asking for favors, just to work and move on.

The old hostler took another long look at the saddle bum in front of him. He didn't take much to what he saw. The few drifters he got up here usually peeled out after he sized them up and read the law. But this gent was staying right there in front of him. Waiting for an answer. A real wild-looking ranny, gaunted down and filthy like a winter-poor bronc, most likely running from something somewhere. But it was the pale eyes that kept George's attention, the violence right there for him to read. And the scars; them too took a man's eye right quick. Hell of a worker this 'un would be, right hand all bent and tore up, bet it don't hardly work at all. Kelleher's face mirrored his conclusions.

Anyone could read the refusal. He'd seen it plenty of times

before, could watch those clear blue eyes take in all the signs. He knew he looked like he'd been dragged and whipped. He had been, but he could work, and would, given the chance. The bright blue eyes took on a frosty glint. The drifter spoke up fast to beat the words he'd heard too often. "No chance, huh? Not even for cleaning out the pens in back, this stable? A fair swap for some grub and the use of the hay pile for the night. Even with this hand I can push a 'barrow." The pain of these words drove deep to his core. He was begging now, but had little choice. There was no place left to go.

He tried to keep the bitterness out, but the anger slipped in. He said the words again, this time shaking not from fear but from hunger. "You'll get your money's worth from me." His tenuous hold on his temper slipped as he watched the shiny white head shake its final no. He turned and walked toward the bright doorway, saddle held tight in his bent hand. Best to get outside before he blew. Just as he neared the door, a voice came from outside, stopping him, breaking into the tension inside the stable walls.

"George, you there, I got them horses you wanted; what do you want done with 'em?" A stocky red-headed puncher in his early thirties led three half-broke horses into the stable and stopped with the broncs milling about him. One dun mare reared back, ears pinned flat, to pull away from the handler. Unused to being confined and spooked by the threatening walls, she flew in great leaps deeper into the stable dark. The tie rope flapped along her sides adding to the panicked flight. As the dun came flying by, the drifter grabbed for the rope and caught it, swung from it, using his weight to slow the mare. His hand found the soft flesh above the distended nostrils and a few quiet words eased the mare's fear. The dun stood, ears perked forward at the unaccustomed sound, one hoof cocked in warning.

The round hostler rubbed his chin, then scratched an offending ear, sighed, then spoke. "Put that fool horse in the back pen, come get these other two. The shovel's by the door, wheelbarrow be out back. You can finish the pens and I'll get you fixed up with some eats. Work out later what you gets paid for putting a better handle on these here broncs, if I decide to take them offa Red here." He turned to the grinning cowboy. "Gosh durn it, you trying to cheat me again. How come you didn't socialize them horses better; you know I'm too old for this." Still holding the two bays, the redhead laughed. As usual, George was making himself out to be the loser. Always ready to turn anything to his advantage. Now they'd compare poverty, hard times, swap a few hefty lies and insults, then head to Rand's to drink some, haggle and swear at each other, drink some more, then settle on a price that suited them both.

Red handed the two bays to the silent man; with an inviting grin he offered, "Good job you caught that dun mare; she's a quick hard-assed lady, but will be a good one once she learns her manners. Too good for George here . . ." Not caring that he got no response, the cowboy grinned again and turned back to Kelleher. "Come on, stop lining up more work for this poor bastard to do. Let's get to business."

George sighed again, slapped his pockets looking for a pipe, then forgot what he was looking for and sputtered at the puncher. "Guess I got me a new helper, knows horses by God, handles them broncs better'n you. What price you put on them; you know I ain't got much hard cash, took on a lot of stock already this spring." The two men walked out of the barn, already deep into their horse trading. George stopped as he hit the sunshine, and turned his round head back toward the stable, tugging at straggling wisps of hair. "What name you go by, mister, if you got one?"

A voice, cracked and uncertain, came through the dim quiet. "Bishop, Holly Bishop."

There was a moment of silence as George rolled the name over in his mind. "Damn fool thing to call a man, damn fool name."

Holly didn't have to be outside to see the old hostler's expression. Surprise, then disgust. Holly brought a twist to a man's face. He'd taken enough beatings with the name, had learned to fight as a kid for the right to have his own name. Damn them all.

Holy slapped the dun lightly on the rump as he passed into the pen. A swift black hoof streaked by his leg as a warning. He grinned slightly. "Move over, gal, I've got work to do. No one's going to bother you today." He hoped the same words applied to himself.

CHAPTER THREE

George Kelleher chuckled as he patted the bill of sale stuffed in his shirt pocket. Red Willis thought he'd gotten one over on George this time, making him pay a pretty price for that dun mare and the two bays. But dumb ole George knew the bays would be worth a good dollar, just needed to have a good handle on them. And if he could read character like he used to—well, that drifter was just the man to do the job. And the work wouldn't cost much. The man was run out, that was easy to see. Cost some food, use of the hay pile, and maybe a bit of cash when he was done. Maybe, too, he could be generous and give the man that spooky mare, be good to get rid of that one. They sure enough would make a matched pair, those two. George chuckled again at his image of the dun and the drifter in harness. That would be a pair to pull hell apart.

George stood by the back of the stable, close to the door, with a wary eye on the office and his shotgun. But he wanted to watch this man work. Bishop bothered him, he carried violence in his face, violence that could easily get out of control, but if the man did his work, then ole George could put up with the worry. He just planned to keep that shotgun greased up and breech full. By the gate of the large pen, he watched the tall man stop, take a deep breath and steady himself on the fence rail, then walk to the smaller pen. The big one was shoveled out, the manure from the past winter now resting on the old pile beyond the fence line, steam rising from the heated pile. The work was getting done and plenty fast enough, had to give the drifter that. George smiled to himself and retreated to his office to enjoy a pipe. Tough work at his advanced age to watch someone doing all that hard shoveling.

The last pen was done, the last shovel of manure rested atop the still-smoking mound beyond the ragged fence line. Holly rested briefly, leaning against the rear of the stable. Damn. He was cold again. Right to the bone. Moving those last loads of horse dung had been a struggle, his knees shaky, arms close to quitting work. Now for something to eat. Holly could envision a steaming bowl of stew, a thick cut of steak, hot slices of bread. He shook his mind clear of that particular picture, a wry smile crossing his thin features. He'd better watch out for hot bread, got him deep in trouble.

A gust of air came from deep inside, to echo the physical weariness that held him. The hard-earned meal and a soft bed in the clean haymow were his. Holly pushed himself away from the obliging outside wall with one foot, picked up the shovel, and headed into the stable. Inside was dark, warmed by the shifting bodies of stalled horses pulling at their evening hay. He laid the shovel against the end stall and walked slowly to the closed office door. But before he could knock, it opened, and George Kelleher, pipe in hand, was waiting on the other side, already started on his talk to the new hand. "—finished all those pens, be guessing you might be hungry; I told Eben Simpson over to the cafe to be expecting you; he'll put your meal on my bill, just don't go to eating everything in sight. Food's good there, not that you look to be choosy. Can sleep up under the hay, no smokes but then I bet you don't have the makings anyway. You can take a couple of saddle blankets, use that old sheepskin coat there. Got a smell all its own, but you don't appear to be minding that. Gets good and cool up here to the evenings."

The words came fast, offering Holly little chance to respond. Kelleher continued to ramble, some of the words making sense to the hungry man in front of him. Finally, Holly reached abruptly for the sheepskin coat that was hanging just inside the door. Kelleher stepped back, the alarm strong in his face, his hand going quickly behind the door. Holly refused to acknowledge the shotgun that appeared in the old man's hand. He shrugged his shoulders into the rank coat and backed out of the small office to turn on his heel and disappear into the gloom. The resistant squeak of the swinging front door came to George, and then all was easy in the barn. He sputtered to himself, left uneasy by the confrontation. "Damned if I'm going to jump each time that ranny moves around here, but he sure enough is spooky, do me to watch close." He absently patted the worn stock of his familiar shotgun, then remembered the pipe stuffed still smoldering into his rear pants pocket and hurried to pull it out. "Fool name for a man, a damn fool name." George sat down in the soiled and tattered chair and worked over the pipe, continuing to mutter.

Holly stopped just outside the door to draw the wooly coat tight around himself. Relief flooded him; he was outside and free. The warmth was comforting against the spring evening. The coat did carry a special smell, a compilation of years of sweat, both man and animal. The bitter tang of blood, dried to rusted spots across the front, added its own touch. A tight smile tugged at his mouth, together he and the garment must put out an odor calling all the polecats and varmints in the area. Fill up this small town fast. He grinned to himself in the darkness.

His hunger had long since gone beyond the sharp stage to a dull ache deep in his gut. He was light-headed, and even in the fast-fading dusk, he could see bright spots just out of range of his eyes, shiny spots that spun when he turned his head to catch them. High in his throat was a strong, demanding pound, reminding him that his heart worked, that his body needed nourishment. A quick turn of his head to catch a drifting spot brought nausea to his empty belly. He took a step forward to catch his balance, and took another step; something came on the warm air still hovering, not yet pushed aside by the strong evening cold from the high snowy peaks. Holly swallowed hard, surprised at the liquid filling up his mouth. Damn. Here he stood, drooling in the dark over something cooking, the smell lying heavy on the wind, while he had earned the right to his share of that food.

His boots made a satisfying ring on the wooden sidewalk. Even their rotting soles could raise a deep thump as he walked quickly toward the small square building carrying the sign "Good Food, Eben and Mary Simpson, Owners." He came to an abrupt halt in front of the building, which was set back from the walk. Inside was dinner, but also inside were more people, and more questions. The few words he had spoken since riding into this town on the tailgate had not erased the lonesome time in the high mountains. His hesitation angered him; he had earned the meal and needed it. Holly reached for the door and yanked it open, the frilly printed curtains covering the glass half-bounced and fluttered as the frame gave under his pull. Once inside, he stopped again. The smell of food was strong enough to cause his tender stomach to flip uncomfortably. Holly shook his head, "Good and holy hell, what's the matter? Get to eating, old son, you've earned it."

By the startled look from the pretty blond behind the counter, Holly figured he was talking out loud. He could feel the beginning of a flush, thankfully hidden by the dark whiskers. The mountains sure made a man even stranger. The small cafe held a homey warmth, with simple round tables crowded with chairs. Most of the tables now held only dirty dishes: piles of plates, glasses pushed to one side, evidence that the rush hour had come and gone, the diners on to their evening's entertainment. The few still seated were at the end of their meal, working on the last bite of pie. Engrossed in their companions, they paid little attention to the ragged man standing by himself at the doorway.

Only the girl noticed Holly's one-sided conversation. A slow, warm smile came across her soft features. Her blossoming figure was enhanced by the starched white apron tied tightly around her waist, pointing up her full breasts covered by a straining shirtwaist, highlighting her slender waist. Holly's discomfort heightened as he found himself responding to the warmth in her smile, the light in her clear blue eyes. He was hungry for everything.

Up against the wall was an empty seat at the counter, a safe place where he could see everything going on in the cafe. Holly's head lifted as the young woman moved to stand in front of him. On this closer look he could see her youth, the fresh unspoiled beauty. Not out of her teens, she had her shiny blond hair pulled back and twisted to stay out of her face, blue eyes bright and shining, mouth ripe with a pout to the lower lip that asked and offered. That wonderful mouth turned to a smile, then formed the words he wanted to hear. "Dinner, mister? We've got stew tonight, and always have steak, hot biscuits, lots of coffee. And hot dried apple pie, all you can eat." Her voice was young too, unlined with worry.

Holly stared straight at the girl, fascinated by her cleanness. He watched and waited, as she took her first real look at him. The blue eyes widened as they took in his battered face, the scars, the hunted set to his eyes. Her brilliant smile dimmed and she took a half step back, one slender hand coming up to fiddle with a loosened bow at her throat. Then her eyes came back to meet his briefly, dropped, and looked away. Spooked. His voice was harsh and raspy: "Stew, coffee, biscuits, pie. Lots of it."

Julie Warner smoothed her ever-escaping hair as she walked away from the counter. She wanted to turn back and look at the dark-faced man again, look without him returning the look. His eyes scared her: pale, almost amber, their stare level and hard. Set deep in his face they were high-lighted by the long hair and deeply bronzed skin. This man was dangerous, scary, appealing. She took a deep breath and let it out slowly, aware of the effect this action created. He was more interesting than the cowboys who flocked around her all the time. Even more interesting than the Hubbard boy, who had grown up back east, and who rode in whenever he could to shyly ask her out for a walk.

"Julie, you want something? Seems I heard the door open; another customer? What is it, dear?" Mrs. Simpson's easy voice broke Julie's wandering thoughts. She answered slowly, "Oh, yes, an order of stew, biscuits, and pie." Then she hesitated, "But I don't think he can pay for the meal, doesn't look like he's got any money. And that coat, I know it's George Kelleher's old butcher coat. At least it sure smells like that old coat."

Julie stepped aside as Mr. Simpson came through the half-door to the large kitchen and smiled at the young girl. A kind man, he was shorter than his wife, with a layer of thinning hair combed carefully over his balding spot. "I see Kelleher's new horse wrangler finally made it in. George was over earlier, said to feed him and put it on his bill. Says he came in from up near the road to Tyson's, got Ollie Kimball out of trouble again with those silly mares he keeps. Sure is a rough-looking one, but George insists he works hard, earns his keep. At least so far. Must be, he cleaned out those back pens in a hurry. Anyway," he said as he handed Julie a bowl and a plate stacked high with steaming biscuits, "George says to feed him so we will. Looks like we'll make a profit on this one, been a long while since he had much to eat. Here, child, let's give the man his meal."

A plate appeared in front of Holly, heaped with hot biscuits. Next to it a bowl appeared, hot steam rising to carry the rich smell of beef stew. A cup of black coffee went beside the bowl, a spoon was put down near the mug. "Here's your meal, mister, enjoy. The pie'll be along as soon's you're done." Holly didn't hear the words; he picked up the bent spoon and dug a big hole in the rich gravy. It slipped around in his mouth, chunks of meat, bits of wild onion, carrots, and slices of potato all jumbled together. He chewed fast and swallowed greedily, already holding another waiting spoonful. A quick gulp of scalding coffee slowed him briefly, to wait while the hot liquid settled, then he went back to shoveling in big quantities of the food. Words buzzed around his ears, ignored in the hurry to eat as much as he could.

Finally a word came through to him; he stopped eating abruptly as if the sense of the spoken word had caught up to him. The girl's voice was clear and brittle. "You know, you'll make yourself awful sick, you keep eating that fast." Holly looked around wildly, then realized she was standing directly in front of him, offering him her good advice. She smiled again at the man, seeking his recognition of her beauty. A frown crossed her unlined features. He had given only a short nod to her, then had gone back to his eating, this time as if the first panic had subsided and he could now enjoy the meal. And ignore her.

Julie stormed back into the kitchen, pouting at the slight she had received. "I don't like that man, he's got no more manners than a wild dog." Eben Simpson smiled at the harsh words from the pretty girl who, in the three years since she had come to them with parents freshly buried in a fever epidemic, had become a daughter to the childless couple. She was young, beautiful, vain, and sweet. And spoiled by all the attention. His smile widened as she continued fussing; someone had ignored her presence, and she didn't like it, wasn't used to it. Usually the cowboys gave her all the attention she wanted. And now Kelleher's wild man had ignored her for a bowl of stew. Eben Simpson smiled at the girl.

Holly pushed the stool back from the counter and turned a bit to look around him. The panic was gone, his stomach full for the first time in weeks. Almost too full. The pretty girl had been right and he knew it. The pie put the finish on the hunger. Now all he craved was sleep. An older man, short, neat, clean, came to stand in front of him, a big smile on his lined face. Nodding to the wiped-clean plate and bowl in front of Holly, he ventured his opinion. "More customers like you and we could fire the dishwasher, cleaned right down to the shine. You're George's new man, right? I put this on his bill?"

Holly offered nothing more than a nod to the small man to signal his agreement, nothing that would continue the conversation. The shiny hair gleamed tight over the balding head, the neat tie in its snug bow at the shirt collar, the bright striped shirt front, the clean cuffs and starched collar, apron only lightly soiled after a day's work. Here was a townman— proper, clean, forbidding. Holly felt his itchy face, the pull of dirty hair, the imbedded sweat and grease of his clothes. The thick warmth of the cafe overpowered him, the smell of the food, the tang of bitter coffee, hot bread. He stood to reach for his battered black hat and was at the door in one easy move, in a hurry to get outside. The panic lessened in the relief of the cold evening air. He walked on a few steps, then stopped to lean against a store front.

It wasn't a bad town, the stores clean, well built, prosperous. Not a bad-looking girl, either. His mind drifted over the pretty blond face, that special warm female smell distinct even among the food and his own ripe odor. He started along the sidewalk slowly, feeling the weight of the unaccustomed food settling hard. Shapes of two men closed in the wooden walkway, taking up all the room, coming out of the darkness. They strode toward him; a heavy-set man pushed past, slamming Holly hard up against the building, rattling the glass in its frames. Stunned, Holly took a harsh breath, his fists clenched. A tall companion to the big man came between Holly and the looming shape, spoke words meant to soothe though the voice behind them carried no feeling. "Excuse the manners, friend. Turner here is too big to fit on this walk sociable like. Didn't see you in the dark. No harm meant."

A light came on from a nearby home, to heighten the long face of the speaker, the narrow jaw, lank hair, loose-held arms. No sign of apology in this man's eyes, but the words eased Holly out of a fight he was sure to lose. He tipped his head in acceptance of the apology, then stood aside to let the two men past. A sickness rode in his belly; a man that size would be a battle anytime, right now he would tear Holly apart. His talkative companion didn't look much like a pilgrim either, his hand rode too close and too easy near his shiny pistol. The food had stirred with the tension, and cramps told him he'd eaten too much too fast. Time to get back to the stables and sleep.

George was waiting for him, standing just inside the front door. Two horses with the sweat barely dried on their dull coats stood in tie stalls, their heads low in exhaustion. "Here, now, you finally back, eating up all them profits already. Them two horses need brushing and oats." A wild hand gestured in circles to the dulled horses. "Water, too, in a while. They belong to the Two Crown and the Judge likes his stock cared for mighty particular. Brush them first and cool them before you grain them, they're mighty hot. That Turner don't know how to ride a horse, could ruin these two . . ." The voice went on, speaking words that meant little to Holly. The name Turner hit a chord, but nothing enough to bother him. He stripped the bit and saddle from one horse, picked up a brush, and started work.

The chestnut was a big-barreled, fine-headed animal who rolled his eyes and evaded Holly's touch at first. Finally the gelding settled into the grooming, stretching and blowing softly as Holly worked over the saddle mark. The paint mare in the next stall reacted the same way; she pushed over to the far edge of the stall and flattened her ears when Holly went near, resisting all contact. The scent of good hay came to Holly as he worked on the tall mare, soft warm hay that offered comfort for a weary man. The brushing done, Holly put a can of oats in each feed trough, dropped in a pile of hay, and checked each horse again before leaving the stalls. They were done, eating quietly. He grabbed two smelly blankets off a rack, climbed up into the mow and rolled deep into the hay. Before the hay had settled, his eyes closed, and he was gone.

George listened from his office and didn't hear any low voice talking to the stock or other sounds of anything getting done. He stuck his head beyond the doorway to listen, already building anger at the lazy bum who was taking advantage of his good nature. The horses stood patiently in their stalls, working at their dinner. From the loft came distant sounds of snoring. George scratched himself on the ear, then tugged at his long nose. Guess that drifter'll do after all. Those horses were done right quick and looked shiny. Locking the office door, the heavy old man went out through the front to turn down the walkway. It was time for his evening drink at Rand's.

Inside the overheated office, the furniture dark and forboding, the slender, silver-haired man turned on his heel, his eyes brilliant with anger. No one in this town was to question his orders, especially not his own lawyer. Once again, Judge Jonathan Breen stated his simple order in short, clipped words that the reluctant lawyer could not help but understand. "Jenkins, finish the contract. Now. Make the bid high enough that Hubbard cannot help but underbid me. I want him to be able to see and feel the profits, to go out on a limb to fulfill this contract. No one else will bid. Turner and Jack have taken my word to all ranchers who might be interested. You need only take care my bid is high, that Hubbard can afford to bid lower. Never mind the rest. It is none of your business."

The Judge stood with his legs apart, hands behind his back in a caricature of the military "at ease." His judicial title was self-ordained; his military bearing, which hinted at a past of glorious service, was also fiction. Jonathan Breen believed his own fabricated life. Slight, gray hair cut short and severe, in his mid-fifties, he had a lifetime of self-deception behind him, and the money to support it. Born into a wealthy eastern family, he had been sent west before the War Between the States in hopes he would become a man. He quickly discovered that hard cash would buy him respect in the young and unsettled land. Now he ruled a large empire of cattle, horses, and men, and everything was the best. Extra wages ensured the loyalty and fealty of his foreman and crew. But it was a lonely life; since no woman could live up to his expectations, he lived alone in baronial splendor.

The Hubbard family had moved into the Judge's valley from the east, and had filed on a piece of range, separate from his holdings, that was made remote by a large strip of marsh and rock. The land was good, rich grazing that ran up into the foothills, ideal for raising high-country horses. The Judge used the piece on occasion when his summer range was dry, but had never bothered to take title to the property. To find a small rancher using his summer range was enough to earn the Judge's enmity. For that same man to have a fine stallion, a horse that all in the valley could see was far superior to anything the Judge owned made him livid with rage. And Hubbard had refused all attempts to buy the horse, but had kindly offered to allow the Judge to breed a few of his better mares to the stallion, in hopes of raising a good stud of his own. This was not enough. The bay stallion must belong to the Judge. And the first step to that end was to be put together this evening by his lily-necked lawyer.

The army at Fort Bradford, twenty miles out on the plains, had put out a bidding contract for remounts. They would pay a premium for solid color geldings, fifteen hands or better, between four and seven years old, broke to ride

41

and sound of wind and limb. This contract called for twenty-five horses, a good piece of hard cash for the contractor. Hubbard's horses were the finest in the area. The stallion reached back to Messenger in his bloodlines, and passed his speed and intelligence on to his offspring. Hubbard crossed this good blood with range mares chosen for their stamina and cow sense. But Hubbard did not have twenty-five horses of marketable age, more like fifteen ready to go. So he would have to borrow to buy the difference, and once he borrowed he would be owned by the Judge, like everyone else in Guffey Creek.

The lawyer tried soothing the Judge, to ease the hot temper and back the man away from carrying out his scheme. Ned Jenkins was not a highly ethical man, but the deal seemed too raw to him. They needed more good solid families like the Hubbards in the valley for the small town to grow and prosper. "Now, Judge, why not let Hubbard go along with his breeding, bet you could buy a good colt from him, raise it for your own. This family has been a good addition to the valley, lots of folks like them. Be a shame to see them lose everything over one horse."

The Judge turned on his whey-faced lackey, surprised at the man's championing of the Hubbards. "You fool, I will have that stallion." The anger in his voice underscored his determination. "Damn Hubbard and his arrogance. I will have the best horses, by God, and no one will refuse me. When he gets that contract, I will make certain he cannot meet his deadline or his debts. Then that stallion will belong to me." The Judge glared at Jenkins, a small, soft man with sparse whiskers covering his upper lip and jaw line, light hair combed over a domed forehead. Jenkins flinched visibly from the power behind Judge Breen's words. "Now, finish that contract. I will sign it, then Turner and Jack will be here to deliver it to the army post tonight. Get to your work and leave Hubbard and the horse to me."

The two men who had brushed by Holly earlier stood at

the door to the law office. The tall one knocked, and the Judge opened the door, his flushed face highlighted in the well-lit office. "Come in, Jack; Turner with you?" Good. When Jenkins is done, I want you to take this paper to Captain Stanfield at Fort Bradford; make sure it goes right to Stanfield's hand. He is in charge and I want no mistakes." The Judge focused his attention on the heavy, dull-looking man who had just walked up behind Jack. "You, I want you to ride up to Tyson's Station, have a few drinks, only a few, mind you, and let it slip that I have bid one hundred twenty-five dollars on the army contract. The word will get back to Hubbard. There are men up there who like Hubbard and will think they are doing him a favor. Be rock sure that no one thinks you meant to let the bid amount slip. Don't make a big fuss, just get the word out." The Judge's distaste for dealing with the hulking man was most evident in his manner of speech, as if the words could keep a distance between himself and the dirty rider who stood too near him, an insulting grin playing on his face. Jenkins wordlessly handed the papers to the Judge, who scanned them and signed with a flourish, to hand the papers on to the waiting pair.

The two left the office, the door shutting behind them with a silent swing. These two liked their work for the Judge; good pay, no hard ranch work, plenty of time to drink. A few heads needing busting, a storekeeper needing a reminder that the Judge was the power in town—whatever the Judge wanted, that was their job. The two men were in deep contrast to the trim, almost prissy neatness of their employer. Jack Levitt stood over six feet three inches, with narrow, stooped shoulders, a long, cavernous face topped by thinning dully brown hair, eyes a matching watery brown. In tan pants, a white shirt buttoned to the top and worn with a black string tie, wearing half-boots and a flat-brimmed city hat he looked like a salesman of some unpronounceable tonic. It was when you noticed the buffed shine on the oiled holster strapped low on his left thigh, the sheen to the gun handle, and the unconscious manner in which he stroked the side of the gun that you took a second look. The eyes missed little; there were no laugh lines around his thin bowed mouth, only severe lines of disapproval. Jack Levitt saw everything, and disliked most of what he saw. Hard cash and hard whiskey kept him content, and the Judge kept him well supplied with both.

His companion was in direct contrast: Turner Allward was almost as tall as Levitt, but big, wide, and meaty, layered with fat. Dirty blond hair combed straight back and trimmed even with his frayed collar framed a dull-red face and ice-blue eyes. He played the fool, unable to think, to make up his mind. Many men had gone down smashed by his thick hands, led on to their suicide by believing they could bait the giant and have some fun. If Turner couldn't handle a man with his fists, Jack and his gun took over. Between them they could whipsaw a man, get him off balance, and finish him with either guns or fists. Alone, each was a menace, together they provided the muscle that kept the small valley agreeing with the Judge's orders.

Turner headed for the stable, to roust out the hostler and get their horses ready. Jack Levitt stood a moment longer, watching the wide back and absently playing with the pistol butt, fondling the warm slick surface. Then he slammed aside the batwing doors into the saloon. They needed a bottle for the night's trip. He wasn't watching as Turner shoved open the stable door and yelled for George to get their mounts.

The loud insistent voice brought Holly partway out of a deep sleep with a start. He rolled over fast and instinctively searched for a weapon, then gathered himself to be ready for whatever was threatening. The shock of so abrupt an awakening left him sick. Standing by the doorway, Turner could see movement in the loft and yelled again, "Get down here and get those broncs. Pronto." Holly stuck his head over the loft edge, stared briefly at the big man, and withdrew his head to slide back into the hay pile. Like a hound, he turned in the warm mound and settled back for sleep.

Turner stood flatfooted on the stable floor; it took a long moment for him to realize his order had been ignored—by the saddle bum he had shouldered aside earlier. The ladder rungs shook under his weight as he climbed the first four rungs. Above he could see a neat pile of hay in which the man was bedded. His back was near Turner, a bony shoulder protruding, partially covered with a smelly horse blanket. Turner's meaty hand grabbed the offending body and pulled Holly from his warm bed. Holly went flying off the loft edge to land hard up against the office door. Glass rattled, threatened to shatter. An angry voice brought him out of his stunned condition. "You son-of-a-whore, I want them horses, now!" Holly looked up at a familiar shape: wide shoulders, thick arms falling away from a coarse body, a massive belly hanging low over fine twill ranch pants, tucked into fancy black boots. Now he remembered Turner.

Holly came partway to his feet, moving slowly, stiff and weak. Turner accepted his downed head as surrender, only to gasp in pain and rage as the dark head piled into his soft hanging stomach, driving the air out in a foul *whoosh* of breath. Holly rolled past Turner with his momentum, then up onto his feet, ready now to carry the fight. Turner straightened slowly. Disbelief fought the unaccustomed pain in his face. Few in this town had dared challenge him this way. But the man in front of him, Kelleher's new swamper, had not followed the rules.

Holly grabbed the shovel he had left leaning on the stall; fighting fair with this giant would be foolish. He swung low and hard, hoping to hit the exposed and tender belly again. An immense hand grabbed the handle, its mate swung at Holly's head. He saw the swing start, raised his arm in defense and the blow connected on his upraised forearm. His shoulder went numb, then pain blossomed from bruised muscle and bone. Holly dropped the shovel and put his

45

anger into a shot at the red face so close in front of him, but was blocked by a huge fist reaching to him and he took a sharp crack on the cheek. The skin split from the impact and he went down, ringing in his ears and a flowering pain radiating from his cheekbone.

Turner's shape again loomed over him. "Damn you, get my horse saddled." The man stepped back again, expecting compliance with the command. Holly stood shakily, rubbing his numb arm, raising an unwilling hand to wipe the blood from his face. To continue the fight was suicide, but the big man's assurance that he would give in tore at Holly's common sense. Temper took over reasoning. Holly tensed and took another shot at the bulk in front of him, surprise taking the blow through those large hands to land on the meaty face, raising an instant blue welt along Turner's jaw. Turner roared in his anger, reached to grab Holly by his shirt, picked him up and slammed him into a support. Face inches from the drifter's, Turner bellowed the order: "Get those broncs now." He dropped the thin cowboy and stood, hands heavy and loose at his sides, unwilling to consider anything less than complete surrender. Knowing it was crazy to continue, Holly took another breath, shuddered, and swung again, this time landing the blow squarely on the offending nose, sending the huge man staggering and drawing a fountain of blood. Rage turned the mountain into a fury. Holly ducked a big fist aimed at his head and walked into a rocklike hand that clamped around his throat, shutting off his breath. Then he felt himself lifted; a post rammed hard against his back, feet just touching the barn floor. A big fist struck against his jaw, sending shards of light and pain through him. Another blow, this time on the side of his head, brought him close to unconsciousness.

A burst of pain in his belly, food gagging in his throat as Turner changed his target, Holly was only just aware of the blood covering his eyes, coloring what little he could see in a red mist. Just before the pain took him completely, Holly

46

heard the voice, a familiar voice. "Easy, there, take it easy." It was the same unfeeling voice that had blocked Turner on the sidewalk that evening. "We don't need this gent pounded to death tonight. Got to get going. George was over to Rand's, be right here to get the horses. Let's get this one out of sight." Thin shoulders pushed between Turner and Holly's limp body, braced up against a post. The flat nasal voice had interrupted the nightmare. "We've got better things to do; leave him."

Turner stepped back to watch as Holly slid down the supporting post and rolled sideways to sprawl on the dusty floor. The smooth-worn wood felt comforting to his hot face, the floor staying steady beneath him. Voices continued above him, the words meaning nothing. Turner frowned. But Jack stayed in front of him. "What the hell is going on?"

Turner's bass voice answered. "This two-bit ranny wouldn't get our broncs when I told him. Bet he jumps next time I holler." A wicked grin crossed the bloodied face in anticipation. Turner took a swipe at his nose with a grimy neckerchief. The two men could hear Kelleher yanking at his own front door, unable to get the stiff hinges to give.

Jack moved quickly, kicked at Holly's inert body. "No need to get that old fool prattling on about this." Face registering no emotion, he rolled the bleeding man deep into an empty stall. They waited as George brought out their mounts, saddled and ready.

Oblivious of the fight, unobservant of Turner's swelling nose, Kelleher rambled on in his fashion about how well the horses had been cared for, how shiny they were. "Never seen them look better, have you boys? I got me a new man who is a winner for sure."

Jack took the reins of his paint, gave George a macabre grin, and told him to give their compliments to the groom. Turner was right behind him, still swiping at his dripping nose as they took their horses outside. Jack swung up on the dancing paint mare, reined her hard, and urged his companion to get going. "We can make the ride easy to Hangman's Bend, split up there." He reluctantly offered to share the bottle with Turner to hurry the man along. The big man hauled his bulk up on the nervous chestnut, cuffed the swinging head with a hard right hand, and rode up to claim his booze. After a long swallow, the two rode out beyond the stable back door, heading up into the looming mountain peaks.

Holly heard someone groaning, tried to find the sound, and realized it was himself when he tried to pick up his head. One eye was swollen shut, blood had dried on his chin, and more blood oozed into his eyes from a loose flap of skin across his forehead. He could make out a shape coming at him from the front of the stall, tried to rise to fight, and fell forward from his knees. George Kelleher reached the man as he fell, caught his limp body and laid it down gently in the musty bedding.

"Good Lord, sonny, you musta tangled with Turner. He likes to use his fists, keeps him in practice. Guess no one thought to tell you the way things is done in this town. You do what those two tell you, they do what the Judge wants. That way we all makes money." George rocked back to sit on his wide backside and study the battered body in front of him, carefully weighing the problems it created. An enemy of Turner's now, a problem for George. He studied the body some more, his mind slowly going over what was involved. The words came slowly to the silent and unconscious man in front of the fat old hostler. "I owe to clean you, Mister Holly, even maybe call Doc Simonson. But then I guess I'll leave you here for the night. And I'll have to think on you staying here long. Could be a bit of trouble. I'm too old for that."

Later, Holly was vaguely aware of shadows moving around him, of something burning across his forehead, and voices soft and murmuring. Then condemning, arguing. Finally he slept.

48

CHAPTER FOUR

Something was tickling his nose. Holly came awake instantly, fighting to open his eyes. They were bound shut. He raised a hand to his face, seeking to remove the obstruction. The hand found swollen flesh, dried crust holding along tender eyelids. He scrubbed gently at the bloody glue. His right eye came open reluctantly, still held with threads of mucus. He was on his back in a corner, head sideways against a stall partition. A rolling eye and curious looming nose looked down at him; the large yellow teeth went sideways in a grinding motion, dropping another bit of hay on his face, tickling his ear this time.

The insistent throbbing in his head and the tightness in his belly holding the damaged muscles brought back last night's slaughter. He could see the red, heavy face, eyes carrying a wicked light, a big hand reaching toward him, blocking out everything else; his head slamming again and again up against a post, unable to return the blows, numbed, distant. He rubbed a hand tentatively across his forehead; a roughness in the skin startled him. It felt like someone else had been at him, stitching the damaged skin together.

Holly picked at the individual bits he remembered, voices talking around him, someone holding his head. But Turner's face stayed in front of his eyes. He moved quickly, summoning the energy to roll over, wedging up against the manger. The horse snorted in surprise at the sudden move. Inches away from Holly's eyes were the grainy lines of old lumber. He held the edge of the manger and used it as a crutch to push and pull himself erect. He was eye to eye with the startled horse. He grinned at the bewilderment clear in the animal's face. "Me too, son, got no idea why I'm your neighbor." He rubbed the muzzle poking at his sore chest, lipping off bits of hay from his frayed shoulder. Holly needed water now, inside and out. It was a long trip to the water pump and trough, but worth the effort.

By the time George Kelleher found his way to the office and unlocked the door, his eyes still bleary from the evening's supply of whiskey, fuzzy hair pushed around his pink skull, he was surprised to find the drifter up and moving. The man's face had been washed clear of most of the dried blood, and he was forking hay down to the stock in neat piles, leaving no waste to drift to the floor. George watched in some amusement as the easy swinging throw of the pitchfork shortened as the man tensed, becoming aware of George's presence in the barn. He was right; this one would be hard to catch out, to sneak up on. Had to be on the run, but George didn't care about that, just that the man did his work.

George had a few words about the evening's events. Holly stood quiet, his face blank as the old man worked up to what he wanted to say. "Tough night, hey, cowboy? And sure looks to be you got the tougher end. Meant to tell about them two what whupped you, best do ex-act-i-tally what they tells you. They work for the Judge and he runs us all. Now hear what I am telling you and you'll get along fine." George drew out the words long and lovingly, letting Holly know about the situation.

The old man backed away from Holly, snuffled, coughed, and spat into the dust. Arms waving in wide general circles, he set off on his morning lecture of things to do. "You feed them broncs, get cleaned up and hit the cafe. Mary'll be expecting you. Good time to start on repairing some gear, got plenty, just been waiting for the right time to get the work started . . ." The voice went on, establishing its routine chatter, leaving Holly to pick out the important bits. He blocked out the sounds, left them buzzing at his throbbing head. He grained each stalled horse, finished shaking down the morning hay, and forked it to the horses outside, churning in the corrals, eager for their breakfast. The dun mare kicked out at the more greedy horses, establishing her supremacy in the herd.

Holly, too, was eager for his morning meal. His belly rumbled, gently in response to its tender condition, but still complaining that it was empty again. Spoiled by the feast of last night and willing for more. And still Holly hesitated at the cafe door, still reluctant to go inside, too conscious this morning of his battered face and body. A man brushed by him, fine whiskers fluffing out in his hurry for breakfast, and muttered a "nice morning" to the ragged man. The smell of hot coffee set Holly's mind, and he pushed aside the door to go inside, once again the frilly curtains setting up their fluttering welcome.

A tall woman, a big smile of welcome on her face, came to take his order. She knew her morning cutomers, and without asking a cup of coffee appeared at his place. She then read off the morning selection. The woman was wide and sturdy, carrying a good supply of flesh, obviously a product of her own proud cooking. He heard the words he wanted to hear. "We've got all you want." Coffee was his main interest. Inhaling the fragrant steam rising from the white chipped cup, he leaned on his elbows, head bent to the aroma, drinking deeply of the bitter black liquid.

This was going to work. This town would be all right. Even with the beating. He had work and food, a place to sleep. The coffee worked its magic, the tension lessened in his body, the aching muscles relented in their stiffness. He even attempted a brief smile at the big woman when she returned with a platter of eggs. She accepted his tentative greeting, and offered him more. "You're George's new helper, right? I'm Mrs. Simpson, Eb, here, and I run this place with Julie's help. Expect we'll be seeing you every day. Good. Eat up, I like to see my food enjoyed." Holly took her at her word.

He worked cautiously all day at the repairs. He sat stiffly, back braced against a wall in a corner of the stable. With the few tools Kelleher had, Holly worked easily with the gear, stitching broken and rotted bridle back together, replacing a crown piece, fashioning a new noseband, reworking a busted rein. Kelleher stayed away after first checking a finished driving bridle. His satisfaction showed in a brief, wide grin, a short chuckle. He could see the profits in front of him. Holly had nothing to say, preferring the rhythm of his work to any conversation, his hands moving with a swift sure touch over the dried bits of leather. When the stiffness got too much, he would stand slowly, easing his back, stretching through the pain. A walk out to the pump helped loosen him, a quick bath in cold water, then a trip out back to relieve himself. By evening much of the major work had been done. Tomorrow he could get to the horses, but tonight he would eat, slowly, then sleep.

The small town was proving easy to live in, the store-keepers only mildly suspicious of him at first. Timmons at the mercantile had kept his hand on his shotgun the first time Holly went inside. George had run out of tobacco and sent Holly to fetch some. He didn't like being an errand boy, but the uneasy truce between the old hostler and him was too fragile to shake, and he walked the short distance to the store.

Timmons could probably make his boast on "everything you could need." The store was piled high in a ragged and rough order, with anything a dreamer could want: lamps, ranch pants, iron skillets, and the bright colors of penny candy lined the counter-front and fought for space with opened tins of crackers, boxes of different sized nails, spools of thread. Toward the back of the store ranged the larger necessities, telling of the varying uses for the land. A few plows shoved in a corner, precious stacks of lumber, glass carefully protected in wooden forms, even a few new items, hinting at Timmons' faith in the future of his town: rolls of barbed wire, the newest type of rifle and shotgun. The walls were stacked with clothes, hats piled on top of each other, shirts mixed in with sturdy denim pants and fancy twills.

Holly made his small purchase and told the storekeeper to put the items on Kelleher's bill. Evidently George had gotten the word around, as the storekeeper took his hand away from his protection long enough to write out the slip for the few pennies worth of tobacco. He didn't smile, nor did he give Holly the usual storekeeper's call to come back. But he was glad for the business.

Holly had kept to himself, away from the saloon. Whiskey had lost its taste for him; he tagged the taste with lost tempers, jails, fights. A couple of times he had stood in front of the bootmaker's shop. But he never went inside. George had found him another cast-off pair of boots with some life left in them. And the sheepskin coat continued to warm him come evening. But his favorite place was the cafe. Eating regular had been lost to him after that paint stomped his hand, and it was a luxury he was willing to stick to a town for, at least for a while.

Holly sighed deeply, a complete, satisfied sigh. His third breakfast in a row, this time steak and eggs, fresh hot bread. And more coffee. He'd even come to the point where hot bread didn't make him check back over his shoulder. Today he would buck out the dun mare. Yesterday he had worked the bays lightly, to get a feel for them. Both were easy, enough buck in them to let you know they had heart, but steady and reliable, solid performers. Good horses, but without the spark of a great one.

The dun, well, she was another matter. Lean neck, good strong back, low-set hocks, heavy muscled gaskin, wide in the ribs for stamina, solid chest and rump for power. But her eyes told the story and signaled the oncoming fight. Large, clear, with an intelligent light. Willing to fight, ready to test man's supremacy, but also ready to learn and learn fast. Holly pushed away from the counter with a short nod to Mrs. Simpson. He felt light, free, a knot of anticipation in his chest. He barely noticed the sidewalk on his way back to the stable.

Fashioning a loop in one of Kelleher's ropes, Holly walked quietly into the large pen where the dun mare stood, now boss of the herd, working on her morning hay. The clean chiseled head came up, eyes quick to follow Holly as he walked to the center. Holding the loop in his left hand, right fingers bent around the coils, he stood quiet, relaxed. Almost without motion the loop snaked out across the pen and settled on the dun-colored neck. The horse lowered her head just as the rope touched her, and it slid off the wiry black mane. With her head still lowered, the dun looked across the dirt at the wrangler. Holly slowly pulled in the line, coiled it, and once again built a loop. He picked out another horse, ignoring the watchful dun. She shifted her attention back to her hay, intent on driving off an intruder with a threatening hoof. The rope slipped over the turned head to settle snugly around the neck just back of her poll. The dun reared in shock, snorted, then came down to stand quietly. The red-headed cowboy had at least rope-broke the horse, even if he hadn't got manners on her beyond that. Holly and the dun looked at each other down the long riata line.

The mare followed meekly out the pen gate and into

another, smaller pen. Here they could fight it out uninterrupted. Tying the dun, Holly opened a blanket under the horse's nose. The dun pulled back, eyes widened, nostrils distended to get the scent of the strange object. But she did not panic. Holly folded the blanket and laid it gently on the rigid back. Ears flat, the dun blew hard to show disapproval, but remained still. She received the saddle the same way, rigid and quiet, as if waiting to use her energy when it counted. Adjusting the hackamore around the clean head, Holly watched the eye. Alert, ready, it signaled the coming battle. He removed the choking rope, loosing the animal in the pen with reins snugged to the horn. He flapped his battered hat beside the dun's face, hoping to provoke a fight, to top off the horse's energy. The mare would have none of it. She shied from the hat, took a few walking steps, then stood waiting for her rider. She wouldn't fight an empty saddle.

"Smart son, ain't you." Holly grabbed the cheekpiece of the bridle and drew the mouse-colored head around to her left shoulder. He put his left foot in the bell-shaped stirrup, still holding the dun's head. Carrying a stiffness from his beating, he pulled himself into the saddle with some difficulty and gathered the reins in his right hand, bending the reluctant fingers around the braided horsehair mecate. He looked the dun mare in the eye, let go of the bridle, and waited. It wasn't a long wait.

The body beneath him tensed; the muscles rippled along the shoulders, the head came high, ears back. Her hindquarters sank almost imperceptably; she let out a bellow and shoved herself high from the corral ground to reach for an impossible height and come back to earth with legs straight, sending shock waves through Holly's loose body. He held the rein tight, and feathered his legs along the dun's shoulders, goading the animal to wilder and higher efforts.

He wasn't disappointed. The horse reached skyward again, dropped her right shoulder as she rose, twisted as she came down almost in the same spot. Holly slipped some in his balance; the dun spun in a circle to the left, sank down again on her haunches and sailed up, this time to drop a left shoulder and twist, almost bending in half with the effort. The mare landed up against the fence, jamming Holly's leg into the railings. She reared, threatening to fall backward from teetering hind legs. Holly loosened his feet, ready to bail out. The dun surprised him, lunging forward in a sky-high leap, twisting again at the top, and landed hard on four stiff legs. Before her rider could set himself again in the saddle, the dun took off, twisting violently as she rose in the air. Holly felt the saddle slip beneath him, lost the feel of the dun's head through slipping reins, and he fell hard to the packed earth, breath gone, head spinning. He rolled instinctively to the fence to get away from an attack. He stopped and struggled to sit up. The silence called to him beyond the ringing in his ears, and he looked around. The dun mare stood quietly across from him, head lowered, sides heaving to draw in air. Watching him, measuring him, eyes clear, ears relaxed, just waiting.

"You won that round, old son. Time to try again." Holly rose stiffly, feeling shaken but not damaged, except for his good opinion of himself. The dun snorted and turned her head aside as Holly reached for the bridle, but made no other move to elude the searching hand. Holly grasped the horn and wriggled the hull, settling everything back in place. The dun eyed her rider and waited patiently as he reached to stroke the sweaty neck, then lightly touched the tan muzzle. "Okay, again." He tugged his hat hard onto his head, pulled at his slipping pants, then brought the dun's head around again by the cheekpiece.

He mounted quickly and released his hold on the bridle as he picked up the mecate. This time the horse did not wait, but went straight to work, pounding hard as she rose in wild plunges, squealing with effort and rage as she reached out with her forelegs, hindlegs deep underneath her body in a squat. This time the twisting, sloping shoulder caught Holly

56

almost immediately, giving him no chance to find the rhythm, and he went flying to land in a roll on his shoulder, skidding across the churned dirt to bury his face in a pile of dust and manure.

Again he rolled, not out of fear this time but to find his balance and get up fast. He climbed the railings, eyes blurry, head ringing, a bitter taste of metal in his mouth. When his vision cleared some, he could see the dun, standing quietly again, head hanging, sweat gathering to drip off her belly and chest. Holly shook his head, shook it again. George Kelleher looked like three people standing to watch the performance. A man stepped forward from beside George, a solid, blocky man, short dark hair, neat rancher's garb, a hesitation in his step. "At least I'm not seeing triple yet." Holly spoke out loud to the dun. Both of them were startled by the intrusion of his harsh dusty speech in the stillness.

The man stopped and spoke to George, his voice clear against Holly's few words. "I thought you said this man could work out a rough horse. He is doing a very slipshod job with that dun mare. We best rework our deal with the bays; I cannot afford to buy horses that have been badly started." Holly's head came up at the harsh words, hot anger fought to the surface. He started toward the two men, then stopped. A slender woman dressed for riding in a dark divided skirt and fitted white shirtwaist, a hat hanging down her back on a braided thong, moved to stand beside the blocky man, her hand resting lightly on his arm.

Taking tight hold of his temper, Holly turned his attention back to the dun. The woman's gentle smile as she spoke to the rancher stayed in his mind, an unbidden memory. A few steps brought him back beside the dun to touch the wet face in a salute. He ran his hand down the damp neck to gather the fallen mecate. This time he did not pull her head around and did not use the stirrups, but slipped up into the saddle and tucked his feet in to urge the dun with his heels. The mare again did not disappoint. She left the ground in a

57

coiled jump, twisting again at the peak, landing hard on stilted legs to jolt her rider. Holly felt his head snap back; a trickle of blood leaked from between his clenched teeth.

Again and again the dun reared and plunged, but this time Holly had found the key and could stay with the mare, going with her rhythm of bucking, watching the powerful shoulders slide easily in the prodigious leaps. The horse began to tire as she reared, the plunges to earth less intense. Rather than egging the mare on to exhaustion, Holly eased up on her head, asking for her to move out across the corral instead of bucking in one place.

With a sigh of relief the mare went from a wild crowhop into a slow lope, circling the corral with her head stretched, sweat running through her dust-covered coat. With a squeeze and a light hold on the reins, Holly brought the mare to a welcome stop, slid off the far side, and went to the animal's head. He ran his fingers through the knotted forelock, down the fine-boned head, and cupped the muzzle in his hands, speaking soft nonsense. He led the dun back to the fence, where he stripped off the gear and scrubbed the hot steaming body with a wad of hay. The mare signaled her pleasure by wriggling her upper lip. Finished, he led the tired horse back into the large corral and turned her loose with a slap on the rump. No black hoof rose to challenge him this time.

Holly leaned back against the fence rails, raised a hand to wipe the crusted dirt from his face, and found his hand shaking. The dun had been a hard one to ride, a real thinker who put intelligence into the contest. Today he had ridden the mare, but it would take more days before the dun would give in completely and take to the training. Something moved near him; he set himself through his tiredness, alert to any danger.

George Kelleher came up to stand near Holly, still talking and gesturing with flying hands to the blocky man who was slow in keeping up with the old man. The young woman

58

walked slowly with the rancher, listening to George's erratic words. George spoke to Holly in uncertain tones, "This here is Mr. Hubbard, uh, Paul Hubbard. Uh, and this here is Holly Bishop. Hubbard here lives out beyond the Judge, just this side of Tyson's Station, up near where you got found by Kimball. He made a deal, we bargained for the two bays, Hubbard here needs them soon, they got to be broke, at least well started, the army likes their remounts . . ."

George's voice went on, searching for the words, filling the air, aware that the two men, the neat and clean rancher and the ragged unkempt wrangler were taking measure of each other and not paying attention to his bluster. Holly watched the rancher, saw the annoyance building as the old hostler rambled in his accustomed manner. His firm voice finally interrupted the tirade, the words carrying a precision and tone that betrayed the man's eastern background. "Yes, Mr. Kelleher, I do want those two bays well started, using no brutality. My son and I will finish them." The words silenced George; then the rancher turned his attention back to Holly. He was blunt and harsh in his statement. "I doubted your ability when I first watched you, but you finally stayed with the mare and did not bully her. I like that. You'll do well with the bays."

Holly barely listened as the man spoke to him. His eyes drifted beyond these two men and stayed on the girl, now standing with two horses. His horseman's eye ran over the horses, as well as the girl; good lines to the body, excellent head, clean legs, high spirited. He grinned slightly to himself as the girl swung her heavy chestnut braid, dark eyes showing anger as she read what this impudent wrangler was doing. Her hand tightened involuntarily on the reins and the two horses felt the tension, lifted their heads in response. Quality showed in both the girl and the horses.

He brought his attention back to the solid man in front of him, reading the quickening anger in the blocky face that drew deep lines across his forehead. His voice got deeper, demanding attention, drawing Holly to the meaning of his words. "I expect those horses by the end of next week. And you will deliver them along with a bill of sale. I will pay half now, as I may not be able to return to town before the drive, but will get the rest to you somehow. Perhaps this man," he indicated Holly with a short dip of his head, "will deliver the horses to the ranch." He left a long pause. "That is, if you can trust him."

Holly stiffened away from the fence. Even George shifted uneasily at the insult. Holly's face hardened; the pale amber eyes glinted with a mounting fury. The fresh scar across his forehead pounded, and his right hand pained as the fingers bent into a tight fist. He stood straight and still for a brief moment, then moved closer to Hubbard, still saying nothing.

The rancher recognized his blunder and the impending battle, but was uncertain how to handle his mistake. Fighting was not in his nature; he expected those he hired to do his bidding, not to fight back. He glanced quickly at Kelleher, but the old man only shook his head, his eyes fastened on Bishop. The bronc rider took another slow step, bringing him within striking distance; Hubbard unconsciously stepped back one step, then caught himself.

A soft voice entered between the two men. A woman's voice, gentle and firm. "Father, I am certain Mr. Bishop will do a good job and will deliver the horses on time. I know Mr. Kelleher trusts him." Her hand touched her father lightly on the shoulder, then slipped back to hang by her side. Holly eased his shoulders, stood quiet, and took a closer look at the young woman, Hubbard's daughter. Her slenderness was deceiving; she was tanned and muscled, hands worn with calluses, light freckles across her face, hair glowing with sun streaks. All the marks of someone who spent a good deal of time outdoors.

Sarah Hubbard turned to the bronc rider, her eyes wide with a smile, to become solemn upon closer inspection of the man she had just championed. She had resented his inspection earlier, but the man intrigued her. So unlike most of the men she had known, what they called a maverick. A slight frown caught her mouth, then she turned to her father, her voice low and serious. "I'm certain he will do fine, please don't worry."

Kelleher nodded vigorously in complete agreement with the girl, fat chins waggling as his head bobbled up and down. The stocky man softened at his daughter's words; he smiled, put an arm around her, and squeezed lightly. Holly backed away. He had recognized her slight frown; the beautiful young woman had taken a good look at him and his appearance turned her away. He walked to the pens, away from the three, feeling battered and kicked by the Hubbards, although only a few words had passed. Uneasy and restless, he wanted to get back to work, to put his hands on a responsive horse and ride out some man-eating bucks. Something violent to ease his anger.

The deepening shadows made it difficult to finish his work. The afternoon had gone to reweaving a new earpiece on a torn crown. Kelleher had wandered in and out as usual. He had stopped by Holly several times, cleared his throat, but never found the words he wanted and left on more important business. Holly kept his fingers at his work, but his mind returned to chestnut hair, bright brown eyes, and a soft, feminine shape. Finally he rose in slow stages, aware of being stiff again. He wondered briefly if he ever would be free of the stiffness; probably not, he thought. The self-pity angered him and he shook his head to put his mind to more immediate concerns. The stable door resisted his push, then groaned and gave way, spilling him outside in a hurry.

A high fluttering snort came on the still hot air, rising almost to a scream of terror. A fine-headed chestnut horse stood on his hind legs, pawing frantically at the man in front of him. Turner, heavy fist wrapped around split leather reins, raised his arm up and back, then completed a powerful swing that landed a loaded quirt on blood-flecked shoulders. The horse screamed again in pain and pulled harder at the reins, tearing his tongue on the sharp Spanish bit. Turner's arm came up and back again, ready for another blow. A stream of curses ran from him, directed at the panicked horse above him.

Holly yelled, as much in surprise as to break Turner's rage and deflect the murderous blow. The bulky man did not even turn his head at the sound of his name. The blow reached to the horse, tearing away more flesh from the raw shoulder. The high shrill scream came again and again as the animal tumbled backward to sit on its haunches, the pain driving all sense of balance from it. Turner lurched forward, eager to destroy the vulnerable animal. A whirlwind came between the heavy man and the chestnut; a flash of bright metal showed as a knife cut the tight leather line. The unexpected release pushed the teetering animal over on its side, and the horse rolled frantically, anxious to be up and free from the menace.

Hubbard's bright-haired daughter spun around to face the brutal tormentor, the small knife in her hand mocking her defenseless situation. Turner raised the quirt to her, drawing back his thick arm for a numbing blow. Holly came up fast behind the man to catch the slippery lash in his twisted right hand. He pulled in desperation, and his unexpected attack from behind lost Turner his edge. His big frame jerked off center; his hand lost its grip on the quirt, and with a murderous look in his eye the red-faced giant turned to face the new aggressor. Holly welcomed the confrontation; Sarah Hubbard had stayed rooted to her spot, too close to danger and too shocked to move.

The two men were head to head; the hulking, thick-legged giant and the tall, thin drifter. Turner stared in fury at the ragged-ass man in front of him. Holly was wired tight and ready, Turner's quirt hanging loosely from his right hand, his pale eyes anticipating the battle. Something in the amber glow shook the bigger man. Turner took an involuntary step back; he recognized the deadly rage in the lean cowboy and did not want to face it. Holly watched the slow retreat. He chose to stay near the girl, allowing Turner his escape.

The sharp click of two barrels of a shotgun being cocked, the double sound of death, stopped Turner's backward march. The sound had come from behind him. A voice spoke clearly, cutting the heavy air in the horse pens. "That is enough, Allward. You will not beat this horse again, or threaten my daughter." Paul Hubbard stepped out of the stable doorway, the shotgun resting easy in his hands. His careful voice spoke to Holly, cutting through the deafness his rage had built around him. "I regret I doubted you earlier, Mr. Bishop. Thank you for defending my daughter's impulses. Sometimes she thinks we are still back in Pennsylvania, where a policeman would come to her rescue." Hubbard inclined his head to include the shaken girl walking toward him. She smiled tentatively at Holly, her thanks shining through the dust covering her pale face.

Holly watched the soft smile come to her lips, wiping out the remnants of fear. Sarah scrubbed at the dust covering her arms and her face, and left a wide smudge on one cheekbone. Holly raised his hand partway as if to reach out and wipe the mark clean. He caught the move, and dropped his hand, to turn his anger on himself for the foolishness. The Hubbard girl stood close to her father for protection, and turned her back to Holly. Once again he felt as if he had been dismissed, cut off from these two people so different from himself.

Turner remained planted where he had stopped his retreat, his eyes holding an angry glare, his body unwilling to act. Paul Hubbard raised his shotgun one more time and gestured with the barrels, telling Turner to move on. Then he took Sarah and walked away with her.

Turner remained unmoving as the Hubbards left. But his mouth moved in a series of silent curses. As the two walked out of sight, the words became intelligible, the sounds just reaching Holly. "I'll get you for this, missy, don't think your pa's pretty manners will protect you for long out here."

CHAPTER FIVE

A slight, nervous man, with wispy hair fussing around his face was speaking to Kelleher, gesturing wildly and looking over George's shoulder at Holly, who was fiddling with the dun. It had been a week since the mare had quit bucking, and he'd been able to teach the horse a good deal. The bays had come along well, almost enough to deliver them to the rancher. Turner hadn't shown up anywhere around Holly; the townsfok had taken to nodding a greeting when he passed. And he was getting fat from Mrs. Simpson's fine cooking.

He stepped aside quickly as the dun mare spooked. George Kelleher stood next to him, and he hadn't heard the man come near. The fat horsetrader had the city-dressed gentleman with him. Kelleher himself looked spooked, and acted as if he had been bitten. "Bishop, Mr. Jenkins here wants a word with you. Lord only knows what kind of problems he's got, but you better listen." Holly led the dun back to the pen and returned, walking slowly and deliberately toward the slight man, stopping just short of him. He looked the man over carefully, watched his face, and waited. The man's restless moves quickened under the eyes of the hard-faced cowboy. His eyes refused to settle in one place; his hands tried to knot the side of his coat.

Ned Jenkins sputtered, coughed over his words, then finally got them going. "Mister, Judge Breen hears you're doing a fair job breaking these horses for George here, understands your work is just about finished. So the Judge wants you out at his place tomorrow to start work on his private stock. Pay is forty dollars a month and found, won't find better anywhere in the valley. The Judge always pays more than fair."

Finished with his speech, the lawyer turned and started to leave. It took him two beats to realize he had gotten no response from the wrangler. He half turned back and spoke quickly. "George can tell you how to get to the Judge's ranch, oh, and he wants the two bays also. Remember, he expects you tomorrow." Holly still said nothing, just looked at the small man, shook his head and went back to the pen and the horses. "What do you mean, no? You don't say no to the Judge," stammered the nervous man, his hands going to his jacket pockets for security. Holly kept his back to the man, feeling anger riding him hard. The lawyer's voice went on, becoming higher as he spoke. "George, you've got to talk with this man; it is ridiculous, I've done my job at least, now it is up to you. He must go to the Judge tomorrow with those two horses." With those final words the man went back through the stable, carefully picking his way around the piles of dung, unwilling to soil his city shoes, and shaking his head at the folly of refusing Jonathan Breen.

Holly spun around as George's heavy footsteps approached his back. "Back off, old man. No one hires me unless I choose. I'm taking those bays out to Hubbard tomorrow, filling your deal for you. Then I figure I'm done here." George's face was white, his mouth quiet. Who the hell was this Judge that folks jumped when he spoke. The hostler looked like a poleaxed steer, and that lawyer was worked up over not much, just some drifter saying no to a job. Holly was glad to be moving out of the valley.

He did some figuring; George owed him more than meals

and the haymow. He touched the old man on the shoulder and watched the round face blanch in fearful anticipation. His words came harsher than he intended. "Figure you owe me some hard cash and a bill of sale for that dun mare." Still speechless at the wrangler's refusal to work for the Judge, Kelleher only nodded his agreement and took off for his office and the hidden bottle. Here was his chance to get the drifter gone before the Judge's boys came around looking for him, this time with more than a beating in mind. He could truthfully tell them he had sent the man out to deliver the bays, and didn't know where he was. That was worth a five dollar gold piece.

A quick pull at his emergency bottle eased the old man's fears. Now he didn't care; he'd pay off the drifter and be glad to see him gone. He watched the dark face tighten as he gave over a shiny five dollar gold piece and a small bit of paper delivering ownership of the dun. The pale eyes had cleared of their anger, and now showed a deep weariness and little else. George surprised himself. He was going to miss this quiet, slow-talking rider, miss the unexpected streak of humor behind the silent face. A man to trust, even if he never let anyone get near. But George would not let his feelings show. "Here, take that old sheepskin, be good up in the mountains, take a couple of blankets too. I'll be going to Rand's, I . . ." For once he ran out of words. Little showed on the thin face in front of him, only a tightening around the mouth as if words were trying to be spoken. George backed away and scurried out the door.

A bleak grin touched Holly's face. George was in a hurry. The whole town was in a hurry wherever this Judge was concerned. It was time for him to get out, and he was glad to be going. The unexpected gold piece sparkled in his hand. Hard cash was a luxury he hadn't had for a long time. A bath and a haircut were the first things on his mind. He'd been washing in the water trough each morning, but that cold mountain water and no soap didn't take much of the grime away.

Scraping away at his beard with the same cold water and a borrowed razor from George didn't suit him much either. Two bits could be thrown away on some hot water and a barber. Supplies from the mercantile first: coffee, flour, beans, some airtights of tomatoes—they'd beat rancid horsemeat and ice water on the trail. Holly knew that the towno folk didn't particularly want him in their stores, especially now that the Judge was after him, but they would take his money. They had the same disease as George, fear, and with Kelleher over at Rand's going on about his refusal to work at Two Crown, the fear would work for him and the service would be faster. He could leave this town sooner.

Holly thought briefly about what had slipped out of George about this contract deal with Hubbard. The whole town knew, although it was supposed to be secret. Now that the bid was set, Breen's two bullies were working to make sure no horses got to the fort through Hubbard. And the town was going to let him get away with the steal. All this so that one man could get his hands on a blooded stallion. He hadn't seen the horse, but it must be one fancy stud. But not worth ruining a family for.

Holly hurried his steps, his thoughts driving him faster. Having things twisted some people, made them greedy for more. He stopped and stood on the slanted steps leading inside the darkened store. There was a sense of distance between himself and the world he dealt with, a feeling that he was safer chasing the wild horses, riding the outlaw broncs, than trying to live with his own kind.

He had to grin at the barber's face when he pushed open the glass-fronted door and walked into the deserted shop. The man just plain didn't want him in the place. He watched bemusedly as the nervous man fussed with his working tools, moving razor handles from here to there, straightening the mugs belonging to his regular customers. "Need a bath and a haircut; shave, too." Holly spoke loudly in the empty room.

The small man jumped as if he hadn't seen Holly come

inside. His voice came cracked and high. "I'm just about to close up, need to close for just the day. Please to come back tomorrow, if you please."

Holly remained in front of the man, his words insistent and strong. "All's I want is what you advertise on your pole out front, a bath and a shave, today."

He walked around the frozen barber and through a door out to the big wooden tub set in the back room. He called to the still unmoving man. "I want me out of here too, sooner than you." With those words acting as a spur, the gray-haired man finally reacted. He hurried to the copper vat of steaming water, drew two buckets, and poured them into the large tub. Holly watched in silence as the man scurried back and forth with buckets, to finally get enough depth in the tub for a good soak. Holly undressed, hanging what passed for his clothing on wooden pegs, and slowly climbed into the beckoning steam.

The barber found himself reluctantly fascinated with his customer. The word had gone quickly around the small town that this man had refused the Judge, in fact, was going against his orders. Such an ordinary-looking man, not large and fierce like Turner and Jack. Sitting in the high-sided tub, his eyes closed, body relaxed, he looked not at all like someone who would have the strength to defy anyone. His long angular body was covered with scars from years of battling horses; knots on his side rode over broken ribs; one collarbone showed an awkward pitch from a badly healed break. The barber turned his eyes away from the white scars crossing the pale back. He did not want to know more about this man's painful humanity. A quiet voice called to him; the request was simple, thoughtful. "Why don't you shave me in here, save time my sitting up in your chair out front, near all those windows. Cut the hair too. Save more time."

Holly heard the barber thumping around in the front of the store, collecting his instruments, and marveled at the man's obvious fear. The Judge carried a pretty big stick to run fear through a simple barber because a drifting bronc rider disobeyed him. He put the small town and its problems aside and luxuriated in the bath. He stretched his full length, the water running up and over his shoulders, carrying whirlpools in differing patterns along his legs. The warmth, the soft edge of cleanness, the sweetish smell of soap, lye mixed with pine, slowly washed away the remnants of the long walk through the mountains, the taste of rancid horsemeat, his own vomit. If being with people meant he could bathe with regularity, it almost would be a favorable trade.

Less than a half-hour later, Holly stepped gingerly from the shop. Clean shaven, lower face white against his darkened forehead, a ring of white around his neck, he looked almost civilized. Carrying the supplies from the mercantile in a burlap bag, he pushed open the cafe door, sending the frills shivering and the bell clattering to announce his entrance. He absently took his accustomed seat at the counter. Vaguely annoyed at the instinctive routine, he shifted seats, and felt an odd relief at the gesture. Julie Warner's young, cheerful voice interrupted his thoughts, to ask what he wanted.

Julie's mouth relaxed, the lower lip slightly parted. She smiled to herself, reading in Holly's changed exterior a relaxing of his guard. "You sure look nice, did you finally find yourself a girl?" She curled her voice around the last words, taking her rightful place as the girl in her question. Now this man would pay attention to her. A giggle came from her; she had finally won him.

Holly straightened up at the teasing implications in the young girl's words. He only knew one response to a woman's teasing, and it was not the way to answer this young one's innocent words. Angered at his own reaction, his voice growled at her, the order almost unintelligible in the harshness. "Coffee, steak, pie." He could not look into the clean young face, did not see the mouth turn to a pout, then to set in anger at his rebuff. Julie blushed, the red staining her

70

soft complexion.

Returning with his order, she stared at the bent head, the shaven neck smooth enough to stroke, the clean pine scent covering his ingrained horse odor, the thick dark hair shining and damp, suggesting a clean body beneath his old shirt. Unused to such heavy pictures, secure only with her childlike flirting and not understanding the thickening response of a man, Julie fought to cover her growing confusion. "Well, if you don't want anyone to say hello, why get yourself all clean and pretty. It sure don't change your attitude any, so why bother? Bet the vermin leave you alone anyways, too nasty to taste good, so why look human if you don't want company?"

Surprised by the strength of her outburst, Julie whirled around and flew into the kitchen to grab a cloth and take long, furious swipes at a counter-top, cleaning away any kind thoughts she had of the drifter. Holly sat hunched and quiet, the food stuck in his throat. Her words and the feelings behind them stunned him. He had done nothing to cause such violent feelings, didn't want or expect any kindness from her or anyone else in this damned mountain town. It was time to be moving. He put down his last dollar to pay for the food; this last meal wasn't going to be on George. The sack of supplies heavy in his left hand, Holly left the cafe, door banging, curtains flying and the steak uneaten.

Holly eased the saddle onto the bay gelding's back, settled it in place, and reached for the cinch. Of the two geldings, this bay was least likely to give trouble leading the other two on the trail. George had agreed—it made no sense to try leading from the dun; there would be a tangled mess when she took it into her head to fight, and George wanted those bays delivered clean, to wherever they went. The second bay, a blocky, solid animal, was strong enough to pull the dun along when she got cranky. Holly roped the two horses together, running a neck rope on them cavalry style, and ran the rope through the bay's halter to his saddled horse.

George worried, "Here, now, don't put any marks on that bay, want them two delivered unmarked. I expect my full payment, why don't you take . . ."

Holly stopped listening, Kelleher would get to the point eventually. ". . . you turn off before the fork to Tyson's Station, follow along the creek for a bit, can't miss their Rocking H sign; Hubbard built himself a nice place up there. Not a bad ride, should get you there by dark." George had put it plainly, he expected the horses to go to Hubbard, yet Holly knew the old man would whine and tell Breen's boys that he had sent the horses on to the Judge.

He swung up on the bay, reined the gelding around, and headed out beyond the stable to the mountain trail. George watched the man go, thought to say something, then changed his mind and decided it was time for his afternoon pick-me-up. He muttered loudly as he shoveled thoughts around in his mind. "Glad the man is gone, guess I be needing to find someone else to work around here, mite easier with a body doing the shoveling instead of me. Getting too old for this kind of work." His mind at ease about the disappearing horses, he closed the stable door and picked his way down the wooden walk to the coolness of Rand's.

The dun pulled and jerked on the neckline, knocking the chunky bay off the trail. Holly reached back with the end of the rope and walloped the mare on the neck. "Quit fighting, you bullhead, just walk along nice." The mare settled sullenly in place, and Holly turned back to watch the trail, aware of the pleasure of being on the move again, especially with a good horse under him. Too bad this bay was going to end up in the army. He could just head up over the pass with these three horses. Slicked up and fattened, he'd bet no one in the town of Elkin would recognize him as the bread thief of a few weeks ago. George wouldn't expect payment for three or four days, give him a good head start. But it would be horse stealing.

The dun mare jerked again, almost yanking the rope from

his hand. Damn bronc. Holly reined the bay up and waited for the two horses to settle out. A touch with his heels put the bay into a lope, the dun leaped forward and fell to her knees from the counterweight of the other horse. The two staggered forward in a seesaw motion, found their rhythm at the lope and eased up alongside the ridden horse. Holly pushed his bay into a gallop, stringing the others behind him. Running them until their sides heaved, he pulled back into a trot for a breather, then on again into a slower gallop.

Holly and the three horses made their way to the fork, one way to Tyson's Station, the other to the Rocking H. Hubbard's road turned right, winding through sparse trees, deep into the hills. He checked the horses for a moment and leaned on the saddle horn. Here was his decision. He gigged the bay forward and swung onto the right-hand trail, up toward the hills. The constant running had settled the edge off the three, and they were content to walk along, snuffling and snorting as if they, too, were glad to be out of the confines of town. Behind him opened a wide valley, ahead the road wound around broken rock and grassy slopes to disappear up into the mountains.

CHAPTER SIX

Miriam Hubbard stood at the back kitchen door, watching the two figures working in the corral. Her husband's dark head was bent, listening to the soothing words their son spoke to a rugged sorrel gelding, held by a taut rope to the snubbing post set deep in the middle of the pen. She could almost hear his words.

"Dad", Paul's head came up to look at his son. "I think he's ready for the saddle now. I've sacked him twice and he don't seem to mind much."

Paul Hubbard stepped away from the sorrel. "This one is yours, Jimmy, you think he's ready, I'll go get the gear." When Hubbard returned with the well-worn saddle and blanket, his son grinned at him, the young face split in a wide smile.

"I like it better when we work with our own stock, they're much better than these broncs you had to buy. This one's all right," he patted the yellow neck, "but we've got one light sorrel that's going to be a real stomper."

Paul smiled at the superiority implied in the boy's comment. Not only did they handle their stock from birth, but Paul was convinced that the bloodlines that came through Tower, his thoroughbred stallion, put a higher intelligence and a readiness to accept man in the offspring.

Standing next to the boy, the father-son relationship of the two was obvious. Paul Hubbard was a solid, stocky man of middle height, with thinning dark hair, dark eyes set deep in his square face, lines of humor around his eyes and mouth. Hard work showed in new scars on his hands, and the heavy muscles bunched under his handmade calico shirt. The son was a younger, newer version, not yet filled in, with hair only shades lighter that showed the auburn tints from his mother. The boy had been born with his parents' love of horses, and showed a remarkable talent in working with the young stock.

The Hubbards had built a simple and sturdy working ranch when they first moved on to their land. They had had years back east to plan and change plans, so their ranch layout was built with ease and economy in mind. The main house was a square building, a big room across the front where the bookwork was done, and the rare treat of company was received. A stairway led to the loft, partitioned into two bedrooms, one for their two daughters, Sarah and Amy, the baby, and the other for Jimmy, just turning nineteen. A large study separated the two rooms. Across the back was the huge kitchen and pantry, and their own bedroom, with quick access to the stable directly across from the back door. In spring this was invaluable, since older mares and those with foaling problems could be brought in for close attention.

The slender woman continued to watch as her two men worked with the reluctant gelding. Her hair was a bright auburn, her eyes a steady gray. Age had begun to catch her, but the energy and enthusiasm for her life showed in the small laugh lines webbing her eyes, the light brown of her face. Her figure had thickened from carrying three children, but she still walked with pride. It took only a warm glance from her husband to send her laughing into his arms. But now worry covered the easy smile in her eyes. The contract concerned her. Paul had accepted the slip that had given them the information about the Judge's bid. He found nothing strange in the skinny, pinched-face drifter who had dropped by for a meal and had left behind the figure from Turner's mouth. It made sense to him that the Judge's bank would lend him more money, even with the amount they still owed outstanding. He saw this as their chance to get free. But she was suspicious of any luck that a person had not made for themself.

Four years ago they had come west from Pennsylvania, where Paul had worked the family farm for almost sixteen years. With the death of his father, they had decided to strike off on their own, taking their share from the sale of the farm. Finding this piece of land was the first good bit of luck, then a major setback came in the almost-fatal fall Paul had taken from the newly built barn. His leg had been crushed, and he was unconscious for four days. Miriam had been hopeful when Sarah had fallen in love with the wrangler hired to work the stock while Paul was mending. But Ward Berringer was too much a fiddlefoot, and only stayed to see Paul walking with a cane before he left, taking Sarah with him as his wife.

Miriam wiped her hair from her eyes, she still did not know fully what had happened, why Sarah had come home so quiet, reluctant to say anything more but that Ward had been killed, roping a bull on a bet, caught by the raking horns. That had been almost three years ago. Jimmy had started working with the horses, getting the young stock ready for sale. But they had had to take out loans to pay for the help and to finish the barn before winter, and to cover the six months Paul had been so ill.

Now the contract offered a way free from debt. But it seemed too easy to her that one of the Judge's men would drop the bid amount up at Tyson's, where word would be certain to get back to Paul. She remembered the anger in the Judge's face when Paul refused to sell him Tower. Paul heard only the polite words, and did not see the fury color-

76

ing the man's face a brilliant red. Still, even with her fears and concerns, Miriam Hubbard was happier in these mountains than ever before.

Sounds of commotion disturbed her revery. The evening meal would soon be ready, and the two men would be hungry. Their youngest child, a delight and a surprise to her parents after eight years with the older two, came running out of the hot kitchen to her mother. Long hair caught in braids, freckles covering her nose, wearing her brother's made-over pants, she still carried the proud look of her mother in the gray blue eyes and bright auburn hair. "Quick, Ma, Sarah says dinner is getting too done, or something like that. I'm hungry now, are Pa and Jimmy done with that old horse yet? I'll go down and get them now?" Amy's questions pushed aside her mother's concerns and returned her to the present.

"Yes, they're just about done, go tell them dinner will be waiting." Miriam pushed the back door open and the heat from the black range enveloped her. "Sarah, let's get those greens cooking and I'll check the biscuits."

Amy's flight to the corral caught her brother and father still working with the sorrel. Her sudden appearance spooked the animal, who pulled hard against the snubbing rope, rearing in fright. Jimmy caught the rope and pulled the horse down, touching his head and crooning to the trembling horse. The little girl climbed the fence and sat breathless at the top. "Pa, Jimmy, dinner's ready, I'm hungry, oh I'm sorry, horse, I didn't mean to scare you." Her clear voice rang across the corral, and the horse pricked his ears in question. Jimmy started to let out his anger but his father's hand stopped him.

"She's only a little one, Jim, and doesn't understand." He looked at his youngest with affection. "Well, you say it is time for dinner, and I bet you don't want anything to eat at all." The small child grinned at her father's teasing, and jumped down to stand next to him.

Hoisting his sister up on his shoulders, Jimmy Hubbard caught up with his father on his slow walk to the house. Only walking showed the limp, the damage from the broken thigh and smashed tibia. Once on horseback, the injury did not show, or impede his riding. Miriam looked up and smiled as the three stood at the back door, splashing ice cold water and laughing. Dinner was ready.

The tree shadows were lengthening and the sun beginning to set behind the high rock walls when Holly came up to the creek trail and followed it. A long stop at the water rested the horses, easing their thirst from the dusty trail. The earlier mud had dried, and a hint of the long dry summer was in the pale film on the horses' necks. It was tempting to camp along the creek, quiet and uncrowded. But his luck would run to losing one of the bays and having to spend the night hunting a stray horse. Best get on to the Hubbard ranch, deliver the two, and be on his way, with no further obligations. He could camp here on the way back.

Coming out of a draw that opened into another flat grassland, Holly reined up. Ahead were lights, the dim shapes of buildings in the dusk, and a wooden bridge to welcome the traveler. A small sign hung from a tree; burned into it was the Rocking H brand. Holly walked the animals slowly across the wooden planking and into the yard. The mare danced on the line, excited by the echo of her footsteps on the bridge floor.

The ranch was sturdy, built with pride. Here lived a family. Holly thought again about the Judge's scheme and shook his head. He pulled up at the barn and slid down from the bay. The mare's excitement grew. Perhaps she scented the stallion. She would be unsafe to leave tied while he went to the house. And soft hints of something cooking was coming on the air, reminding his spoiled belly that he had missed two meals this day. He smiled at himself, spoiled so easily.

He took the horses inside, untied the neck ropes, and put the animals in standing stalls. The grain was easy to find. Hubbard was a methodical man and the feed was carefully stored in bins in its own neat room. It was easy to find a brush; the bay wore a saddle mark and a bit of work would remove it. He fell into the rhythm with the brush, the sounds of the horses feeding, a light wind pushing at the barn walls. He could relax here, let tired muscles ease.

A sudden movement slipped beyond the row of stalls. By instinct he crouched down, the horse stirring restlessly at the abrupt act. Something metal rapped against the wall; a door opened beyond the light. He waited, cautious. His rifle was still in the scabbard, still unloaded. Town living had softened him. Another sound as metal hit metal. Holly slipped toward the back of the stall; the bay lifted a hoof in warning. A shadow came up on the wall, lit by a swinging lantern. He watched a figure come along the line of stalls and pause to look at the dun mare, who half-reared against the tie rope, the banging metal spooking her. A few more steps and Holly lunged out of the stall, tackling at knee height the dark figure he could just see.

They went back together into the loose hay. An arm swung wide; something hard cracked at the side of Holly's head. Stunned, he loosened his grip on the legs, which kicked hard at him, catching him in the knee and thigh with pointed toes. Something wet and warm poured over his shoulders; he fell forward onto the body beneath him, driving his opponent further into the hay. His head sunk into soft warmth, and a confusion of memories came unbidden to his mind.

A sharp voice broke the fog. "What in hell are you doing, who are you, damn you, get off me, all the milk is gone, you . . . what are you doing in our barn, get off of me." The last was said in rising anger, and Holly could recognize the woman's voice. He rolled over and sat hunched up, rubbing at the stinging on the side of his head. The girl continued to rage as she struggled to get out of the thick hay pile. "What do you think you are doing, planning to spend the night or just take what you can find? Do you usually knock people down in their own barn? Oh damn you for all this."

Sarah Hubbard reached the light she'd dropped when the intruder had brought her down. It had landed upright in a depression of hay, unhurt. For some reason this made her even angrier. "You could have burned the barn, you fool. Let me look at you, I'll . . . oh." Her voice quieted. The lamp held close to his face highlighted the invader, the bronc rider from George Kelleher's, her defender against Turner Allward. The man opened his eyes at the close light; she saw anger, pain, and something unsettling in the amber eyes. His shirt was covered in milk, which she had just taken from the cow, milk running from his hair, pooling in his shirt collar. Some of the liquid had rivulets of blood threading through it.

"Ma'am, I'm sorry—"

"Mister, I didn't mean to—" Both spoke at once then stopped, waiting for the other. Holly looked at the girl briefly, then nodded and closed his eyes against the invading light. "I really didn't want to cut you, I just swung the bucket and I guess the pail cut into you. I am sorry." Sarah heard herself apologize to this intruder, and her temper started to rise. She knew she still was in this man's debt, but her anger caught hold and took over. "What am I doing, why are you in our barn in the dark, why did you attack me, what is going on?"

Holly took a sharp breath and looked at the girl. She was as beautiful as he remembered. Strong, female, opinionated. He could see her fury building and tried to explain. The words weren't there. "Miss, I came here to deliver those horses. You surprised me so I jumped you." He took another deep breath and released it. "Sorry, too, for the milk." A flash of memory came to him, another warm barn, a lady in long skirts, soft hands holding his, teaching him to milk their cow. He shook his head at the unbidden thought and immediately paid for the action. Flecks of milk and blood came away on his hand when he gingerly explored the pain.

The lantern accentuated the woman in front of him, high-lighting the outlines of her figure. A man's shirt tucked into worn ranch pants, high swelling breasts pushing the shirt, a slender waist flowing into wide hips, long legs. Sarah became aware of the roving glance, and the anger in her brown eyes flashed brighter. "I didn't exactly expect company when I came out here to do my chores. You don't belong here, this is my home."

Don't belong anywhere, the thought jumped into Holly's mind. To push it out, he picked up the fallen bucket. "I'll apologize again if that's what you want."

He rose stiffly, conscious of the stained shirt and his own growing anger. This woman disturbed him, right from the first time he saw her. Made him too aware of her. Sarah remained standing directly in front of Holly, as if challenging him, her eyes glowing with their own anger.

His hand rose with the empty bucket, a silent pleading gesture for forgiveness. Sarah reared back, instant fright fighting her anger. "Don't you come near me again. I'll tell my father to expect you up at the house, and you better have a good explanation. Don't you take anything, you hear me . . ." The young woman turned from her attacker and fled, leaving Holly confused and alone.

He rubbed the corner of his ear. His reception up at the house should be a winner. He rolled some hay into a wisp and used it to wipe up the milk, already drying on his shirt. He would smell pretty come morning. Be a perfect match with Kelleher's sheepskin. Baths may feel good, but their effects didn't last long. He kept his wandering thoughts away from the disturbing woman who had shattered his isolation. He continued his clean-up, dunking the hay swipe in a bucket and sponging at the dried blood. Attempts to straighten his shirt and brush the hay from his jeans only made him feel more like a penitent begger. Finally he made his way to the brightly lit ranchhouse.

A knock on the front door opened it instantly. Paul Hubbard's first words were accusing, brittle, at odds with the soft clipped sound of his eastern-shore voice. "You brought the bays, I hear. Didn't Kelleher tell you to come to the house, or don't you know any better?" Hubbard's eyes went over the rider, taking in everything in great detail, as if checking against the previous opinion. Holly stayed at the doorway, unwilling to accept any proffered hospitality. At the quiet, bitter words, Holly's temper rose hot and heavy in his throat, making the words come thick. He did owe the man a few words of explanation.

Pale amber eyes shielded themselves from the probing of the deep-set dark ones. Holly spoke too loudly. "Mister, these broncs are just green broke, didn't trust them to tie while I explained. Apologized to your daughter, owe you one, too. But that's the end of it." He took the piece of milk-stained paper from his shirt pocket and handed it to the now-silent rancher. "Kelleher wants his money pronto." He thought again of the Judge's scheme, almost spoke his thoughts, then retreated. Too entangling. This family would take him apart. He nodded curtly to the rancher and stepped back away from the door.

Before the dark claimed him, a woman's voice, a new voice, came from inside, clear and insistent. "Just a minute, you need that cut tended to, and supper, you'll want a meal before you ride off." A lady who could only be Hubbard's wife, a gentle smile on her face, moved next to the blocky rancher. She put out a hand to pull Holly back into the large room. "You must be Holly Bishop. I've wanted to thank you for helping Sarah in town. You've made your apologies; there is no need for you to leave now." She turned to her husband. "Paul, it looks like he came off second best in the argument. Sarah is fine, and he is the one needing attention."

As the gentle-faced lady made her plea, a small girl

82

bounced into the room, running up to her mother, eyes wide in excitement. "Sarah's in the kitchen saying bad words and looking mad. She's just like she was before she ran away with Ward." A young man followed, Hubbard's son. He put a hand on the thin shoulders and tried to hold the child. She twisted her body and slipped next to her father to look up at Holly with shining eyes. "You look funny, you're bleeding. You mad, too, or something, mister?" A simple question from an unknowing child. Panic took Holly's mind. There were too many people, all crowding, pushing, wanting to know. Wanting him trapped inside. He had to leave.

"Mister, my mommy won't hurt you." The little girl's face had lost its high excitement, was now drawn and worried. This man was hurt and no one was helping.

Miriam Hubbard watched guardedly as the hunted, panicked look left the drifter's face, replaced by the simple wants from fatigue and pain. He was responding to the simple request from Amy to stay and be cared for. She wasn't used to people like this rider: hard, lonely, withdrawn from civilization and its simple courtesies. She put her hand on the hard-muscled arm, feeling the immediate tense response to her gesture. "Do come in to the kitchen, Mr. Bishop; let me clean out that cut and there's supper you can have." Miriam Hubbard turned away from the drifter and started across the big room, clearly expecting him to follow. The rest of the family backed away as if to give him plenty of room, then trailed behind to troop into the kitchen.

Sarah stood with her back toward the intruder, stirring something on the black stove. Her mother offered a chair; near it were a bowl and some white cloth. Holly sat gingerly on the chair edge while the woman cleaned away the bits of hay and dried milk from the shallow gash behind his right ear. She was appalled at his battered condition. The almost-invisible white line to his notched ear, the horrible right hand. Leaning over to finish the cleaning, she noticed the newly stitched line across his forehead. "Looks like you've been fighting someone else recently." She lightly touched the rawness. "Looks like they might have won." Unstrung by the evening's events, Holly glared at the woman, her face so close to his, her eyes, so much like her daughter's in their steady look, held a glint of teasing which softened the words. Confusion flooded him; reacting so quickly to the gentle words as if they were an insult. Miriam finished her ministrations and patted the tense shoulder.

A plate of food was slammed down in front of Holly. Sarah's voice startled him in its fierceness. "You knock me down and attack me in my own barn, then get brought in here and treated like a lost colt and I have to serve you supper. Here." A plate of cold biscuits bounced onto the table; a fork and knife followed. "Get your own coffee." She swung through the door, pushing past her father and brother as the two men came in silently and sat at the table, joining Holly with a cup of coffee. The silence lengthened. Finally Hubbard spoke.

"You can spend the night in the barn. I want to see you work those two bays come morning. Kelleher promised they'd be well started, and I don't want any surprises. I've got just shy two weeks to fill that contract, and don't plan to waste time. Good night." Holly pushed back away from the table, nodded his thanks, and stepped out the back door to make his way in the dark back to the barn. Outside, away from the crowding of that family, brought him instant relief. Almost as bad as being locked in the small hole in prison, the same closed-in feeling, too tight, too many demands. A familiar pile of hay in the barn welcomed him; rolling in his blankets he was asleep instantly.

"Is he the bronc rider Mr. Kelleher told you about?" Jimmy asked his father as they sat companionably at the table.

Paul Hubbard answered slowly, speaking his doubts of the man. "Kelleher said he never did get used to this man, said he always looked to run at the nearest noise. Always wondered if he was wanted. He's got a touch with the wild stock, though, about half wild himself."

"And lonesome," added his wife. "He doesn't know how to act around people at all." Another moment of peaceful quiet.

Then Amy's childish voice spoke high and clear. "I like him, he's got funny eyes."

At the sound of her voice, both parents moved from the table to put their family to bed. One by one the lights went out and only Sarah was left awake and alone, sitting in the dark, remembering her short-lived marriage, and wondering about the man sleeping by himself in the barn.

CHAPTER SEVEN

The ornate white house stood out sharply in the shadows, its double-storied elegance unique among the ground-hugging dwellings of most of the ranches in the valley. Judge Breen had insisted it be built this way, to remind him of his family home. It had a manufactured air of dignity, with high, double glass doors set back from the front veranda. Inside, the Judge paced vigorously up and down the heavy dark room he called the library, paneled with books lightly covered with dust. His pace was carefully structured in time, each step counted and recounted.

A plump woman, dressed in dark colors relieved only by a long white apron, knocked at the library door. Her voice was toneless, impersonal. "Judge Breen, Mr. Allward and Mr. Levitt are here." She waited for a short moment, anticipating the timing of the Judge's response. Nothing could disturb his pacing.

"Let them in, now, Mrs. Hutton, and bring the coffee. And the bottle."

He resumed his pacing, not breaking stride as the two men entered his room. "He never showed, Judge, and I checked with Jenkins; he did deliver the message to Kelleher and the drifter." Jack Levitt kept his voice even, clean of all expression.

Turner giggled, "Yeah, we had a talk later with old George, he did tell us Bishop heared Jenkins out, told him to forget it. Old George said the drifter was to take the two remount horses out here, then he was figuring on leaving the area. But he ain't never showed, we figured—"

The Judge interrupted brusquely, dubious of any thoughts Turner might have. "Tomorrow you two will go to the Hubbard place, check carefully, and see that the bronc rider does not remain there, if indeed he is there at all. Do not let anyone see you; get at him while he's off the place or there alone. Of course, if he has gone, the problem is solved, except for the return of the horses. I trust you two know that he must not be allowed to stay there and help Hubbard. I repeat, he must not be allowed to remain. If he has gone, scout around the horse herd, note how many horses there are, and how close you think Hubbard is to moving the horses to the fort. Also, check for ambush points; do some good ground work. But for now, leave the Hubbards alone. That's all. Mrs. Hutton will have your whiskey for you when you leave. Good night."

The Judge turned his back on the two men, their signal for dismissal. He resumed the pacing, to wait for the coffee, oblivious of the hirelings. Jack and Turner let themselves out; this was their routine: the evening report, tomorrow's duties, and the bottle. Once outside, Turner took a long pull from the whiskey. "Tomorrow ought to be interesting, partner." He grinned devilishly at Jack's forbidding face. "We got license to roust that drifter any old way we choose, yep, mighty interesting." Levitt said nothing, just reached for the bottle.

Holly rolled over quickly and came up in a crouch, reaching for his rifle tucked under the blankets. Something had moved, and he couldn't pinpoint the distraction. He straightened slowly to become aware of his surroundings. This was not Kelleher's livery, where a strange sound could mean trouble, but the barn at Hubbard's Rocking H. He listened again; the noise that had awakened him was someone milking that cow again. A morning and evening chore.

He relaxed slowly, feeling foolish. He sure was causing a ruckus over a milch cow. Putting the rifle down with his gear, he went outside with a bucket and pumped up some bitterly cold water. Resting the bucket on a stool, he took a very brief morning wash. His shirt collar smelled of sour milk, and the side of his head was tender—sweet memories of last night. The air was clean, the sun just sliding up behind the trees in back of him, and a pervasive smell of coffee came from inside the house. Breakfast. Raking his fingers through thick, tangled hair, and trying to pick hay from his shirt, Holly headed to the back door.

A cheerful voice greeted him. "A cup of coffee, Mr. Bishop, and some breakfast." Miriam Hubbard's flushed face peered at him through the back door, and her gesturing hand offered him the hospitality of the warm kitchen. "Please, do come in, my husband and Jimmy will be right in from their chores."

Holly remained outside, still reluctant to enter their home. These people were too fast for him, they had accepted him without judgment and offered their home, their food, He was out of place here, and had no business being with a family when his presence would only bring trouble. "Ma'am, I'm better off out here, steps'll do me fine. Don't want to be a bother. Thank you just the same."

Miriam stopped her work in the kitchen. Coffee pot in hand, she took a long, studying look at the man on the other side of the door. He was right; he was an outsider on their ranch. The wildness deep in his face promised a temper and an edge of violence unknown to them. His manners hinted that he had known better at some time, but now he lived close to the edge, more an outlaw than just a drifting cowboy. For a swift moment she felt fear, then she breathed deeply and made her choice.

"Please, come in. Never mind Sarah's assessment of you last night. I know you would like a cup of coffee. Takes the chill away." She held out a full cup and gestured once more to the heavy plank table.

The open and honest smile offered Holly something he rarely saw, true kindness and compassion. He took the steps slowly, opened the door, and came to sit where she indicated. The cup rose stiffly to his mouth and he drank deeply of the bitter, burning liquid. "Pure honey," he murmured. And louder, "Thank you, ma'am."

"At least call me Mrs. Hubbard," she countered. This young man appealed to her; beyond his awkward and ragged looks lay a hint of gentleness. She hoped Paul could use him with the stock. It would be interesting to learn about him.

Standing near where Holly sat, to stir the eggs frying on the black stove, Miriam reached out and lightly touched the cut behind his ear; his quick threatening response of raised hand and angry eyes startled her, and she stepped back abruptly. Smiling sheepishly at his own behavior, Holly offered a flag of truce, "At least there will be milk for your breakfast this morning with me out of the barn. The bucket should make it to the house." Miriam accepted the offering, and called for the rest of the family to come and sit.

The silence was companionable as breakfast ended. Sarah had not come in from the barn before they were done. Her mother knew what was bothering her daughter, and would talk with her later. Paul spoke softly, ending the silent meal. "Amy, go get your books. Your mother's got lunch ready; I'll catch up Spreckles for you. School time." The small girl wiggled out of her chair next to Holly, and ran from the room.

As Paul shifted his weight in preparation to stand, Holly broke his self-imposed quiet, to pay for the meal. "Just tell me where, I'll get the pony."

Paul settled back, eased his leg out in front of him, and smiled. "Thanks. There's a red paint pony, about fourteen hands, in the side pen with the two-year-olds. He needs to be roped up, still man shy. I'll be out directly and we can get to those bays. Want to see them go before you leave."

Holly spoke his thanks and went through the door, glad to be outside again. The little girl ran to catch up with him, and ask him more questions. A good breakfast, yes. But to sit with a family made him uneasy; all the years of running, stealing, fighting, and the ugly death of his father came back to wipe out the good feeling left near the black stove. Running was all he had learned from family. He crossed to the barn, and found a good rope among Hubbard's carefully stored gear. He fashioned a small loop with his left hand. The paint raised his head as Holly came into the pen. He recognized the man and was instantly alert. "We're old friends, paint," Holly spoke to the pony, as much to ease his own concerns as to sooth the old gelding. He carried the rope in a low, dragging loop and walked slowly across the pen. The two-year-old geldings raised their heads from their morning hay to inspect the intruder. The rope whirled, the loop cast out, and the paint stood caught.

Hubbard sat, the last bit of coffee waiting in the bottom of his cup, and watched as the remote man walked with a peculiar horseman's grace across the barnyard, head bent to listen to all the thoughts Amy was trying to give him. The image of the twisted hand came before his own thoughts; he wondered how the man dealt with a rope. He'd obviously learned to compensate, but how, and how well? The question pushed Paul away from the breakfast table and outside to watch.

The pony followed Holly willingly into the barn. A flicker of movement showed Sarah heading back to her kitchen, carrying a full bucket. Amy was waiting inside the barn with her old braided bridle, a big smile on her shiny face. "Isn't he wonderful? He's my friend. Nobody wanted him 'cause he

90

was too old and they couldn't bridle him. Daddy said I could keep him if I learned him to bridle. We spent hours petting him, and now he loves me and I ride him to school every day."

It was easy to bridle the pony, who rolled a wise eye at the tall man and only snorted his displeasure. He boosted Amy up on the broad back and opened the barn door for the small child and her paint. He had nothing to say, but stood flat-footed and disarmed as the little girl leaned down and kissed his whiskered face, then kicked her pony and trotted gaily across the wooden bridge, the paint's even, heavy hoofbeats clattering in the clear air. Holly stayed at the barn door and watched her ride away.

Paul Hubbard walked with his hesitating step up to the drifter, and watched as the man tensed and turned his eyes on him, those flat, expectant, alert eyes. Hubbard spoke to ease the tension, unused to such intense reactions. These quick reactions of a man constantly posed against danger were new to him, a shock and surprise he wasn't sure he liked. He used his words to try and cover the antagonism he felt toward the man standing in front of him, the one his small, precious child had just kissed.

"Good job with the paint, I thought that hand might hamper you, but obviously it doesn't." Paul was instantly aware he had stepped over another boundary, as he had in questioning this man's integrity earlier. The drifter did not move, but his tense body vibrated with instant anger; his face tightened even more. Paul could read the distrust and fury in the clear pale eyes. He wasn't certain what he should do next, so he blundered on, mouthing his way through the impasse. "If you work half that well with the bays, maybe we can use you here with the stock. You must know about the army contract; well, we need to get those horses moving as soon as possible." Paul witnessed a battle going on in the drawn face he did not understand. Almost as if the man fought within himself over an impulse to attack, to hit out at the words.

Such discipline was unexpected in such a ragged saddle bum.

Hubbard turned to his son, walking toward the two men in the early morning warmth. He could put aside the moment's indecision, and leave it to take care of itself. "Bring out one of the bays," He turned back to Holly, all business now. "I take it the dun mare is yours, she acted only part broke so I put her alone, didn't want any scuffing up with the remount stock."

A faint grin crossed the tight mouth, and Holly spoke casually, "Yeah, she's unbroke, we're a lot alike."

Holly took the bay and tied him snug. He gave the broad back a quick rub with a brush and smoothed the blanket over the shiny expanse. Swinging the saddle into place, he tightened the cinch and reached for the bridle. Slipping it on the red-brown head, he rechecked the gear and led the horse outside to a large corral. Holly put his hand over the near eye, tugged his shapeless hat down hard, and slipped up into the saddle before the bay was ready. The horse gave two almost-gentle bucks, snorted loudly, and lined out across the pen at a long trot. Holly put him into a reining pattern across the center, stopped the bay and spun him, then urged him into a lope to haul to a quick stop in front of Hubbard and his son. He slapped the dark neck. "He's a good one; the other ain't so good, not so smart or smooth, but they'll both do."

Holly dismounted and handed the bridle to Hubbard. He was done now; he had kept his part of the bargain. The offer to work had been shunted aside and forgotten. This man could no longer use his words or his family to find the soft spots, dig his way in, poke at the distant past. Back in his mind, Holly felt the pressure of knowing about the Judge's deal. It would destroy this family, and most of all the proud young woman who angered him. She would lose again.

He didn't want to hear the words coming from Hubbard. They put up a contest within himself he did not want. "Bishop, that bay rides well. How about I give you a bonus when we deliver the stock to the fort. I need you now. Best I can do is bed and board until the contract is paid. You work with us till then. A deal?"

The decision was taken from him before he could think it over. Holly was as surprised as Hubbard when the words came fast from his mouth. "Which horses you want started now?"

Leaving Holly to work on the unbroken stock milling in a pen, Jimmy Hubbard walked back to the house with his father. His unformed face radiated anger and despair. "But Dad, this man's taking my work. I'm the one to finish the stock, you said I've been doing a good job."

His father answered carefully; he knew the boy's pride was the issue. "Son, this will give us a chance, we can get some of the chores we've neglected done, check fence, put in supplies. I need you with me for the chores."

"Dad, that's farmer's work. I aim to be a bronc rider, not a plow jockey." His words dug at Paul. His young son was reaching to be a man and wanted to prove himself. Mending fence didn't offer excitement; topping off a bucking horse made him feel a man.

"Jim, listen, I need you. There will be more broncs and more contracts. Tell you what, now that Bishop is working the stock, come to town with your mother and me today. I want to see Collins at the bank about another short loan, and your mother needs some things at the mercantile. We can work out the chores when we get home." Jimmy accepted the peace offering; he could visit with Julie at the cafe, and maybe work up the courage to ask her out for a walk.

Holly roped out a tough, wall-eyed sorrel with three white legs. The bronc's long ears went flat back at the sight of this man. He was a fighter. Snubbed tight at the post, the sorrel still lashed out sideways at Holly, who grabbed an ear and twisted it lightly, getting the horse's attention. He ran his hands down the shaggy, pale mane and rubbed the tense, drawn-up back. "You're going to be a tough one, son; guess

93

I'll start you first." He was barely aware when, not too much later, the three Hubbards drove out of the yard on their way to Guffey Creek. The sorrel outlaw took all of his attention.

A sorrel hind foot whispered past Holly's ribs, evidence that the horse was still willing to fight his touch. The sacking out had only been partially successful. He stood back from the animal, saddle blanket in hand. The horse suddenly picked up his laid-back ears. Something out in the brush had caught his attention. Holly followed the horse's rigid gaze. Out beyond the bridge a slight movement showed. He walked deliberately into the barn, slow and casual, as if to pick up some forgotten equipment. Inside, he quickly picked up his rifle, checked the chambers. Full and primed. Whatever was out there didn't want to be seen, and that meant trouble.

He went out the back door, which couldn't be seen from the creek, and watched the sorrel, still tied to the post. The gelding was rigid, watching with widening nostrils as he tried to catch the scent of the potential enemy. A quick scanning told Holly he could go around the far side of the building through the series of pens and, using the cover of the high rail fence, work his way up to the creek. Bushes offered protection there, and he could try to pick up the sign of who or whatever was out there.

Through the pens, using the restless horses as cover, Holly crouched down and looked back at the motionless sorrel, head riveted toward the water. The stream was high from spring runoff, so it meant wading across with his rifle held high, using the bridge as cover. Whatever was in the bushes had stayed on the far side of the bridge. Holly worked his way into the bush, careful not to break branches or move loose rocks. He stopped, listened. The sounds of horses stomping restlessly came to him, a snort, followed by a low whicker. Two horses, from the sounds. Quietly parting the thick brush, he spoke to the tied animals, and loosened both cinches. These were horses he knew, a fine-headed chestnut and a spooky paint mare. Ahead were Allward and his companion; he owed them and this was a good time to start.

The two errand boys sat uncomfortably at the back side of the ranch house. They had seen the Hubbard buckboard drive out. And no noise came from inside the house. That left the drifter alone, right where they wanted him. They could wipe up the ground with him, turn the remount herd loose and place his body in their path. They'd be gone before Hubbard returned. Turner poked Jack in the ribs. "Guess this is our lucky day. Judge might spring for an extra bottle this evening when he hears what we done." Turner looked over Jack's shoulder and his face tightened in shock.

Bishop loomed above the two men, rifle pointed in an easy wave at them. "You two, up and quick. You sure don't belong here." He motioned with the rifle barrel toward the barn. Turner shoved Jack hard and stood up. Bishop stepped back, well out of his long reach. "Move. Now." His words were hard and clear.

The three made a silent procession to the corrals. At the fence, Holly nudged them up against the railings, the round steel hole covering them carefully. With a bleak smile, Holly set out what would happen. "The Judge sent you two, for mischief. If he still wants me over at his place, he'll have to send better. Tell him that. Now get." He gestured toward the creek and the horses. Turner reached forward in unthinking rage. The quiet click as Holly cocked the rifle stopped him. His voice was low and full of promise. "Anytime, Turner. I owe you. Anytime." He scrubbed his forehead with his right fist, the rifle held easily in his left, and balanced against his hip. The edge in his eyes matched his voice. Even Turner could read it. "Come on, try."

Turner's voice rose to cover his retreat. "You can't put the Judge off like this; he'll get to you, you bastard." His voice carried in the still, noontime heat. Inside the house, Sarah Hubbard heard the distinct sounds, reaching her as she sat. The front door squeaked softly as she pushed it open to investigate the sounds. She had heard Holly earlier talking with the horses, but had not wanted to see the fighting. But this was a different voice. She saw Holly walking behind two men, heading toward the creek, a rifle riding easy in his hand. She called his name, softly at first, then loud and startling. All three men stopped in their path to the water. Holly half-turned in response to his name, taking his attention off Jack for an instant. The man spun around and struck at the rifle. Turner came back on his heels and slammed a heavy fist at Holly's turned head. It connected with a crack on his right ear and Holly went forward and down in the dust.

He rolled fast to the right, holding hard to the rifle stock. Jack dove at him, hitting full force onto Holly's chest and driving the air out of him as he tried to rise. The two flew back, Holly still desperately holding the rifle. He ducked as Turner came up beside them and aimed a kick at Holly's ribs. Jack took the brunt of the blow and went sailing over Holly's head. Holly continued the roll, landing at Turner's feet. The rifle was thrown aside as he grabbed onto a huge boot and shoved violently up and backward. Turner thudded to the ground, and dust shot up in a large cloud. Jack made a leap for the cast-aside rifle; Holly saw the movement and went after him. They reached the rifle together. Holly doubled his right fist and laced all his anger and strength into the blow aimed at Jack's narrow belly. The man doubled from the blow, and Holly hit again at the exposed neck, using the rifle as a club. Jack went down in a heap, rolled to the side, and lay still. The force of the blow shook Holly; his right hand and arm were numb.

Turner was slow getting up, but murder showed plainly in his face. Holly could see Sarah's figure on the porch as she watched the destruction helplessly. He upended the rifle and pointed it at Turner's massive chest, backing away from Jack's still form. "Go ahead, Turner, you can still try." Holly's voice remained quiet; only the quickened breathing

96

and bloody face showed the effects of the fight. Turner stayed put. These odds weren't to his liking. The rifle barrel traced a pattern in the air, a tight figure aimed at his chest, showing him his own potential death.

Holly let out a long-held breath. "Take him, put him on his horse, and get out of here. Tell the Judge to go to hell, just for me." Turner hauled Jack into a sitting position and slapped the narrow face hard. Getting no response, he hauled the unconscious body over his shoulder and staggered with it to the creek bed. Holly made him cross through the water, pushing the big man's temper. He watched in silence as the red-faced man floundered with the loosened saddles, dropping Jack hard onto the ground as his rig turned under the horse's belly. Jerking savagely at the paint, Turner got the saddle done up, dropped Jack over the seat, fixed his own hull, and cuffed the chestnut as he mounted. The two horses jigged slowly out of the brush and onto the road to town. Holly watched until he could no longer see them.

The rifle barrel was too heavy. He let it point to the ground. His back ached, shoulders sagged, and the bright hot day came back into focus. His eyes cleared and a thirst hit him. Before he could get to the pump, Sarah Hubbard's voice interrupted him. "Mr. Bishop, please come to the house and I'll fix those cuts." Her voice carried no disgust, no proper distaste for the brutality of the fight. Her request was well meant. Holly unconsciously felt the side of his head; the cut from last night's ruckus had reopened and been enlarged by Turner's first blow. His shirt was covered with blood; his right fist ached, the knuckles split and oozing, the scar tissue shredded. Still, the blows to Jack's belly and head had felt good. A release for his anger.

Holly walked heavily to the back steps near the kitchen and sat. "Come in, please, I can work better on you in here."

Holly shook his head gently in refusal; the move was painful. "Out here is best, miss. Not right for me to be in there

97

with you." He remained stubbornly seated on the steps, the sun warming him.

Finally, the back door opened, and Sarah came down to sit next to him, a pan of water and some cloths in her hand. Close to him, her clean smell was like perfume. And her voice was soft and soothing this time, as if he were an injured animal. "Whenever we meet, it seems you get a good blow to the head. This didn't do yesterday's damage any good. Hold still." Something burned into the cut. Her chestnut hair came close to his face as she bent to inspect the other damage. Holly could inhale her smell, the warm female smell, a rich sweet smell that made him wince with longing. He took another short, deep breath as she dabbed at the open wound. "This needs a stitch or two. You're going to look like my grandmother has been near you with her needlepoint work."

Sarah looked into the drawn face as she spoke the words. The pain and longing she saw hurt her. The man turned his face away, shutting his eyes against further invasion. "I've stitched heads before; my husband was a bronc rider, too. I've had lots of practice." No pity asked for or given in the declaration, just matter of fact. A moment later, Holly could feel the tug of a needle pulling at his scalp. He was too numbed to react to the pain. A burning on his hand, another tugging pull. Sarah sat back, satisfied at her work. "You'll hold together for a while; just stay away from the Judge's men, and milkmaids." She smiled to show the words were a joke. Then she turned serious.

"Why were those two here, something to do with the contract? What did they want? It couldn't be anything good." Holly gave no indication that he had heard her questions. For a brief moment she sat, warm and quiet, with him on the steps, silent and easy in the afternoon sun.

Holly could sit near this woman forever. He shrugged his shoulders in answer to his own unspoken question. He had no right to sit here. He stood up and looked down at the shining hair. "Thanks for the nursing. That bronc must be mad as a scorched cat, tied there in the sun." He backed away to pick up the rifle and walked to the corral. His thoughts were active and confused. "Those two will be back, or will try something else. Hubbard needs to know about the contract, and his friends in town ain't going to tell him. Damn. I'm getting caught in this. Don't need other's fights, got enough of my own. Best get my work done and get out of here." He realized he was talking out loud to himself, and grimaced at the folly. Leaning the rifle up against the corral gate, he spoke to the angry sorrel. "Here we go again, friend." He continued talking to the horse as he walked into the corral. The enforced period of being tied had done nothing for the bronc's temper. Ears back, two hind feet lashed out at the wrangler. Holly grinned ruefully.

Hugging her legs, Sarah watching as the man and horse worked on their mutual distrust. "He's as wild as that mustang," she thought. She smiled to herself at the challenge. He did intrigue her, the dark under his quiet surface, the manners at odds with the roughness. Her husband, dead almost two years, had been a wild one too, but he was open in his wildness, his blond hair flying when he topped a bronc, yelling his pleasure to the wind. He had whirled her off the ground and kept her laughing. Yet before he died, she had learned there was no gentleness behind the laughter. She had had to follow him, to leave her injured father. He would never give to her. This man, held in check by his own iron will, stirred some of the same feelings in her. She responded to the hint of kindness beneath his roughness, and wanted to dig at him until he smiled.

Enough daydreaming; Sarah stood up. Holly had saddled the sorrel, and was preparing to mount. Unwilling to watch, the young woman walked inside her home. He would be thrown, and would mount again and again, until the job was done. She did not want to watch.

CHAPTER EIGHT

Turner's big frame twisted uncomfortably in the saddle. Some of the blows Bishop had landed put up a hurting complaint, but his pride hurt more. He looked back at his so-called partner, hanging head down over the saddle. The Judge wasn't going to like their evening report this time. But, by then, he would think of some way to get his own from the drifter and fix Hubbard so he couldn't meet the contract deadline. Turner rode in silence, picking over ideas and discarding them.

Head bouncing at each step, Jack began to struggle. Why in hell was he upside down. Finally he recovered enough to yell for Turner, his voice startling in the quiet afternoon. "Goddamn it, Turner, get me off this mule."

Turner yanked hard on the chestnut's mouth and came to a dead stop. He took his time dismounting, and walked over to stand next to the back of the yelling man. "Took only two good punches to drop you. Try and explain that to the Judge."

Jack's head rolled back and forth on the paint's belly; he bellowed in rage and frustration. "Haul me off here and do it quick or I'll explain this to you with the side of my pistol." Turner grinned maliciously at the threat and grabbed for Jack's shirt. Picking up the thin shoulders, he slid the angry man off the other side of his horse. They faced each other across the saddle. Jack's face was swollen, filled with blood from traveling wrong side up. Turner grinned again at the sight. Jack made a threatening motion with his left hand toward his gun, and discovered his pistol had slid out at some point. One more thing to get Bishop for.

From inside Jack's saddlebag, Turner offered his working partner a drink from his own bottle. "This should ease the pain, but nothing's going to make me feel better till we get that saddle bum between us again and pound him into little pieces." Lowering the bottle, Jack passed it over the paint's back to Turner, who laid his head back and took a long, deep drink. His whole body shuddered as the crude liquor hit bottom, then he wiped his mouth and stuck the bottle back in the saddlebag. He slapped the saddle for emphasis, and the paint jumped at the sharp sound. "Let's get mounted and do some checking. I got me an idea while I was waiting for you to recover from those light taps Bishop handed you. That bog between the Judge's and Hubbard's, there's fence around it now on Hubbard's side, but they ain't had much time to check there since they been working on the remount broncs. Let's us head up there, see if some of them posts could be persuaded to loosen up and we can shove in those geldings up to their bellies in mud."

Jack turned over the idea. Looked good, even coming from Turner. Even if it weren't the remount horses they put in the bog, time would be lost for the Hubbards, and it would put them behind. Not bad. "Okay, Turner, this may be a good one. Let's move." The two men remounted, Jack stiff and sore from his upside-down ride, turned their horses off the road, and went down through trees to circle up beyond Hubbard's ranch to the bog. An hour later they came over the rise, and could see a small number of horses grazing in the narrow valley below. The bog fence was at the southern end, winter loose and waiting for them.

They rode closer, cautious not to spook the herd. "Well of

101

all the luck. Must be eighteen or nineteen geldings here, bet this is the remount bunch." Jack's face held an unaccustomed smile. He dismounted and removed his boots. "This is going to cost the Judge extra," he muttered as he stood in tattered gray socks. Leaving the paint, he walked gingerly across the remaining grass to the wooden fence-line. Their luck held. Several of the posts were bent with winter snow and winds, cracked and loosened at their base. The rails had started to shift and slide, weakening the sections. Grabbing one post that leaned precariously, Jack shook it, rocking it back and forth. The rails pushed down and made a wedge against the two posts holding them. One post broke at the ground line, to fall away in Jack's hand. He dropped the rotted wood, and went to the next section. This post held better under the pressure, but finally gave way and lay on the ground. The stacked rails rolled free, spreading out across the grass in an erratic fan. The rails in the next section of fence were also freed by the broken posts, and dropped and scattered from their confinement, breaking another post off by their weight alone. Jack's trap was ready.

The tall, angular man walked back to Turner, his gray socks now muddy brown. Pulling his boots back on, he remounted and sat for a minute, carefully watching the herd. They had grazed closer to the two saddled horses, their curiosity aroused by the strangers. "By God, Turner, we are in luck. These broncs are all shod. We can ride right into the herd and haze them over the rails. Put them dead in the bog."

The two men spurred their horses toward the herd, scattering the geldings. Several horses laid their ears back and trotted away from the newcomers. One bright chestnut went near the downed fence and stopped, snorting at the unfamiliar shapes on the ground. Turner slapped his rope at the nearest bronc until it broke into a nervous, shuffling trot and went closer to the chestnut. Slowly, the horse herd was drifted near the downed fence; only the bright red horse's continued snorting kept them out of the bog.

102

Jack made a short cast with his rope and struck the red horse on the neck. It spooked sideways and stepped over a pile of rails. Two others followed the gelding. On unfamiliar ground, the horse stood braced, sniffing and checking. Jack gave a great whoop and threw his rope again, striking the horse hard on the rump. The red gelding leaped forward, took three running strides, and went sideways up to his chest in the deep bog. The two bays balked at the edge of the soft footing, but Turner followed Jack's lead and spanked the two in. The remainder of the herd scattered; two more horses went over the downed fence but stayed out of the mire, and several others milled at the railings.

Jack and Turner put their horses at a lope back up into the hills. They were satisfied with the work. "That looks to be a right good mess; Hubbard'll be at least three horses short by tomorrow. Let's leave this here, and tell the Judge." Turner chuckled at his own handywork. Jack wordlessly reached in back of his saddle for the ever-present bottle, took a deep swallow, and handed it to Turner.

In the bog, the three horses struggled frantically, their eyes wild with terror, the sweat glistening on their necks as they fought to free themselves. Two horses still free of the sucking mud stepped cautiously back over the downed fence and rejoined the grazing herd. The horses went back to tearing at the lush grass, only occasionally glancing at their downed companions. Only one horse glanced up as the chestnut and the paint loped out of the now peaceful valley.

It took three spills from the sorrel before horse and rider came to an understanding. More of a truce. Holly walked slower now, stiffened by the fight and then the spills. The right side of his face showed a dark spreading bruise from slamming up against the snubbing post on his first dive from the sorrel's back. The horse was equally subdued, his coat darkened by heavy sweat mingled with dust. He had gone over and down twice in savage attempts to maim his rider. Both times, Holly had bailed out and been back on the horse before the animal could get to his feet. It had been a violent contest, but now Holly could reach over and slap the damp neck without those yellow teeth trying to shred his shirt sleeve.

He stripped the gear from the sweaty horse and grabbed a handful of hay to fashion a twist. The sorrel wriggled his lip in pleasure as Holly scrubbed the hot back. Then the horse's ears pricked up and Holly turned to see the buckboard coming across the wooden bridge. The small shape of a little girl was wedged between her parents on the front seat, and her paint pony trailed behind, led by Jimmy sitting in back. The team moved at a smart trot, eager to be home. Holly put the sorrel out with the others, and waited at the barn. Hubbard drove up to the house, got out, and helped his wife, while Amy climbed over the seat and slid onto the paint's broad back. Jimmy turned the team and brought them back to the barn to unhitch.

"What happened to your face, did you ride that old sorrel? I know Jimmy's scared of him, thought he would get thrown." Holly held the paint as Amy slipped off, her face solemn with concern.

Her brother's face flushed bright as he heard the careless words. He'd had enough of this man today. First taking his job as bronc rider, then Julie talking only of the dark-faced man who had eaten there every day, now his sister telling the world he was afraid of a horse that same man had just ridden. Fists clenched in building rage, the boy intruded between Holly and the old gelding. "You leave my sister alone, leave everybody alone. You ain't got no right, coming in here and taking my job and my girlfriend."

Holly backed away from the outraged boy, his mouth tight, his eyes bitter glass. Between the two warring men, the small child stood in bewilderment. Holly was caught—challenged by the youth, bound to the small girl. Jimmy landed a roundhouse punch on Holly's face. He rocked back with the force, and the thin hold on his blossoming anger split, leaving him wild. He reached for the youth in front of him, one hand drawn back for a murderous blow. Amy's shrill scream shook him. And Holly let his arm drop, opened his clenched and aching fist, leaving himself wide open to the expected blow from Jimmy which sent him back against the solid body of the paint gelding, blood spurting from a cut lip. Holly waited stolidly for the next blow, his eyes distracted by the frightened little girl.

A steady voice reached between the antagonists. "Son, stop, can't you see the man is not fighting back. That is enough."

Jimmy's eyes went from the hated face to his father's familiar one. Unable to look for long at the disappointment he saw, he turned back to Holly and let his anger flow. "This man has taken everything away from me. Ain't fair." Holly stayed up against the paint; a dusty hand wiped across his mouth left a bloody smear of dirt. The boy spun on his boot heel and headed for the house, the undiminished fury showing in each step he took, heels hard against the solid earth. Amy started a question, but her father picked her up and hugged her briefly, then set her down.

"Put Spreckles away and take your school things to the house; your mother needs you." She knew better than to question further, so she left the two men alone.

Holly watched as the small child ran across the yard, books swinging from her arm. Running to her home and her mother. Damn this family; they clobbered him on the head, stitched his wounds, smiled at him, and then punched him in the face. Hubbard's voice caught his wandering attention. "Jim's just finding out he's a man; if you can leave him be he'll work out something with the girl." Paul leaned against the door, a remembering smile on his face. "I still remember how mad I got when Miriam showed interest in Charlie Evans. She told me later it was to get my attention. Worked too." He paused, "You okay now?"

The two stood silent. Hubbard rolled a cigarette, offered the makings to Holly, who took them in silence and rolled a smoke of his own. Hubbard relaxed, and looked at the blood-smeared man beside him. This was a hard one for him to figure. The man had a touch, should be working his own stock, not just drifting and fighting. Such a life was beyond his understanding. He noticed the darkening bruise on the gaunt face. He probed gently, "Finish that sorrel yet? Looks more like he tried to finish you."

Holly shifted his weight, uncertain how to begin. The day's events had changed the world for him. He was going to break his own rules for survival. He had to. "Hubbard, we had a visit today while you were in town; Breen's two errand boys came to roust me out of here, didn't work but they had a good try." Paul straightened; something more was coming. This man didn't volunteer anything unless he had to. Holly found it hard to continue, but a small girl's bright eyes, a kind woman's hands battled against the years of silence. And Sarah's warm smell, her light touch. Turner had it in for her, left alone the man would get her somehow.

"In town they know something, that Breen rigged it for you to get the contract. He bid high; no one else bid. He's bought up your loan personal, put his two boys against you to guarantee you won't deliver. He wants your stud horse and aims to get him."

Paul Hubbard dropped his butt and ground it under his heel. He looked sharply at the drifter standing next to him. "If that's true, I'm in deeper trouble. Took another short loan today to cover stock and help. Thought it went too easy, but I didn't want to question the good fortune. That's why town was quiet today, why no one wanted to visit. They all know what's going on and don't have the courage to call the Judge on it. They're just going to sit and wait." His voice crackled with mounting anger. "Damn it, we're so close. Just have to fight the best I can. We can bring the remount stock in closer, keep guard during the day." He shook his head, disbelief fighting despair in his face. "Bet I won't be able to hire extra hands for the drive; the Judge will see to that. Damn."

The silence returned. The late afternoon warmth over the small mountain ranch had turned hard and sharp. Holly ran his hand over his face, wincing as he touched the bruise. "The sorrel is done; the three left are easy. If Jimmy can give me a hand, we can top them tomorrow easy. Leave soon and take a different trail to the fort, keep the Judge off balance. Make the drive fast, get out early and finish the horses near the fort. No one can bother you there."

Hubbard nodded his agreement, and pushed away from the door as if he had come to a major decision. "Good. Yes. Quick, catch two horses and we'll go bring in the remount herd. They're up in Long Valley. I'm going to the house; Miriam needs to know what's going on, and I need Jimmy here as a guard while we're gone." Without looking back, the stocky rancher hurried unevenly across the yard. Bishop's suggestions were good; instead of trailing through town, they could slip out behind Tyson's, and be on the plains before the Judge's boys knew it. "Miriam, Sarah, Jim, you too, Amy, come here." He reached the kitchen door.

Holly caught up the sorrel again, and pulled out a tough-looking gray. Hubbard's gear went on the gray, and he was just done with the sorrel's cinch when the rancher came storming back to the barn. Face grim in determination, Hubbard led the gray out and mounted without a word. He headed out into the main pasture and put his horse into a fast lope, Holly right behind him. In five minutes, the two men reached the narrow opening to the long valley. Holly could see the horse herd bunched at the far end. Paul eased up his gray for a moment as Holly caught up to halt his sorrel beside the restive gray. The rancher spoke rapidly: "We'll bring the horses out of here, put them in the two big corrals for the night. You and Jimmy finish the broncs in the next two-three days, and then we'll go."

He touched the gray into a long trot, eager to get the herd moving, and Holly moved the sorrel just behind him. As they came up on the herd, it was obvious something was agitating the horses. The main herd was spooky, milling around, heads up. Only a few were still grazing. Paul saw the downed horses first. "Good Lord Almighty." The words came in an explosive gasp. "The fence is down." The riders pushed through the herd up close to the fence. Holly slid from the sorrel and made his way over the scattered rail to the bogged animals. They were exhausted from their efforts to get free; two were lying half on their sides, the ground around them torn and furrowed from their fright. The third gelding had only his head and shoulders above the mire, quarters sunk deep into the muck.

Paul shook out his rope and threw it to Holly. One muddy bay lifted his head to eye the intruders. Holly dropped to his stomach and wiggled across to the animal, drawing the rope with him in his teeth. He patted the muddied neck in reassurance, and slid back along to the quarters, which rose just above the mud. Running his hand down the rump, Holly could just get the rope snugged around the horse's rear. He worked his way around the back of the horse, fighting the pull of the churned mud, and was able to push the rope all the way around the animal's submerged body. It took some slaps before the horse would raise his head to let Holly slip the rope over his neck and push it down by his chest. Holly looked back at Paul, who had set the sturdy gray in place and had taken a dally around the horn. He was set and waiting.

Holly nodded. The gray moved back to tighten the rope. The bay suddenly started struggling again. The horse leaned against the pull of the rope and struck out with his forelegs. A flailing hoof struck near Holly and he rolled out of the way onto solid ground. The bay fought this new enemy with squealing fury, and the gray kept backing, the rope always taut. With an airy gasp the mud let go its hold and the bay

108

found his front legs on solid ground. He dug in more; the pull on his quarters infuriated him and gave him the energy to lunge forward. The bog loosened its grip and the bay came up free.

Holly picked up the muddy loop where it had slipped off the bay, and worked his way over to the other bay, head raised to watch his companion trot unsteadily away to rejoin the herd. Repeating his efforts, the second bay was soon free. The chestnut's eyes rolled in fright as Holly wriggled his way to the animal, sunk deeply in the bog. Paul brought the gray in closer. "We may lose this one, Holly. Can you even touch his rump?"

Holly's reply was muffled by the mud sticking to his mouth. "Throw another rope, going to tie myself to that tree stump behind him, try to push him out while you pull. Hope it works." Holly could feel his body being sucked in by the greedy mud as he worked himself nearer the rotting stump. He wrapped the tossed rope around the bottom, then around his waist. At least he could pull himself free if they went under. If the stump held. The chestnut's rump was totally submerged by the soupy mud. He would have to shove the rope deep into the slime, hoping he could reach the quarters and work the rope around them.

Holly felt in back of the stump. Part of a branch came to his searching fingers. Pulling it forward, he tried stuffing the rope down toward the horse's backside with short jabs of the stick. The horse lifted his head and whinnied in protest as the sharp end jabbed into his back. Holly slithered around the horse to the right, poking all the time with the stick. The mud kept pulling at him, trying to bring him under. Using the rope he pulled himself back to the stump and then along the left side of the sinking animal, repeating the poking. He had to hit the chestnut hard to get his head up, the rope finally resting near the animal's chest.

Paul stepped the gray back to tighten the line. The chestnut didn't even bother to raise his head at the pull. He had given up. Holly went hand over hand back to the tree stump, the mud pulling stronger against his tired arms. Back braced against the stump, he shoved his feet deep into the mire. Paul watched, and before Holly could speak, he reined the gray back sharply, giving a strong tug to the dying horse. Holly pushed hard with his feet against the mired quarters. Feeling a slight give in the mud, he pushed harder; the gray took another step back.

The chestnut finally raised his head. He too had felt the give. His legs started a weak thrashing, loosening the mud and inching him slowly forward. The gray took another two steps back and brought up the slack. The chestnut made two mighty plunges, then quit just short of solid ground, nostrils distended, gasping for air. Paul moved the gray back again, Holly reached for the stick and beat the emerging back. The horse squealed in fury at the pain, made another leap, and was out. The rope slid off him and he stood trembling, and free.

Holly was half-submerged in the liquid earth. One boot had been sucked off in the last push. Shirt torn. Mud covering his eyes, thick in his ears and mouth. Hubbard's voice called him. "Hold it, I'll come out."

Holly spat out some mud, "Don't." He could barely hear his own voice. "Worse out here now, all stirred up. Throw me your rope." His breath came quickly. Something struck him, Hubbard's rope. He fumbled with the knot holding him to the stump; his fingers were thick with mud and could not get a grasp. He wiped his hands on a bit of swamp grass and worked the knot again.

"Okay, now, pull." The gray horse backed up once again, pulling Holly slowly through the mire onto solid earth. Once more, Paul Hubbard dismounted, winding up his rope as he came to the figure lying in the high grass.

He looked down at the man trying to scrape through the muck on his face. "The horses are all right, how about you?"

Holly looked up through a muddy mask and offered a

110

silly, lopsided grin. "Guess I wasn't meant to be a swamp creature, sure need my Saturday bath now."

The two men walked slowly back to their saddle horses. Holly limped on one bare foot. Paul worked some thoughts over in his mind, then spoke out bitterly. "Those posts weren't that rotten. I checked them a few weeks ago." He stopped walking.

Holly sank to the ground and pointed at a large, round impression off to one side, an impression that looked vaguely like a footprint. "Could be someone here in their stocking feet. Could have been the Judge's boys; they were out here earlier." Hubbard's face stiffened in shock and growing anger. He swung up onto the gray and waited. Holly stood by the sorrel, still tired enough to stand quietly, and rested his head on the warm neck. The long day had caught up to him also. Paul Hubbard waited with the cowboy in easy silence. He was learning not to intrude.

In a moment, Holly mounted, and they turned the horse herd to home. Once the animals were started, Paul rode up alongside the bronc rider and glanced over at the man. Under the drying mud he could see lines of exhaustion etched deeply on the thin face, which was pale under its splattering of dirt and mud. "Thanks, Bishop." The man's head came up, his face turned to his companion. A brief nod was the only reaction. The two horses jogged slowly in the later afternoon light, toward home.

CHAPTER NINE

The Judge was rattled, angry. Jack and Turner were not on time for their evening report. He resumed his customary pacing, breaking stride now and then to check out the window. Each step across the room added to his growing rage. This campaign was not going according to his plan. His lawyer, Jenkins, that twittering fool, had come to the ranch today. And in his chattering foolish way he had warned the Judge that some of the townspeople were angered by his actions against the Hubbard family. Even George Kelleher, that ludicrous spectacle who thought he knew horses, even he had the nerve to argue with Jenkins, telling him the Judge was wrong to force the Hubbards.

And the Simpsons at the cafe had looked at him with a questioning eye when he ate at their establishment last. Perhaps it would be his last meal for a while at their restaurant, until they learned who owned this valley and the town. These people must not question his actions; they must do exactly what he commanded, and only then would he continue to support their businesses. Otherwise, without his patronage, the town would wither and die. Mrs. Hutton's timid knock at the library door broke into his thoughts. "Yes, send them in now." He turned to pose in front of the fireplace, taking warmth against the evening chill.

"Gentlemen." The Judge's words rang with ironic formality. "You are late. I therefore assume you have good news to report, some furtherance of our campaign." He looked the two men over carefully, took note of their battered condition, and smiled. "Ah, you have had to resort to fists. I take it the drifter was at Hubbard's or that you met up with him on the trail. He is on his way out, correct?" This last was more of a question than the Judge intended.

Jack Levitt stepped forward and cleared his throat. "Well, Judge, it wasn't that simple. We did find the cowboy at Hubbard's, in fact, working on a bronc. But somehow he snuck up on us. Turner here got into a fight and would of finished him, but the Hubbard girl, that older one, came out. You told us not to involve the family directly, so we let him get to his rifle and we left."

They had practiced this story on the ride back to the ranch, figuring the Judge wouldn't question it once he heard about the fence. "That ain't all, Judge," Jack pushed on, actually interrupting the Judge's beginning tirade. "Turner here had a good idea. We went roundabout from the ranch over to that bog, and sure enough the remount herd was in the valley. We tore down sections of fence, made it look like winter damage, and hazed three horses into the bog. Left them up to their bellies with the others hanging around. That should put Hubbard behind for a good while. We'll get the drifter later."

His judicial anger at the crass interruption was mollified by the rest of Jack's report, so the Judge relaxed enough to sit down. This report finally sounded like some progress was being made. And no one could put the blame on him. "Well, done, gentlemen; you have earned your pay this day. When the business is completed satisfactorily, we will discuss a bonus in some form. I suggest tomorrow you carefully reconnoiter the valley again, make certain your efforts succeed in their intent. And you must take care of the drifter. He has done enough damage, blocked our way enough. Now, I suggest you retire to your quarters and do some more planning. That bog fence was excellent. Good night."

Jack and Turner stepped off the back steps into the dark. Turner taunted his companion. "Think you did a damn good job of playing down how that hardcase wiped you out today. You sure can bend the facts to fit."

Jack gave it right back to Turner: "Didn't notice you piping up to describe how Bishop got the drop on you any too fast." Then his voice lost its faint suggestion of teasing; his long face hardened. "Tell you now, I get that bum in my gun sight and he's gone." Jack pulled the cork on their evening bottle and had his usual long drink, wiped his mouth, and almost cracked a smile. "That sure feels better, eases my belly and my mind." Turner grabbed for his share, but Jack turned aside and took another long pull. "Bishop's time is short. I can see his head through my sights. Pulling that trigger will be 'most as good as this here liquor."

Turner put one meaty paw on Jack's shoulder and pressed hard. "Give me that damned bottle."

Miriam had watched her daughter as the two men came in from gathering the horse herd. They could see the horses trot into the corral. Even in the early dusk light, they could see by the riders' silhouettes that something had happened. Paul rode stiffly, his back rigid as if braced against an enemy. The bronc rider was slumped over his mount, riding against the motion of his horse. Sarah and Jimmy both started out to the men; Miriam put her hand to Sarah's arm, gently. Her voice soft and full of concern, she spoke to her daughter. "Let Jimmy help, we can wait." Sarah's eyes sought her mother's, worry etching her face. She nodded her assent.

Jimmy came bursting back into the kitchen. "Ma, someone drove three of the horses into the bog, tore down the fence, Pa says. He and Holly pulled them out. Pa's arguing with Holly; he needs a bath but won't come to the house. He looks funny."

His father came in the house carrying two buckets. "Need to do a good cleaning job, Miriam. Get me shirt, pants, and such. Not much left of Holly's clothes. And a pair of boots, too. Lost one in the mud." He sat down heavily. "Looks like the Judge is serious about us losing the contract. Someone pulled that fence down and tried to make it look like the posts were winter broken. Holly found a stocking footprint near the fence line. Tomorrow we'll have to put a guard on the herd, bring them back each night. Amy," he looked at their youngest, listening with eyes wide and shining, "we'll need you these next few days. And you, too, Sarah. We're in this until the end."

Holly had scraped most of the dried mud off, and wanted to bathe in the trough. Paul refused him, insisted that he come to the house. "All that mud won't do the horses any good in their drinking water," he teased. Holly only looked hard at the man. He spoke flatly, the harsh words deliberately ambiguous. "I don't belong in your house, too dirty."

Paul pushed the words aside, refusing the message. "Come up to the house; I'll go ahead and tell Miriam what you need." Reluctantly, Holly came up to the house after scraping more of the mud off himself. Uneasy at facing the family members, he knocked softly at the back door. Miriam Hubbard opened the door and faced Holly, who had backed away out of the direct light. But she could still see him. Dried mud stood in sharp relief in the lines on his face. His shirt was molded to his body, underscoring its gauntness. Bits of dried blood mingled with the dirt and grass on his neck and shoulders. He frightened her eastern sensibilities.

And her look of shock and horror startled Holly; he retreated even further from the kitchen door, looking to run. But her kind voice brought him back inside. "Please, let me wash that cut, and then we'll leave you to a hot bath. Supper will be ready for you when you are done. Please." The woman was offering him a part of her family. "There's even fresh cream to go with the pie. Please come in." Sarah Hubbard came to stand at her side, with a bowl of water in hand, steam rising from it, soft cloths tucked under her arm. Holly could not meet those two sets of imploring eyes. He came inside to sit stiffly on the edge of a chair closest to the door to outside.

Miriam had her daughter hold the warm cloth to the reopened sore. The rag came away clotted with mud and bits of blood. Unmindful of the tension in the battered man, Sarah leaned closer to work over the raw wound. Holly shied away from the touch. The light became too bright, colors too intense, the clean scent of the girl invaded his senses. His control slipped away.

He swung out, hit the bowl, water spilling as it crashed to the floor. He stood up fast, panic strong in his face. "No!" He was out the door before anyone reacted.

Paul Hubbard reached the door first, to look outside and then back toward his astonished family. "Best we leave the man alone. I'll take out food and clothing." Sarah knelt to pick up the scattered pieces; she checked each fragment carefully, going over in her mind what had just happened. The eyes stayed with her, the fear, the wariness. Her father's voice broke her concentration. Then Jimmy pestered her, wanting to know what had just happened. Sarah only shook her head in mute refusal.

Then Amy spoke out plaintively, "What happened to the bowl, why did Holly run away from us. Pa says I don't go to school tomorrow. Why?" Activity returned to the kitchen. Amy's mother reassured the little girl that supper would be soon, that all was well.

In the safety of the barn, Holly stopped running, still shaking from being trapped in the kitchen. He had to get out of this valley. Footsteps sounded outside, a hesitation clear in their pattern. Then Paul Hubbard's voice came quiet through the dark. "Brought some food and clean clothes." Hubbard came inside and put down his bundle. Something

116

clattered, smothered inside the clothing. Hubbard reached out to touch Holly; he stepped forward to evade the touch. Then Paul's voice receded, the barn door squeaked. "I left a bottle with the clothes. Thought you might be needing a bit of comfort. See you in the morning." The rancher stayed a bit longer by the door, then walked out into the dark, back to his family.

The liquor bit hard as Holly took the first swallow. He choked and coughed, wiped his mouth and had another swallow. It had been a long time, but this was one time he could use a good drunk. He would finish the bottle, then take his bath in the trough and sleep. He sat down and leaned back against an upright. It took a moment to find a spot on his back that didn't hurt when it touched the post. Another drink and the stiffness wasn't so hard to bear. Another two pulls and he couldn't even feel the blood still leaking from the cut. People sure are determined to rap me upside the head; guess they want to knock what brains I got to some other place. The thought was an odd comfort.

He was numb and content, even his head had stopped aching. The lantern in the barn burned low, almost out of fuel. Better take that bath now, he thought, don't want to make another trip to the house. Sarah Hubbard drifted through his memory; he shook his head violently and stood up. The barn whirled, and Holly put out a hand to lean on a post, missed, and went down to his knees. He rolled over on his back and laughed. Managed to ride that sorrel today, but got throwed by a barn floor. He struggled up and tried standing again. Needed two more legs, but this time he found the right post even though the barn ducked and spun. Another drink from the half-empty bottle and his world moved back into place. It was easy getting out of his shirt. Not much left of it, and only one button to hold things together. Same with the boots, much easier if you wore only one, half as long to take them off. He giggled and sat down hard. His pants took the longest to get off, the buttons were

117

stubborn and thick, would not let go.

Holly shivered in the night cold. The black water in the trough looked like ice, but the caked and dried mud itched infernally; had to choose between two bad choices. Like running or stealing. Outside was bitter cold; best go back and get another drink. He walked into the barn door and bounced back to stand and curse the idiot that closed it. The remains of the bottle were inside, but he could not find the door handle. To hell with it, on to the bath. One foot over the side and in the water. My God, it's cold. Balancing to get the other foot in, he slipped and sat hard on the mossy bottom. Seem to be doing a lot of sitting tonight. He snorted.

Soap. He needed soap, never did have any soap, at least there wasn't any in the pile of clothes and whiskey. The reminder of the liquor hurried him. To hell with the soap. The mud came off reluctantly in the hard mountain water. Handfuls of sand helped scrub the imbedded clay from his body. Did a good job of reminding his bruises and sores to start paining again too. This taking a bath was a poor idea. His teeth began to chatter and goose bumps covered his body. Time to get out, get a drink, and get warm. Those last mouthfuls of whiskey tasted good already.

He laboriously climbed out of the makeshift tub. The mountain air drifted around him as he stood, dripping water forming a small puddle at his feet. Must look like a skeleton, he thought, and snorted again at the picture. Sort of like Ichabod Crane. The barn door was a long walk across the yard, but this time he found the handle and pulled the door open without much of a fight. Inside, a fairly clean saddle blanket became a towel to rub him dry. The roughness was reassuring. Gave him the smell of a range bronc, a pleasing smell.

The extra clothes huddled in a small pile and caused him more trouble than they were worth. Nothing wanted to button. The pants kept going on backwards, and the boots didn't fit worth a damn. Too much room. Finally he wrestled

118

the garb into covering his body; his reward was another drink. He reached for the bottle. But a movement from the rear of the barn flickered just outside his narrowed range of vision. Holly stood still. Not going to catch him attacking that girl again. Damn cow should give its own milk, not need to have someone pull at its teats every day. He shook his head, damp hair sending a frozen shower.

Something was really moving in the dim light. Holly tried to pull his mind alert. The icy water had shocked him into partial sobriety. He was not going to allow anyone to sneak up on him tonight. He reached for the rifle, which was now loaded and ready. A low, sweet voice came from the rear of the barn, by the empty stalls. "You don't need that for me, Holly." It was Sarah Hubbard, her throaty voice startling in the dark. If the girl had been standing there the past few minutes, she had watched him get dressed. The thought of her eyes on his nakedness aroused him. The woman had no right to invade him. He would teach her some manners.

Sarah Hubbard now stood in front of him, a fall of rich chestnut hair down her back, the loose strands softly touching her face, enhancing the glow from the lantern. Her nightdress was designed to cover and hide, but the gentle folds slid easily over her breasts, then dipped in to follow the rounded belly and hint at the flow of leg from full hips. The garment shifted and pulled as she swayed, offering Holly a complete knowledge of her body. He took quick, angry steps and reached to grasp her arms, his hands tight and demanding on her flesh. Sarah's eyes widened as she felt the fury in his touch. She could see the violence in his raw eyes. The empty bottle told of his drinking, and now she felt her own desires heightened by fear. The face before her held anger and something else glittering in those pale hazel eyes rimmed with fire.

She hadn't meant to spy, but sleep had come slowly, refusing to take away her memories. Her thoughts returned over

119

and over to Holly's flight from the kitchen. Her father had taken out the clothing and returned with nothing to say. Dinner had been eaten in silent worry. Jimmy was confused but no one was able to ease his thoughts. Amy hardly ate, too excited at tomorrow's beginning adventure. And later, Sarah had come down from the loft; her sister's shallow breathing as she slept only underscored her own inability to sleep.

She sat in the kitchen, rocking slowly, letting her thoughts roam, eyes on the starlit yard. The stark white figure that danced across the yard and climbed into the trough with difficulty could not help but catch her attention. Even at a distance the long body was much too thin, had more the appearance of a scarecrow than a man. The drifter had remained in the tub a long time, to the point where Sarah feared he was asleep. She slipped out the back door intending to wake him. But by the time she had gotten near the trough, he pulled himself out and over the edge, to stand motionless for a short minute, heading then back for the warmth of the barn, his steps unsteady and loose.

She knew better, but she could not help but stare as he wandered in the yard. She knew nothing of this man except his passion for freedom, his refusal to be bound by another. Yet she stood watching him, intrigued by what she saw and knew. A strong man, emaciated, scarred, pale, shivering. But a man whose quiet gentleness with animals she would like extended to herself. The lacing of white lines across his back, the knots alongside his ribs, the long dark furrow down one thigh. She would like to touch each scar, to know what had happened. To know him.

Sarah slipped inside the back of the barn while he wrestled with the obstinate front door. The dance he went through trying to dress in her father's old shirt and pants made her swallow her laughter. She knew that one sound would send him to find her. She sobered. And moved in the shadows, hitting the side of a stall, catching his wandering attention.

Holly's grip on her arms tightened; without resistance she met him to offer her body up against his. She could feel his heart, could feel her own. In the middle of rising excitement, of feelings she thought buried with her husband, pity came to her. The flat bones of his chest were exposed and vulnerable under his half-buttoned borrowed shirt. A hand, the twisted and bent hand, touched her face and lifted her chin so she could no longer hide in the folds of his shirt. Holly bent down and covered her mouth with his. A demanding pressure opened her mouth and drew her closer. Her arms, freed from his grasping hands, wound around him, conscious of the frail ribbing that supported him. She was in a dream, she was protected; she was on fire.

Holly broke the kiss and backed away from the swaying woman. Even drunk, he knew he was wrong. Breathing was impossible; his mouth was thick and swollen, his heart raced. He could not face the young woman, but when he turned away she was still there in front of him, her eyes bright, those firm breasts lifting with each intake of air. He shook. "Miss, go; get out of here. I've no business with you." Holly's voice was both sober and brutal. Sarah wanted to touch and reassure him, but the memory of his earlier bolt from the family was too strong. Time would bring him to her again, and without the alcohol he would know the feelings were real.

The gentle smile on Sarah's face tore at Holly. She should be hating him, yet the smile lingered and grew warmer. "Good night, Holly." Her voice stayed with him as she left the barn. He watched her walk lightly across the yard to the back door of her home. Home. That was the word that separated them. The security he could never give. Holly kicked at the empty bottle. It shattered in tiny dancing spears.

CHAPTER TEN

Paul Hubbard stood at the fence and watched a dark brown gelding work across the pen, the rider gently guiding the animal's awkward steps. "That's the last of them, Holly. We can finish these on the road." Paul grinned as the bronc came to a neat stop by the gate. He couldn't keep the enthusiasm from his voice. "By all that is holy, we may have a good chance after all. We're ahead now, and no one's bothered us these past few days."

Three days had gone since they'd pulled the stock from the bog. Amy and her older sister rode out every day with the herd to the long valley, and stayed with them as guards. Sarah had reported something up on the rocky side of the valley on the first day; she placed a shot halfway up the wall to scare the intruder. Nothing else had come near the herd since then. Amy was enjoying the release from school. She could ride her pony all day, and Sarah packed a special lunch for them both. Almost like a holiday.

Holly and Hubbard's son had declared a truce, and worked together on the remaining stock. Holly's hangover the first day had been worked out with sweat and dust. He was more uncommunicative than before, rarely looking at anyone or speaking more than a few words. His silence fed the boy's anger. Jimmy still did not know what had gone on that night; all he knew was his sister's face when she looked at the man, his father's growing trust as he worked along with the drifter, and his mother's growing distress. Jimmy focused all his confusion on Holly, blaming him for all the unsettled feelings. Paul watched as the boy took out his anger on the horses; gone was his gentle touch, his empathy with each animal. He attacked the horses, raking them with harsh spurs until his father took the bloodied rowels away, his face stern.

Holly patted the damp brown neck, the horse lowering his head with a groan. Hubbard stood outside the railings, watching with evident satisfaction. "Jimmy and I are heading to town; we need supplies, and you certainly need some clothes." Paul spoke to his son, "Better put in a rifle; we may be needing protection." His voice came hard and flat; he was finally learning to protect his own. "We'll pick up more shells."

Holly swung down from the brown, stiff and uncomfortable in the boy's presence. Paul asked, "What do you need, shells for your rifle, got a handgun?"

Holly kept his head in the horse's belly as he fiddled with the cinch. "Nope, no handgun, just that .30-30, needs more shells." He pulled the rigging off the brown and dropped it over the fence. Still with his back to Hubbard, he spoke, "I'll check over the gear, get ready while you're gone."

Hubbard studied the tense back for a moment longer. "I think you need some new boots, and maybe pants. Don't want you getting tangled up in those britches you got now." He almost laughed. The drifter looked odd in his borrowed gear, the pants too short and bunched at the middle, the shirt flapping around his bony shoulders. Holly's head spun around at the teasing, his eyes flared bright with temper. For a moment Paul was startled by the reaction, then Holly took a visible hold on his anger, mumbled an inaudible "sorry," and walked off leading the brown.

Jimmy checked his father's reaction. "He sure has a short

fuse, Pa, wish he was gone."

Paul returned his son's glance, following the boy's eyes as he glared at the disappearing back. "We need him, Jim, and I think he needs us but won't admit to it."

Miriam watched as the team took her husband and son out of the yard and across the bridge. The dust settled, and she still remained on the porch. Their home was a beautiful place, and the next few weeks would determine if it would continue to be theirs. She sighed and brushed an errant wisp of graying hair from her eyes. A horse moving fast came from the valley. It was Amy's paint, his stubby legs moving faster than ever before, driven by his rider's urgency. Her thin voice came across the yard, "Help, Pa, Holly, help." Miriam picked up her long skirt and flew across the yard.

Holly shoved open the barn door, bridle in hand, and reached for the lathered paint. Amy struggled to speak. Holly put his hand on her leg, "Take a deep breath, bright eyes, it'll come." Her mother was there, terror strong on her face. It must be Sarah.

"Someone took a shot at us, someone tried to shoot Sarah, the horses are running all over, she's out there with someone shooting at her, she told me to come get Pa and help." Her words ran together in fright. Amy looked around her for her father. She slid off the paint, and her mother swept the small child up, arms tight and comforting.

Miriam's voice eased her fear. "Holly, I'll get Paul's handgun, be right back." Still holding her little girl, Miriam ran for the house. Holly disappeared into the barn, grabbed his rope, and caught up the dun. The gear went on fast, and the woman reached him as he mounted, to give him a pistol which he shoved into his waistband. "I couldn't find the holster, here are extra shells. Oh Holly, take care of Sarah."

Holly kept the rein on the dun short; the horse fidgeted and spun around. One hand on his rifle, jammed hard into the scabbard, he spoke to ease the mother's fears. "It's me the Judge's two want, not Sarah. She's bait. Surprised they weren't here earlier." With that he whirled the eager horse around and dug his heels hard into her ribs, giving the animal no chance to get her head down as they tore across the field to the valley entrance.

The dun plowed to a stop just short of the narrow opening to the valley, crossed by a wooden gate, left open in Amy's flight for home. A light breeze pushed the swinging wooden barrier. It complained of the motion. Far inside, Holly could see the horses bunched near the bog. A rifle spoke from half-way up the rock wall to his left. Another shot followed, answered by a flash of light from the bog end of the valley. The horses jumped at the noise, spinning and kicking in fright. Sarah was holding her own, and now he knew where one of the marksmen was. The tumbled rocks offered space to hide. There would be another rifle on the opposite side of the valley, waiting for the rescuer to show himself.

If he was careful, and quiet, he could climb his way up the rock wall, unseen by the sharpshooter on the east side until he entered into the fight. Surprise would give him an edge. Once he fired, though, his position would be open to the hidden gunman, a chance he would have to take. He couldn't leave the girl at their mercy. He was certain it was Jack and Turner. No one else in this peaceful range would use the Hubbard girls as targets. One good shot would take out half the enemy force; the rest was up to luck.

Working his way up the rock wall took precious time. He had to be careful not to dislodge any loose rocks, give himself away. Another shot went toward the end of the valley, giving the marksman's position to Holly. A deep slit in the wall offered him a good place to move around and yet be in good cover. Almost to the split a boulder was wedged sideways, blocking his path. He reached above blindly, left hand searching for a hold, right fist closed hard around the rifle, pistol shoved deep in the folds of his loose britches. He just needed a handhold, anything that would hold his weight.

125

His fingers found a deep gouge in the rock; he dug into the crevass, then sought a brace for his feet. He lifted the rifle and shoved it into the crack, leaving himself weaponless. His feet found a step in a straggling bush, roots wound into the rock wall. He pushed hard, and landed belly-down in the crevasse, the pistol driven into his belly, but still secure. Kind of a poor man's holster, these bunched pants.

Holly turned so he could look out over the valley below him. Close to the edge of the split he was exposed, but he also could fight back. Above him to his left a brief glimmer of blue told him he had gotten close to the sharpshooter. A shot rang out just beyond him; a moment later another shot came, near where the first one was fired from. Whoever was up there could move around some, hidden securely by the rock facing.

Holly would wait for the blue flash to show again, take a chance shot and at least draw fire away from Sarah. In order to fire above his position, he would have to crouch close to the edge of the ledge, offering a fine target to the rifle he knew was across the valley waiting. If luck held, he could take out one rifle and draw fire from the other, exposing his position. Another flash of blue drew his attention. The man was getting restless, spacing his shots closer, impatient to draw Holly into the valley trap. Holly waited, letting the short temper work for him.

In time Holly could see the shape of an arm, the blue flash, a bright shirt sleeve. Holding his rifle high, he rolled up into a sitting ball, took quick aim and squeezed his shot. The blue jerked and he heard a muffled yell. The echo of his own shot was hard and bright in the close space. A bullet whined past his ear, striking the wall behind him and sending rock chips flying. He could pinpoint the flash from across the valley floor, on the curve of the slowly rising tree-covered slope. Another shot followed, searching him out in the rock ledge. Time to get out of this trap now that he knew where both opponents were. Another shot. This one hit the wall beside him and angled off, raking a burn across his neck. He flinched at the instant pain, then hunched down and moved to the back of the ledge. That was too close.

His rifle leaped from his hand, the stock shattered by another searching bullet. Broken pieces slipped from his numbed left hand to bounce down the rock slide to the floor. He heard nothing from the man above him, but now the rifle across the floor spoke in rapid succession, each bullet deep in the split, bouncing from the walls in crazy angles. Either a direct hit or a richochet would find him soon. The burning line on his neck warned him. The one across the way was good and would soon find his mark.

Acting on instinct, Holly rolled out of the split, tightening up in a ball as he hit the slope. Trying to protect his head with one arm and holding his other across the handgun in his pants, he hit hard on his right shoulder, then bounced and rolled down the wall. Slamming into rocks, then caught for a moment on a scraggly tree trying to grow against the odds, he broke the fall's momentum. But he landed hard on the floor on his belly, right hand still clinging to the handgun, stunned by the force of the fall but basically unharmed. He waited: still, unmoving, each moment loud and clear. His breathing sounded harsh to him in the quiet. Blood seeped from the neck burn and spread in a thin trickle onto the grass. He was waiting, tensing his muscles at the magnified sounds. There was no action from either side of the valley.

Wait, listen, he counseled himself, wanting to stand and confront the snipers. A distant nicker from the dun came to him, a warning. Someone was moving. Footsteps came through the ground, hesitant; a long time between each step; watchful steps. Holly could count each stride, and wanted to hurry the distance between them. Everything was bright and clear, the blade of grass near his face sharp and defined. Distinct. The dun nickered again, moving restlessly in the grove of trees.

A snap close to him. And another. Holly rolled suddenly,

pulling at the pistol in his pants, cocking it clumsily with his right hand. In a continuous motion he was on his feet and firing. The man standing so close to him fired, the bullet going wild to chip the rocks in back of Holly. He fired three times at the figure; finally the tall, cavernous shape folded in slow motion; the body shifted backward from the force of the blows, arms flailing at the unseen foe as if to deny it entry into soft flesh. Jack Levitt landed on his back, arms and legs wide, and lay still. A bright red stain widened across his chest, blood pumped from a hole in his throat. More spread from just above his belt buckle. Luck had been with Holly.

There still was no movement from the rock wall, no return fire. Either Turner was too hurt to fire or had pulled out to leave his companion on his own. Holly stooped and picked up the rifle still clenched in Jack's right hand. This one would replace his own shattered weapon. He left the man's six-gun alone. Levitt's eyes had rolled up into his head; his mouth was pulled back into an unaccustomed grin. Irreverently, Holly thought that for the first time maybe Jack was some-place he liked. Looking down the valley, he could see Sarah coming out of the treeline leading her mount. He raised the captured rifle overhead. She gave an answering wave with her rifle and swung up on her mare to come join him.

Holly checked once more up into the rocks where he had seen and fired at the blue sleeve. Still no movement. Turner would have to wait. His dun looked up in anticipation as Holly approached, her soft nicker reaching his ears. With no warning something slammed into his back, along his ribs. Turner had been waiting.

The sharp report of the bullet came to him as he fell. Too late. His fall sent the dun plunging back on the reins. Holly's breath came short, deep lancing pain taking hold with each attempt to draw in needed air.

His back was numb; he was sliding into darkness. He knew there was something he had to do, so he tried to push up on his right arm. Even the barest of movement brought

128

spasms of agony. Bright flames went through his side, dulling his mind. The blackness beckoned; he could feel a pool of blood underneath his stomach. He was floating, drifting, all feeling gone. If he did nothing but lie still the pain would be over. Holly stopped fighting and dropped to the earth to lie still on the damp ground. Each beat of his heart added his own life fluid to the richness of the valley floor. His eyes closed in relief and acceptance.

But there was something he had to do. Sarah Hubbard. Down at the end of the valley, mounting her mare, responding to his signal that all was well, riding into Turner's trap. He shook his head feebly at the thoughts, and the pain coursed down his side to bring him back to the present. He groaned and rolled over on his left side. The intensity of the pain shocked him. He cried out, and the sound of his own voice came to him. The dun mare snorted violently, and shifted against the tied reins holding her.

Holly could see a stirrup hanging just within reach. The mare's restless stirring brought it even closer. Holly spoke softly, trying to calm the horse, soothe her, make her stand quietly. She stuck her nose near the bloody man, listening and checking. Holly touched the soft muzzle and stroked it gently, whispering nonsense. The mare relaxed; she knew those sounds. Holly shoved himself to a kneeling position, holding his right arm tight to his side, his forearm across his stomach. Blood continued to drip from just under his ribs all along his side. The stirrup looked to be far away, the horse a looming mountain too high to climb.

Sarah Hubbard. He grabbed for the swaying leather, caught it on the third try. The dun pulled against the pressure and snorted, made uneasy by the uncertain moves. Holly held hard to the stirrup and climbed up the fender until he could reach the saddle skirting. He was almost standing now, the dun shifting beside him, just barely willing to accept her rider's odd actions. Each breath tore more pain from him. Lights and circles spun in front of his eyes. He could focus on one thought; Sarah Hubbard was inside the valley, alone with Turner.

One foot found the stirrup; the left hand reached to the horn. Holly leaned forward, placed his weight in the saddle, and pulled. The movement was too much; sweat dripped from his face, nausea threatened to tip him over. Another deep breath, and again the agony went through him. Sarah. That thought kept him going. Setting himself, he leaned and pulled in one motion to raise himself over the saddle. The dun danced against the pull and her steps pushed Holly into the saddle. Dimly he realized he had not yet let go of the pistol, which was still clenched in his right fist. A death grip, he thought. Hell of a time for bad jokes.

He lifted the reins and the dun started down the valley. He kept the mare to the open trail, hoping to draw Turner's fire. What mattered was reaching Sarah. Ahead a shape came near his horse, other forms barely visible behind it, some floating free in his mind, some putting one foot in front of another, mimicking Jack's death waltz. The blurry shapes came closer, and the dun nickered in recognition. One of the forms spoke loudly, the sound sweet and clear. "Holly, oh Lord but I thought you were . . . who shot you . . . oh Lord."

Sarah stopped her mare, and the horse herd milled around her. The apparition in front of her shocked her badly. She had seen the spill from the rocks and had watched helplessly as Jack Levitt walked with rifle in hand, pistol held loosely in the other, toward the downed man. Then the sudden roll, the upward spin, the gun smoking fire. Shots, Levitt's fall. She had watched all this in disbelief. Then Holly had turned to her and raised his arm, telling her all was well. He had disappeared into an aspen grove; she hadn't heard the shot, but someone had gotten to him. His right side was covered in blood. She could see the thick liquid welling from a line at his ribs, dripping off into his boot. He rode hunched over, arm tight to his side.

Holly looked painfully at the woman as she rode up beside him, edging her horse closer. This was why he'd gotten up, and her face told him he was right. That she was important to him. Then memories and shapes from the past interfered; he could care, but he could not let her know. The pleasure in his eyes turned brittle and he straightened slowly in the saddle. "You've got the horses. Good. Turner's still up there. Levitt can wait. Let's get these broncs home." The harshness of his own voice shocked him as he stumbled over the words. Pity and anger fought in Sarah's face as she watched the wrangler. His anger had closed off the pleasure she had glimpsed in his eyes, leaving her nothing.

Her mare whirled around and in two strides was flying down the valley to circle around behind the horses. The dun struggled to follow, but Holly held on to the horn and reined the mare to the far side of the herd. The geldings took the path left for them and picked up into a gallop toward the ranch. Sarah followed at a gallop. The herd bunched wildly as they came to Jack's shrunken body lying at the base of the steep rock wall. They swerved and raced around him on their flight out the narrow opening.

Holly kept the dun to a lope, jerking with the motion, fighting the darkness that wanted to take him. He slowed the dun even more as they came near the main corral. The Hubbard's buckboard stood empty in the sunlit yard. Paul and his son were throwing gear on two horses. Sarah yelled to her father.

The two men stopped to watch her bring in the herd. The horses filed into the big corral and settled slowly from their excitement to dig into piles of hay. Sarah rode to her parents and dismounted, gesturing wildly as she told the story, then turned to watch the lone horse walking toward the barn.

Paul met the dun and put his hands on the reins to stop the mare. His hand went out to Holly for support. "No." The word turned the rancher away. A shake of Holly's head released more pain, his face tightened not to show the effect.

131

The initial shock had gone and he had had time to explore the wound. A slice of flesh taken from his side just between two ribs, a long deep slice starting at his back. Not fatal once the bleeding was stopped, just painful and messy. All he wanted was to get to the barn, clean the burning slash, and then sleep in his hay. But the Hubbards interfered.

"Jim, quick, get your mother. Tell her what's happened; she'll know what to bring. Quick." Paul Hubbard kept his hand on the mare and watched the tight-faced rider carefully, searching the shining eyes. Pain had clouded their clear amber lights, but the wariness, the keep-away look was still there, easy to read. But he tried again. "Holly, you took that bullet for us, now let us take care of you. It won't cost you anything."

Holly shook his head, battling the pain. Then Amy was there, her high voice intruding into his tired mind. "Pa, help him, it's awful. Do something." Holly winced at the fear in her voice. He straightened in the saddle and tried to smile, to ease her concern. The effort cost him dearly. Quietly, everything let go; he could hear nothing, and he slid from the saddle before anyone could help him.

CHAPTER ELEVEN

Something was different. Sarah woke with a start and looked over at the pallet where Holly lay, now quiet and still. She rose wearily from the chair she had slept in, and reached for his forehead. At the touch of her hand his eyes opened. He looked up at her, smiled faintly, and closed his eyes in sleep. She left her hand resting on his forehead, stroking the thin face. Now his skin was damp and cool to her touch.

He had frightened them; he had fought her parents when they tried to get him inside the house. All he could say was "barn, hay," and would not step inside the kitchen. He had fought her father's restraint while her mother cut away the tattered and soaked shirt to expose the wound, a deep furrow along his right side. Even in shock and pain he had resisted their help, relenting only when they fixed a bed of hay for him in the small grain room in the barn. The bullet had hit the lowest rib in his back and had followed the curve, leaving a long, ragged hole. Blood covered everything by the time her mother had cleansed the open wound and was able to stop the bleeding. Fever had set in, leaving him restless and semiconscious. Eyes wide and bright, skin dry, burning to the touch, he'd fought his ghosts until the early morning hours. Sarah had sat with him until the fever eased, then sleep had claimed her. It was the change in his breathing that had awakened her. The fever had gone.

Holly struggled to sit up. The soft hay shifted under him. A sharp pain in his side stopped the struggle. Waiting, he felt it subside into a throb, harsh but bearable. He tried to sit again, made it this time and sat with his head hanging against the dizzying whirl. He couldn't stay here; there was too much still to do. Someone had put him in a nightshirt; it caught underneath him, pulling him back against the mounded hay. A deep breath, a sharp pain. Another deep breath, the pain was less. His trembling hand reached for the chair back, to use it as a crutch. With the chair held unsteadily in his grip, he was able to pull himself erect. This too was bearable. The wound ached but it was no longer the all-consuming fire. Now he didn't even have the borrowed shirt to wear; he thought back over the battle; must be one good-sized hole in the shirt now. He'd be down to skin soon. The looseness of the nightshirt amused him. Guess he was next to naked now.

He tried a step. His legs wobbled and threatened to quit, then stayed firm. Standing with his feet wide apart and one hand on the chair, he listened, trying to determine where the Hubbards were, what was going on, how long he had been out. The distance from the pallet to the grain-room door looked a long way, but it was the only way out. He pushed the chair ahead of him; it scraped along the dirt floor and then caught on something. Now the distance was measurably shorter. Holly gambled and let go of his support to take the few steps that brought him up against a post. He leaned his head on the solid wood, settling the spinning room. One good breath of air or a shove, and he'd be flat on his back again.

Holly raised his head. A startled face was close to his. Paul Hubbard stood there, foot raised to step inside the small, sunless room. "Guess you are awake. Sarah came to the house saying your fever broke, and that you'd opened your eyes. She's asleep now, sat up with you all night. How do you feel?" Holly didn't want to answer questions, he wanted to know what had happened, and what would happen now.

His voice came out raspy and uncertain. "How long I been out, any trouble with the Judge, you got the drive ready?" Holly's voice wavered, betraying his weakness.

Paul put a hand on the thin shoulders and steadied the man. "Best set back down. Miriam made some soup just for you; a bowl will help you back on your feet." He firmly backed Holly to the pallet and eased him back down. The wounded man wanted to resist, but the soft hay was too inviting. His burst of energy was gone, leaving a returning sense of weakness. Words came to him, but he was unable to speak them easily.

Finally, he looked up at the rancher. "Thanks for putting me back together. Jack set me up good, almost worked. Sorry for the trouble." He hesitated a moment, then spoke again. "Thanks." The word wasn't enough, but it was all he had.

Hubbard's words eased the tension. "You came in with the horse herd yesterday, just after noon. It's about noontime today. I rode back this morning but there was no sign of Jack's body. Even I could read the tracks that Turner left getting out of the valley; looks like you got him too, but not too bad. Only a bit of blood on the rocks, a lot more near where Jack was. Jimmy went into town this morning. We wanted to let folks know what their great 'Judge' has been doing before he sets out his own version. We don't want any trouble with the law."

Paul sat in the chair facing Holly and watched the man's face. His color had faded to a pale gray and his eyes now held a feverish glint. "You best stay down. Miriam'll be spooked at me if you get fevered again. She'll blame me for talking too much."

Holly lay his head back against mounded hay; a grimace came sharp across his face. His voice was soft. "Glad you got your boy to help with the broncs; it'll be a while before I can sit a buck worth much." The two were silent, each considering what the next few days held. Holly knew the horse herd had to get moving before the Judge replaced Jack with another killer. And concern sobered Paul's face. The drive had to be soon, and they would be a man short without Holly. It would be a week or more before that gouge healed enough to allow him to ride, perhaps even longer. The herd had to move before then. Leaving Holly behind with Miriam was the only answer, yet he hesitated before accepting this inevitability. He depended on Holly's good sense and quick action.

Holly could watch the conflict work on Hubbard, and recognized the cause. "Be up tomorrow—sleep and some food will see to that. Can't top the wild ones yet, but I'll be there for the drive. Just give me today." His voice faded, his eyes shut. Hubbard rose and pushed the chair aside to leave. Bishop had read his thoughts too clearly. He opened his mouth to clear the situation, but the words were slow in coming.

His wife came into the room, carrying a tray and some clean bandages. "Time for him to eat, and rest. Let me check the cloths. Paul, now out, don't bother him with anything now. Just let the man sleep." Relieved of having to speak his mind, Paul let himself be gently shoved out of the dark room.

The soup was good. Hot and thick, lifegiving. More of it, and a good rest—these would put him back on a horse. Mrs. Hubbard pushed Holly back down on the hay. He could feel his face turn red as she pulled up the nightshirt to check his wound. His embarrassment touched and amused the woman. Then her face clouded. Dots of fresh blood colored the white bandage. She scolded as she cleaned the raw wound and replaced the dressing. By the time she was done, Holly was asleep, face pale but relaxed.

Her husband was waiting outside. They walked to the back of the barn together, each searching for the words to voice their concerns. Finally, Miriam spoke. "Paul, what

136

now? He certainly won't be fit enough to ride with you in three days, never mind going tomorrow. Is Jimmy back yet? I wonder what the Judge will do next?" The questions mirrored her concerns for the family. So much would be settled in the next week, and so many things had gone wrong.

Paul pulled his wife to him and held her silently for a long moment. "We're not done yet, my love. There is still time. We'll be all right."

Jack's paint half-reared in refusal, and Turner's heavy fist struck the mare between the eyes, momentarily stunning the rebellious animal. The shock of the blow traveled up his arm and caused a flare of pain from the bullet slash high up on the fleshy part of his forearm. He cursed the man who had shot him, then cursed the inert body of his former companion. "Greenhorn, you knew better than to walk up to a downed man without shooting him again. You got what you deserved." Hauling the horse up tightly by her bit, Turner attempted to load the body over the saddle. The dead man's shirt ripped and his body fell back to the ground, sending the twitching paint back harder. Turner stood and cursed the snorting horse, the dead bag of flesh at his feet, most of all the drifter. Only the need to remove the evidence of their assault kept him from leaving Jack there to rot. The Judge would insist on disposing of the corpse properly. Hope he has a good wake, with lots of whiskey. The prospect made Turner look more favorably upon the body. This would be one bottle he wouldn't have to share.

He kicked the unprotesting hulk and grabbed it by the belt. The handle held and he was able to throw Jack over the paint's back. The mare stood, shaking, the blood smell assaulting her nose, but fear of blood was less than her fear of the man holding the reins. Turner mounted the chestnut and led the dancing paint out of the valley, and around the back of the rock wall to the Judge's ranch. The deal had gone bad. The only high spot earlier that day had been watching the drifter go down under the bullet to fall hard to the valley floor. That satisfaction no one could take from him. It had been his bullet.

Now the planning was up to him. He could do better than Jack. Jack would have stayed to shoot the woman once Bishop was dead. But Turner knew better. The Judge may have a hold on the town merchants, but they would not stand for shooting a woman. Taking shots to keep her pinned, to set a trap, was one thing; killing her was out. Now he could ride back to the Judge, with the failure of Jack's ideas riding with the dead body. Turner already had his plan. Best to ambush Hubbard with the herd on the trail, scatter the broncs and keep the crew from rounding them up. The Judge would have to give him a tougher bunch than those ranch hands he hired. He needed hard cases who didn't flinch at rousting women. He was betting the Hubbard girl, the one who tried bossing him in town, would be riding along with her pa. He had special plans for her.

He'd send a man to hang around town, watch if the herd comes through. Have another up to Tyson's, just in case. And he'd be hiding above the ranch, and do his own watching. Be an easy few days lying up behind that house, a bottle or two to keep him company. The Hubbards would be shorthanded, their bronc rider dead and the word out so nobody signed on with them. Be against the Judge's orders. A big smile covered his meaty face as he yanked the horses up in front of the Judge's corral. Tossing the reins to an indifferent puncher, he said nothing about the paint's burden, just nodded and walked to the main house. The cowboys who worked for the Two Crown had learned not to get curious; it was bad for their health.

The Judge listened to Turner, his face somber. He could turn his anger on Jack, the utter carelessness, the stupidity. The man had been hired because of his supposed expertise. And to be put down by a mere wandering bronc rider, to be beaten by an amateur, and a handicapped one at that, was a fitting end for a fool. He picked up his pacing, oblivious to Turner's demand for a bottle. Up and down the room, the same number of steps in each line of march. "How dare you, how dare you demand of me, when you cannot even carry out the simplest of tasks." The Judge stopped abruptly, finally aware that the big oaf in front of him was actually demanding, not asking.

Turner stood still, legs apart and arms folded in a parody of the Judge's "at ease" stance. "Judge, that drifter's down and gone. His body warn't there when I got Jack's, but sure was a mess of blood where I dropped him. Ain't my fault Jack was no good. Those were your orders to me, to get the drifter." Turner placed a heavy sound on the "me," letting Breen know that he, at least, had done his job.

"Hire me some men, four good ones, tough enough to do what I want. Jack never could plan nothing." Turner's harsh interruption of the judicial tirade, his refusal to follow military procedure, shook Jonathan Breen. He wanted that stallion, he wanted the Hubbards wiped out and his town returned to him, but it was to be done in precision, cleanly, by military campaign standards. It now was messy, out of control, but he could not stop yet; he had not gotten his prize, and Turner was his only logical solution. "Yes, certainly, hire all the men you deem necessary to do what must be done. But get that stallion for me." The last words were shouted.

Judge Breen stopped himself, appalled at his lack of control. His voice lower, more controlled, he spoke to Turner. "Now, let Mrs. Hutton clean your arm, and I'm certain you would agree to a bottle of whiskey." The Judge turned away at the sight of the widening, vicious smile. He had just handed this ruffian free rein, and he did not want to know what the man planned to do. He only wanted his horse.

Pleasure flooded Julie Warner, an undeniable warmth,

but she let only a bit of it into her smile. Jimmy Hubbard had come into town this morning, and now sat in front of her, talking nonstop. He looked tired and hungry, but his brown eyes glowed with delight, his arms flew, as he described the events of the past few days. The pretty girl in front of him was listening to him, just him. But Julie's smile dimmed as she paid attention to the tale. Her voice was husky when she spoke. "Let me get Mr. Simpson; he'll want to hear what you've been telling me. This is terrible, how could the Judge turn those men on you and your family? What does he have against Mr. Bishop, it's awful that he was shot."

Julie hurriedly pushed through the swinging door into the kitchen, missing the scowl that replaced the delight on the boy's face when she worried about the bronc rider. Wherever he went, people were concerned for or angry about this man. Never mind how Jim Hubbard felt or what he did. His anger grew, fueled by those few kind words. The fears of the past few days burned into a deeper anger and resentment.

Julie and Mr. Simpson came back through the door, followed by Mrs. Simpson. Their faces mirrored the concern he had seen in Julie's; damn them, he thought, shocked at his own words; they care more for that useless drifter than for me and my troubles. Simpson questioned him carefully, starting with Jack and Turner coming to the ranch to threaten Holly and drive him away. Jimmy resisted telling the tale, but the words were pulled from him by the air of authority he felt in the older man. Townspeople came in for mid-morning coffee, to become involved in the tale of the events at the ranch. Soon the boy found himself surrounded by people, their low whisperings of concern and dismay at the words giving him importance. These folks were listening to *him*, not to his father or that damnable drifter. They wanted to hear what *he* had to say.

More people came into the cafe, but Jimmy had no more to tell. He knew that Jack's body had been removed before this morning, but nothing beyond that. The gathering crowd wanted more details; they wanted plans of retaliation; they wanted to hear that the Hubbards would fight back. For the first time, the townspeople felt united in their distaste for the Judge's high-handed actions. His financial importance did not buy this kind of treatment of a family—a good family—hardworking and a fine addition. Jimmy started to retell the story, wanting back the silent attentiveness as these people listened to him speak. The red-headed horse trader, Red Willis, interrupted the boy.

"You told us all that, but what do your father and Bishop plan to do now? Sounds like Bishop made himself a part of what's going on; bet they got something in mind." Willis was one of the small local ranchers whose easygoing nature had allowed the Judge to assume control of the area. All he wanted was to hunt his wild horses, sell them for a profit, and keep his shack and slab-wood barn together. "Damn it, Jimmy, something's got to be done about this; can't have the Judge running everything around here. He's taking too much this time." The voice of the crowd was louder, more insistent, drowning out the boy's attempt to continue the story. Jimmy raised his voice above the crowd's, determined to gain their attention again.

"We do have a plan. Pa's going to drive the horses out beyond Tyson's Station instead of through town. It'll take longer but he bets the Judge's men won't be expecting him to do that. Then out on the plain it'll be clear sailing to the fort." Julie realized Jimmy's mistake and reached out to hush him. The boy pushed her hand aside and continued, not wanting to lose the crowd again. "We'll get those horses out the hard way and surprise the Judge. You'll see."

The men in the crowd became quiet, knowing they had heard more from the boy than they should have. Red Willis grabbed Jimmy's shoulder and spun him out of the silent crowd to one side. "Son, you just put your pa's plans right out where the whole town can see them. They kinda lose their surprise that way. Some snake will carry the tale to the

Judge." Willis thought for a moment. He had really been the one to push the kid by asking for more when the boy was dry. "Guess I owe your family an explanation." He grabbed his hat and shoved at the boy, forcing reluctant steps that brought them to the door. "Say your good-byes to the pretty lady, kid; I'm taking you home." Bewildered by the hustle, and unable to resist the strong hand in his back, Jimmy only saw Julie out of the corner of his eye. She stood alone by the counter to give him a brief smile. Then he went flying through the doorway, Red Willis right behind him.

Another left just after them, waiting until they had mounted and ridden away. He rubbed a dirty hand over his unshaven jaw, then pushed his shapeless hat down on his head. A slab-sided mustang, head hanging, stood just across the street at a tie rail. What he had just heard would be worth at least a new horse to this Judge. The man mounted, jammed in his spurs, and loped out of the small town.

CHAPTER TWELVE

The dark bay stallion bugled his challenge to the intruders. His call echoed across the high pasture, insistent and demanding. Paul Hubbard reined in his gray gelding and sat, watching the magnificence of the horse. He had come up here with no plan, just wanting to see the stallion and the band of mares, to watch the long-legged new foals run with their stilted grace while investigating their world. These horses were his future and his family's; their exuberance reassured him that the coming battle was worth the price. This herd was the foundation for his life. The gray moved restless beneath his rider; he knew the stallion would tear him apart and wanted to leave his territory. Paul eased the gray with a slap on the neck, and spoke to the alert bay. "At least the Judge won't send someone to take a shot at you. You're too valuable to him."

What to do next rolled over and over in Hubbard's thoughts. Bishop insisted he would be riding with them in a few days. But seeing the man lying still, face pale and drawn, made it difficult to believe he would be up and riding. The trail to Tyson's and onto the plains was steep and rough. Tying the horses head to tail instead of loose-herding them made sense, but the trail would demand a fit rider. Sarah would be going with them, and Miriam and Amy would stay behind to care for their ranch stock. And Jimmy. The boy would be a good hand if he let go of his unreasonable reactions to Holly. The drive had to be made soon, and it was no place for fighting. The contract held a specific date and they must meet it.

Paul turned the gray to pick his way back down the slide toward the ranch. He still had no solution to the problems, but he felt immensely better for having visited the stallion. The bay horse stood and watched their passage, triumphant once again in protecting his band of mares. His high scream echoed against the rocky walls and followed Hubbard down the trail.

Amy bounced into the grain room, book in hand. "Holly," her whisper was loud and excited, "you awake? I can't come in unless you're awake, Mommy says." Her clear whisper reached Holly's sleep-heavy mind, and he turned to see the shining face. The small girl came and settled in the chair. "I brought a book to read to you, Mommy says you probably would like some company and this would be a good way for me to keep up with my school work. Miss St. John says we must read aloud every day. Can I read to you, this is Sir Walter Scott's *Ivanhoe*, and Papa says it's a really good book." The slight smile on Holly's face encouraged Amy, so she opened the book to the second chapter. "Let me tell you what's happened so far." Her high voice outlined the plot, familiar to Holly, one he remembered his mother reading to him. These memories didn't hurt, and he lay quietly to listen to the childish voice read the familiar words.

Sarah stepped into the small room. "Amy, you're needed to gather eggs, and round up those hens; they've escaped again. Quick now." She took the book from her sister and glanced at the cover and smiled. "I'm surprised you can listen to this; Amy hardly knows all the words."

Holly lifted his head and watched the small child leave. "That's all right, I remember the book and she's done fine."

Sarah's dark brown eyes brightened at this bit from his

past. She spoke softly, so as not to scare him, "We know so little of you, and yet you've helped us so much. I never did thank you for coming to get me. My husband . . ." her voice trailed off, and bitterness replaced the easy look in her eyes. "Ward never cared for my family, wouldn't stay and help my father when he was needed, wanted only to chase his own dreams." Her face softened with memories. "I loved to watch him ride; he practically lifted the horse with his energy. He could make a stable nag into a race horse. He just swept me up and made me into a race horse. I couldn't bear not to be with him." The realization of what she was saying came to her, and she stopped.

But the drifter just lay there, no judgement on his face, listening to her fancy. Sarah found herself blushing; she had never talked like this about Ward, not even to her mother. The words were too painful, but they came out so easily in front of this silent and bitter man. Needing to take the talk away from herself, she asked a question of the injured man. "Your name intrigues me; why would anyone name a boy Holly? I'm sure others give you a hard time about the name."

The answer was slow and deliberate, as if explaining to a child. "My mother was taken with the name in a book. She showed me the pictures of the windmills, the canals, the people in wooden shoes. She fought with my father about the name. Holland may be a strange name, but she liked it." The usual bitter set to his face had softened for this brief time. Then he looked hard at the woman standing so near him. "That's a long time ago, gone, just like your man. Don't matter now."

He pushed himself into a sitting position, the exertion causing a spasm of pain across his face, sweat beading on his forehead. "Your father said he brought back some clothes from town. I need them. Got to get up." Sarah recognized the anger; she had gotten too close when he spoke to her of private things. "Miss, best get me something to wear, can't ride in this damn dress." Legs under him, Holly pushed

145

himself erect as Sarah backed away.

At the door she turned to take a long, steady look at this man fighting the pain to ride with her family. "I'll get the clothes, be back in a minute."

If he waited and let the boy speak first, Red figured it would make the kid come face to face with what he'd done in town, speaking out about things he had no right to. He watched the boy's father come down from the trail to the high pasture. Paul Hubbard sure sat a horse right, and the long free strides of his gray stirred Red's trading instincts. Man could do well selling this kind of stock. Better than those mustangs.

He watched Hubbard's face change as he recognized the rider with his son. A smile lightened the worry, as Hubbard put his gray next to Red's grullo. "What brings you out here, Red? Not much to trade now, but we can talk in a few months. I've got some good young stock that needs breaking, and plan to get to them after this remount business is settled." Hubbard's face sobered at the reminder of the battle to come.

Red spoke quietly, careful with his words. "Thought I might just happen by, seeing you be short of hands for the drive and all. Busy time for you, but I ain't got much pressing. Quite a tale your son had to tell in town." Paul sensed something more behind the neighborly words than Red was spelling out. He started to push for more, but the horse trader turned the questions by gesturing to Jimmy. "Your boy here done got some things to talk about with you. If'n you don't mind, I'll put my bronc up for a bit and see the missus about a cup of coffee. Long ride out here." He dismounted and walked the grullo past the boy into the cool interior fo the barn, leaving the son to face his father alone.

Stripping the gear from his horse, and securing him in a stall, Red went through the back of the barn, admiring its solid construction. The pole corrals and the stock in them were meant for permanence. At the back door to the house, Mrs. Hubbard met him with coffeepot in hand. "Why, glad to see you, Mr. Willis; we haven't had a visit in quite a time. Do come in and set. Coffee's hot, and I'm sure Paul will be right up from the barn." This was a lady to Red's way of liking; she took in the facts and laid out her welcome.

As he entered the kitchen, he noticed a tall, thin man leaning in a doorway. Shadows made it hard to see for a moment, then he recognized the drifter who had grabbed the dun mare back at George Kelleher's. Red nodded a greeting. "Ain't seen you in a bit; heard you met up with a bullet. Don't look too dead to me." The silent man tipped his head in acknowledgement.

Red took the offered seat, and smiled his thank-you to the lady as she put hot coffee in front of him. "Biscuits, too, Red, when they're done, and some raspberry jam from last summer. I've been heating some soup for Holly." Red took a deep sip of the coffee and looked around the kitchen. These folks had the heart of their family in this house and their horses. Damn shame that the Judge was so set on ruining them.

He glanced briefly at the man still standing in the shadows. "Join me; this hot coffee and those promised biscuits will set easy. You sure look as if you need the fodder." Holly sat slowly, keeping a wary eye on the red-headed puncher.

The back door slammed open; the boy came in followed closely by his father. Tension was in both faces as Paul stood by his son. "Miriam, get Sarah and Amy, please. Jimmy has something to say to the family and I want everyone present." Holly started to rise at the words, a half-eaten biscuit in one hand. Paul motioned to him and Red to remain. "You two stay. Holly, you're already committed to the drive with us, and Red, you know what is going on. I want this done clean." Jimmy's face was high-colored in embarrassment. He felt like a school kid, apologizing to the class for a prank. Made to face everyone and confess. But what he had done was no prank, and he was truly sorry. His mother returned with the two girls, and the three stood up against the back wall, their eyes on him.

"Jimmy, go ahead. Tell us what happened in town." His father's face held both anger and concern. The boy started to speak and found he couldn't. The room was too hot, his parents too near him, crowding him. He cleared his throat and tried again. "I got to town and saw Julie at the cafe, like Pa told me. I told her all of what happened and she made me repeat it to the Simpsons. Then more folks came in. And I got to tell them all about everything, the horses, Holly shooting Jack, everything. They all listened to me and asked questions. Then they all got started talking and forgot about me. I . . ." He stumbled over the next few words. "I wanted them to pay attention to me again. I know it was wrong, but I told them we were going to leave tomorrow or the day after with the horses and go out back of Tyson's." He swallowed and looked away from the rising anger in his father's face. "I told them all about our plans and they listened to me. Red got me to shut up, made me come home. I'm really sorry."

Jimmy stopped abruptly and looked at the floor. The room was quiet for a long while, then the drifter spoke, matter of fact, casual, accepting. "If you start now, this afternoon, and go up the old trail through Badger Pass to Cottonwood, Turner will lose time finding the herd. He's expecting you to go out tomorrow in a different direction. I came over that pass, followed the trail. Not easy, but it's passable. Can find it again no trouble. Red here'll keep quiet. That ought to give you a day's start. Set a guard behind the herd, lead them single file, push them. You can get through." Silence greeted his long speech.

Red smiled at the words. This was bringing the fight right past the enemy. He liked it. He spoke up. "Mr. Hubbard, Ma'am, I rode out here today not just to keep Jimmy company. Want to sign on for your drive. Got nothing going

148

on, only two broncs to my place and both lame. Figure to make the drive with you, if you'll have me."

Paul Hubbard's shoulders relaxed, and his face rounded in a big grin. These two men would make the difference; the drive would work. "Miriam, quick, get some food set. Jim, catch up my gray and pick yourself a good mount. Sarah will be wanting her chestnut mare." She nodded her agreement, catching the mounting excitement from her father. "Sarah, get your things ready, best bring some bandages and medicine, take care of Bishop here and any other problem. Let's go." Enthusiasm brought the family alive. They hurried to their different chores with a quickened purpose. Holly pushed back his chair and stood up, the tightening in his face against the pain barely noticeable. But Sarah noticed, and Red noticed. It would be a tough ride for this man, and he would be needing help. The two exchanged a brief look over the intervening table and watched the cowboy walk slowly out the door.

Red thanked the lady of the house again for the coffee and biscuits. He'd kept eating while the kid talked; he'd heard the story before. Had managed to finish off six biscuits. Ought to hold until supper. The whole shebang was turning out pretty interesting, be good to get out from under the Judge. He'd been pushing too hard lately, riding right over good folks. He'd druther ride with the cowboy. Even in bad shape the man was a fighter. Be smart to do a bit of baby-sitting on the drive. With a great show of disinterest, Red walked behind Holly to the barn, watching each step and ready to put out a hand.

At the barn, he caught up with the man. "You probably will be wanting that dun mare, 'pears to me she might throw a couple of bucks. How 'bout I top her for you, don't want to mess up that new shirt too soon." Red's offer struck Holly's pride; he could ride any horse, especially that dun. But the truth behind the offer was undeniable; a mishap now and he would hold the trip back or leave it one man short. He spoke

149

words he rarely had need of. "Thanks, would help."

Holly put his gear on the dun mare; next to him, Red companionably saddled his grullo. No words passed between the two men. Once the mare was tacked and done, Holly gave Red the reins, and his mouth twitched into an awkward grin. "She's fresh, and likes to drop that off shoulder. Never use spurs on her; just ride it out, and keep fanning." Red accepted the reins and the advice. He could like this man given time.

The mare put her heart into removing the new rider, but found there was another top hand on her. Coming back to the ground to stand quietly on four legs, she turned her head to check out Red's booted foot and snorted. Red slapped the mouse-colored neck and laughed. "Thought she was a good 'un, and she sure is."

Two horses, the sturdy gray gelding and a deep bay, came through the barn, led by Jimmy. "Pa says once we're saddled up to go out to the home pasture and bring in the stock."

Red remained on the dun. "Kid, you and I'll go get them broncs, no need getting too many hands out there and crowding things. Be back in a shake."

Before Holly could protest, Jimmy slipped up onto the saddled bay and the two gigged their horses into a high lope across the corrals, stopping only briefly to open the large gate. Red let out a wild whoop and their mounts responded by leaping into a full run, tails high. The herd could see them coming, and immediately took flight, heading around the pasture at a full gallop, some letting out tremendous bucks in mid-stride. Jimmy went to the outside of the herd and Red stayed behind them, chasing the stragglers. Within minutes the horses were headed to the corrals. The boy rode in with the herd, his bay gelding prancing at the restraining rein. Red stopped to close the gate. Both riders pulled up in front of Holly, eyes flashing, heads high in excitement. Jimmy's face no longer had the soft look of a child. He was a man doing a man's work.

Red slid off the dun mare and handed the reins back to

Holly. "Did a right good job on this 'un, going to be a great drive. Wouldn't mind seeing the Judge's face when these here horses make it to the fort." Red's enthusiasm lit his whole face, the shining pleasure of working with good stock and clean country. Holly found it hard to share the good spirits; Turner was still out there with the mind to finish him. Once the herd got started, there'd be gunhands out looking for them. Wordlessly he stared at Red, his eyes flat. A long look passed between the two, then Holly took the mare to the barn, slipped the bit, and loose-tied her. Time to gather what gear he had and get ready.

Red stood for a long moment and pushed his hat back on his bright hair. Damn. That cowboy could come down hard without saying a thing. Yeah, it was time to pack and get serious, but there was something magnificent about bringing in a good herd that needed to be celebrated. Jimmy came up to stand next to Red, and followed his gaze to the disappearing back. His words came unexpected and violent. "I hate him. Whatever he does here gets my pa and ma upset. Leaves Sarah all weepy. Never gives an inch. I hate him."

It took Red some time to find the words and figure the angles. "Kid, go easy. That gent's seen more'n you ever will. Fighting back is all he knows. Take a listen and do what he says." He slapped the reluctant youngster on the back. "So let's get our gear wrapped up and pack them horses. Here comes your pa."

Paul was pleased to see his son with the flame-haired wrangler. The horse trader was a good addition to their crew. Round faced, stoop shouldered, below-average height with an accentuated bowlegged walk, the man was a godsend. Jimmy was beginning to grow up, and the easy-going horseman was helping the process. And then there was Holly, walking slowly out of the barn to join them.

"Red, you divide those horses into bunches of seven. We'll be taking a couple of extras in case the army rejects any, plus

151

enough horses to get home on. Tie them head to tail. We'll need to pack grain for the crossing up to Cottonwood. Not much graze there, so Bishop tells me." He turned to include the silent man. "Holly, I want you to get us started on the trail to Badger Pass, then backtrack to look for followers. Turner will figure out soon enough what we've done and we'll need cover. It should only take him a day to realize we didn't go out by Tyson's." Holly nodded in agreement.

Red and Jimmy spoke as one. "Yessir, sounds good."

Miriam Hubbard's voice called across the yard to Holly. Leaving his few belongings wrapped in the sheepskin coat, he went through the barn and out the back, walking quickly to the kitchen door. Instinct told him someone was watching, and the less he was exposed, the less chance of being shot. His rifle was carried easily in his left hand. Inside, Mrs. Hubbard was waiting with more cloths and hot water.

"I want to put extra padding on your wound. I told my husband you were in no shape to ride today, or any day for the next few weeks, but he said you insisted on going along. And we do need you." She stopped and looked at the young man, trying to catch his eye. He averted his face, unwilling to meet her gaze. "I do want to thank you for all your help, and to apologize for the trouble we have caused you." Holly felt as if her words should have come from him. He stirred uncomfortably; she had made her point. Her hand on his shoulder gently pushed him into a kitchen chair. "Sit, Mr. Bishop, we will at least make certain you are well cared for now, and well-wrapped for your ride. Take off your shirt."

The shirt unbuttoned, Holly shrugged his shoulders to drop the garment. Unexpected hurt ran through his side. He tried to hide his reaction, but it twisted across his face. She gently took the shirt collar and eased the sleeve from his left arm. Then, carefully, as if undressing an infant, she pulled the sleeve down his right arm. Sweat covered his face. He put his head down, cradled in his left arm, his breath coming in shallow gasps. A hand lay lightly on his forehead, touching the heat of returning fever. "Mr. Bishop, you cannot—"

His voice came muffled by his arm. "Ma'am, just get me bound tight and leave me be. Going time'll be soon, and I best be ready." He remained silent, head on his arm, while she pulled the stained pad away from the raw gouge in his side. His lean body stiffened against the tearing, but he remained silent and still.

Looking up from bathing the inflamed wound, Miriam Hubbard met her daughter's eyes. Concern was strong in her face. Sarah walked quietly to her mother and took the stained cloth from her hand. Motioning her mother away, she knelt down to continue the washing. A low moan escaped from the tense body when she pulled the extra pad from his back, where the bullet had started its damaging path. The hole showed bright red with fresh blood welling around the white rib edge. As she worked swiftly to bathe and rebind the angry sore, Sarah marveled again at the punishment this man had taken. His dark hair was so close to her, she wanted to cradle his head to her breast, to give him comfort, to touch his face and ease his pain. The intensity of what she felt reached Holly through the misting pain. The soft gentle hands gave him pleasure. Angry at himself for reacting to Hubbard's wife like a range stud, he raised his head, eyes blurry, mouth white.

It was Sarah kneeling to work on him, her face so close to his, her hands gentle on his side. An involuntary groan came from him; he straightened in the chair and moved away from her. They faced each other. Sarah touched her hand to her mouth and then reached to touch Holly's face. Her hand stopped in mid-air.

Holly's voice broke the moment. Harsh from pain and wanting, he spoke. "Lady, you best get to finishing your work and let me go. This ain't no good." Sarah bent her head to her work, layering the pads of white cloth to his side and binding them tight. A smile softened her mouth. They had days.

Less than one hour later, the horse herd was ready. In loose order the long line moved out over the wooden bridge,

153

to turn right along the creek. They would follow this line as if heading for Tyson's, then, just before the station, they would swing onto the old track leading up Badger Pass. Holly knew the turn. He had found Kimball and the mares stuck in the mud there. They would hit the area in late afternoon, and would be able to get partway up the pass before it became impossible in the evening dark to follow the trail. A cold camp tonight, and then move on early the next morning. Pushing the herd this way, they would make it almost to Cottonwood the next evening, well ahead of anyone the Judge could send to find them.

At the head of the string, Paul Hubbard was fighting with reluctant stock pressed into service as pack horses. Half-broke, carrying the dead weight of supplies was against their nature, and they took easily to fighting back. Sarah sat her mare easily; her line gave little trouble. Jimmy rode high-shouldered and tense with excitement, and his dark bay echoed the tension of his rider, taking short steps and jigging with nervous energy. To Red, the drive was simple, old hat. His horses gave him no trouble. He rode easy, rolling a smoke as his grullo jogged comfortably at the head of his line.

Holly kept the mare ahead of them all, glad to be out and alone. His side bothered him less if he kept his right arm tucked hard against it. The pain was constant but easy to take. Once he found the trail and rode to the back of the horses, he could set his own pace and worry less. Anyone chasing the herd would have to ride over him first. Whenever he looked back, he caught Sarah's eyes watching him. He worried more about Turner. At the ranch it felt as if someone watched from high in back of the house. He felt vulnerable and exposed in the yard. Several times he had stood just inside the barn and watched the rock spill above the ranch house. He could see nothing, but he knew someone was there.

CHAPTER THIRTEEN

"You got it, mister." Turner had grinned as the drifter once again looked up at his hiding place behind the rock slide. "You bet I'm up here watching. Going to stay here till you move out them horses, then I'll meet you at Tyson's and have a big surprise for you. Got extra special plans for you, bud, and that high-flying pretty gal who got her eye on you; know just what I am to do with you both."

Between Hubbard's ranch and Tyson's Station, the sweet grazing land turned into harsh rock-strewn hills, where few wild things lived by choice. Trails led through the area, now faint and hardly used. Those riding them traveled by night. They cursed the sharp rock that lamed their mounts, and the barren vegetation that offered little to eat for man or beast.

Turner found the wasteland ideal for what he had in mind. Just above the Hubbard house was a crumbling rock wall, offering excellent hiding. He had ridden to the overhang after lifting three bottles from the Judge's vast storehouse. Jack's burial had been brief, and Turner had ridden off that evening, using the darkness to cover him while he worked his way down the wall to slide into the shelter offered by the rock. All the comforts of home; shade, whiskey, a good view of the ranch, and time to plan.

There were surprises as the day progressed. Red Willis

showed up with the Hubbard boy; looked like he planned on riding out with the Hubbards. Turner didn't mind. They'd come to blows over his treatment of the chestnut gelding that Red had sold to the Judge, and Willis swore he'd not let Turner get his hands on another good horse. Having the bandy-legged cowboy riding with the herd gave Turner a chance to bury him while they drove off all those good horses. But the big surprise had been the drifter. He'd come out of the barn, stiff and slow, but he was there. Turner had seen the blood run across his back, had gloried in the man's slack-limbed fall to the ground. Guess this one was tougher than he looked, but him being down below only gave Turner another chance to wipe him out. And the Judge would never know.

The drifter was spooky. Kept looking up into the hills as if he knew Turner was there. A few times Turner thought he'd been spotted, but the man had moved on, uncertain but suspicious. It sure looked like the Hubbards were planning to move out soon—the horses saddled, the herd close in and ready. And the drifter, checking and rechecking Turner's position, as if he could see through the rock.

Turner stretched his arms above his head and leaned back. The string of horses made its way slowly out of the yard, horses kicking at each other, biting the rump in front, generally resisting the move. The line turned along the creek and headed right to Tyson's, where he wanted them to go. Turner reached for a bottle and finished what was left, flinging the empty high and wide. In a bit he'd pick up his horse and make his way down the slide, cross their trail, then head back to the Judge's. There were men already waiting at Tyson's. They couldn't be traced to the Judge's crew at the ranch. Even Tyson didn't know or care who had hired them.

A malicious grin crossed Turner's red face; the Judge would think it was for wages when he went after the herd and wiped out a few riders. Let him think that. Turner wanted that bastard drifter for the first night he'd refused to get the horses, and the time he'd snuck up on them at Hubbard's and driven them off the place. He'd pushed Turner around enough. The man wasn't big enough to tackle him again. One hand around his throat and he could strangle the man, or crush him, wrap both arms around his ribs and crack him like a toy. The pictures were endless. Turner pushed himself up from the rocky ground, not caring if he was exposed to anyone below. Only two females left behind, nothing they could do to him. There was plenty of time ahead for what he planned. That range bum would look like a smear of supper by the time he was done with him. And Red Willis, too.

The chestnut whinnied piteously as Turner walked toward the horse. Damn him, thought Turner. The animal had twisted on the short rope allowed him and had stood through the day with no graze or water. Turner cuffed the horse. Stupid horse, couldn't even stand and graze without getting messed up. These fancy-bred horses might look pretty, but they couldn't take care of themselves. He wrenched the horse around and mounted heavily, then put the spurs to the tired animal who struggled through the spilled rock, occasionally stumbling and throwing Turner partway from the saddle. He finally let the horse drink his fill when they crossed the creek, his mind occupied with plans of revenge. When the horse lifted his head, Turner drove in the spurs again and the horse plunged out of the water and kept at a fast lope back to the Two Crown headquarters.

Since Holly had come down through Badger Pass, the spring winds had changed the trail. Where there had been deep mud, only a few small puddles remained among the rock basins. He rode the dun in a wide-ranging circle as the herd approached the turnoff. The deep holes made by Kimball's wagon and team were only dents now in the drying earth. Quick to spot them, Holly turned off Tyson's trail and began searching for the faint marks that would lead to the trail. Looking up at the mountain peaks ahead, a rider would think them impassable, as Badger Pass could not be seen from the main trail. The deep slot through the rugged hills hid behind another swell. Ranchers found the path too rough for good livestock, so it had become only a memory in the minds of a few men still living. Luck of a sort had brought Holly to the other end. Now that luck would be passed on to the Hubbards.

His eyes caught another marking in the rocks. A few strides more on the dun and another scar on the floor appeared. Here was the trail, starting out through the scrub-pine forest and heading for the high rocks. Holly reined the dun around and loped slowly back to the resting herd, to ride up alongside Hubbard. "Trail's ahead. Pretty clear once you get on it. Best I stay behind, wipe out the herd signs. Just keep your eyes on the marks, points toward the vee in the hills ahead, keep moving straight toward it." He sat motionless on the dun. Hubbard started to speak, but the rider anticipated him and touched his knee to the dun and angled away from the gray. Faint words came back to Paul. "Get moving; I'll send the others along."

Hubbard's gray was reluctant to enter the dark, bristly woods, and the string of horses used this reluctance to set up their own rebellion. The light was fast fading and the spring chill gave a hint of the evening to come. Hubbard fought it out with his gray, and put aside trying to speak with Holly until they made camp. Jimmy swung his set into line behind his father, and at last they were all moving in the long line. Jimmy felt the relief of being out on the trail. He was doing something, not just protecting his own but acting on a plan, taking the first move. He could almost forget his mistake back in town. His thoughts and energy were needed here to handle the half-broke horses. He liked the action, and he was ready to meet all the challenges.

Red waited while Sarah pulled her string in behind her brother's line. She halted briefly while Holly rode past her, but he kept his eyes from touching hers and pushed his mare for a faster trot. When he reached Red's grullo, he pulled in the mare and the two men stayed head to head, waiting for her to move along. She sighed and pushed her mare into a quick trot to catch up to Jimmy.

Red's concern for the line rider showed. "You doing all right, or need a hand?"

Holly did not respond immediately. He sat the dun and stared carefully at the red-haired man, weighing what he saw. As it came time for Red's string to join the line, Holly spoke quickly. "Okay, now, Red, but come night, I could be needing some help. If I don't get into camp by midnight, send someone out looking. 'Spect I'll be needing a push come then." He shifted in the saddle to check the trail in back of them, where the hoofprints of many horses had churned and dug into the soft ground, marking their passage. "Soon the Judge's boys will be after us. Need to have everybody ready to fight." He hesitated; the words came slowly, painfully, words rarely used in his solitary existence. "I'll be needing your help." Red knew this was a first for the drifter; poor bastard, he don't know we all need help.

Holly kept the dun mare steady as the herd settled into the trail, each tugging and fighting their string. His shoulders sagged. God, that line along his ribs felt like a firebrand on his side. What he had to do loomed large before him. Dismount. Tie the mare secure. Wipe out as much of the broken ground as possible. A big band of Mexicans with brooms would come in handy for this job. He chuckled at the picture of them up here in the mountains. Didn't fit. Images floated in front of his eyes—horses thundering across a burning yard, Sarah in her nightdress, Turner's blond hair hanging over Kelleher's bald head. Holly shook himself to remove the pictures; a chill went through him. The fever had come back and had picked the wrong time.

He rode back out to Tyson's trail. It took a long time for him to dismount from the restless mare. He tied her where she couldn't be seen from the main trail. A large boulder offered a seat. Gratefully, he leaned against its bulk, warmed from the day's sun. A chance to give his side a rest. Dampness along his ribs let him know the barely healed wound had broke open again. Breathing came hard, and lights spun around his head. He sat for a moment longer. Remembering what he needed to do was difficult. Holly leaned his head against the hard surface of the rock; it felt soft and comforting.

He jerked awake. Something moved just off to his left. By the sun's position he had slept some over an hour. The last bit of light was leaving the foothills. Higher up near the pass, the horse train would have been in shadows for quite a while. Standing came easier; the rest had done some good. A broken branch made a good enough broom, and he worked hard for twenty minutes raking the branch across the tracks.

Back by the dun, he looked down the swept trail, just visible in the fading light. The tracks weren't easy to see, wouldn't fool a good tracker. But then the Judge and Turner expected them to be going across to the station from here, not turning up this forgotten trail. Holly grinned to himself. Tomorrow, when they didn't show at Tyson's, someone would come flying past this spot, backtracking in a hurry, hoping to read their trail. Even if the tracks were found, the herd still had a good head start, and there was no way to cut off the trail before Cottonwood. Hubbard had gained a day or two.

Holly untied the mare and put his foot in the stirrup. The last half-hour's efforts had used up the respite given by sleep. It took a short breath and willpower to steel himself against the pain as he mounted. The evening's cold got to him as the mare moved out. He weighed the effort needed to dig out Kelleher's sheepskin and decided it wasn't worth it. After ten minutes of keeping the mare to the edge of the path, Holly moved her over onto the trail and touched the horse into a trot, giving her free rein. The dun put her nose to the trail and trotted with her head down, moving like a bloodhound as she followed the scent of the herd. The rider's face tightened against the jarring pain. At this pace they would catch up to the herd before dawn.

The trail made its way slowly up through the foothills deep into the mountain range. Paul Hubbard kept looking back over his shoulder to check on the riders and the remount string. His daughter showed signs of fatigue; earlier he had ridden back to her, offering to take her horses. Her back had straightened in the saddle. "No thanks, Dad. I can take my share." He smiled now at her refusal. It was good that she wanted to stay part of the working crew. Her determination was the first positive sign he had seen since she had come home from her marriage.

Once the sun went behind the hills, the trail became harder to follow. Dusk took their light, and the horses began to stumble frequently, unable to pick their footing in the rough track. Only Red, at the tail end of the string, still sat his saddle with an easy swaying motion. He had been raised to long hours on horseback. Paul reined in his gray and watched the line of horses come to a ragged halt. To his left an opening in the pines and rocks looked a good place to make camp. They had watered the herd less than a half-hour ago in a muddy stream and filled their canteens. A cold dry camp would be unfriendly, but necessary, this first night out.

Tonight they would rope off one end of the small opening and picket the string. Grain would do them instead of grazing; nothing much grew up here, as Holly had warned them. Once again, Paul owed a debt to the rider. He had warned them of the Judge's scheme to take Tower, had defended Sarah and Amy, and knew of this trail, long-forgotten locally. Paul wondered briefly when Bishop would catch up, but put aside the concern as he dismounted. The man would be in later.

Sarah's mare gave a deep sigh, as relieved as Sarah to have the burden off her back. Sarah rubbed the steaming back with a clump of grass. The mare sighed again as the grass eased the itching from the wet saddle blanket. She laughed at the expression on the mare's face. "Too much hard work today; guess we're both soft." The mare wrinkled her nose in return. The smell of oats had come to her. She whickered her anticipation of supper. Sarah reached for the nosebag her father held out.

He spoke, tired eyes filled with pleasure. "A good day's ride. A good start. Tomorrow will get us through the pass and close to Cottonwood Pass. Glad you rode with us, Sarah. We needed you." She smiled at her father standing solid and broad in front of her.

The brown horse flinched as Red's practiced hand slid down the hind leg. Concern mounted in Red's eyes. The other horses he had checked were fine, but this brown gelding, brought in at the last minute, wasn't holding up well. Swelling and heat in his near hock told the tale. Good conformation made for good horses, and this one was sickle-hocked, ready to break down. Red straightened up and saw the Hubbard boy watching him. "Keep an eye on this one tomorrow. Lucky your pa brought a couple of spares, may have to put one in the sale string." He shoved his hands deep into the small of his back, took a big yawn and a long stretch. That felt better, made all the kinks loosen and relax. Now he was ready for supper and a good sleep. He grinned at the kid.

Paul Hubbard came to stand with them. Red extended his grin to his new boss. "I'll be taking first watch, kinda want to be up when Bishop rides in. If he be late, plan to ride back a ways looking for him. That's what we agreed."

Paul marveled at the easy acceptance between these two men. He felt the distance from the hard-faced drifter and the short-legged puncher, as if his eastern manners kept him apart. The faint sounds of supper, a clink of tin pans, brought the three to attention. "Let's grab some of what Miriam packed and get to sleep." Red nodded his assent to the boss man's words. Jimmy passed them, hurrying to the sounds of food.

Red laughed as the boy passed him. "Hungry, ain't he, still growing, by the looks." Red watched the lanky youngster dig into the meager portions offered by his sister. "This trip'll put some extra savvy on him, stretch a few muscles."

A rueful grin touched Hubbard's face at these words. "We're all going to get extra years on us from this trip. Don't know about you, but I don't need a whole lot more years of this kind." The two grinned at each other, and Paul felt he had finally made contact with the cheerful cowboy.

Sarah beckoned to them, offering a pan holding cornbread and cold bacon. "Supper."

Later, Red took the first watch. His eyes, used to the darkness, could make out the shapes of the sleeping crew. He took a careful look around camp and then beyond the immediate area. Still no sign of Bishop. And the night was getting mighty cold. By his reckoning it was getting toward midnight, and the man was overdue. A few more minutes, and he'd take a bronc out, do some backtracking. Probably find the man asleep up against a rock somewheres.

A sharp sound brought his attention back to the area. Something was moving over by the sleepers. Red loosened the thong holding his gun. He didn't usually carry a six-gun, but figured this was a time to be needing one. He heard the sound again, and saw a shadow move toward him. It came closer, and he relaxed his hand on the gun butt and settled back down on his perch. Sarah Hubbard came to him, wrapped in a torn blanket. "Mr. Willis, has Holly ridden in yet? I'm worried."

Well, ain't that a surprise, he thought. This pretty girl is full of surprises. First she goes flying off with the blond bronc stomper, and now she's worried about this high-line rider. The comparison came to him. No one in the valley had liked Berringer; he rode his horses cruelly and pushed them hard. Red suspected he'd be that way with his women too. Now Bishop was different. Gentle with the wild ones;

163

probably be that way with a woman, if one could get close enough. He didn't blame Miss Sarah for her worry. The man drew you to him without trying.

Red shook his head. "Sorry, miss, no sign. Thought I'd go out looking, a bit worried myself." She started to speak, wanting to explain her concern, but Red held up a cautionary finger. "Someone's coming, hope it's Bishop." The two waited, listening for further sounds. A quiet clip of shoe on rock, another clip, then a more steady pattern of hoof steps. A rider slumped over his horse came out of the shadows; the horse stopped abruptly and snorted at the two shapes near the rock.

Holly felt something on his leg and brushed awkwardly at it with his left hand. A warm soft hand took his; he heard Sarah Hubbard's voice speak to him. It wasn't a dream. "It's all right, Holly; you reached camp."

A man's voice, familiar to him, followed her. "Come on, son, just slide down that mustang and we'll get you set in a nice warm spot." Holly shook hard with the night cold as Red pried at his fingers laced in the mare's tangled mane. "Come on, man, step down and have supper." Red's voice reassured him. These voices were ones he could trust. His fingers loosened their grip and he slid into Red's arms.

Red hefted the lax body over his shoulder like a sack of feed. The damn fool didn't weigh much more than a newly born calf. When he put Holly down, his hand came away sticky. "He's leaking again; that's bad." He quickly realized that Sarah had anticipated this, and was there with water and fresh cloths.

"He's feverish again, Red. We've got to get him warm and we can't have a fire. He's got to get warm." Red nodded his agreement. He knew what the woman was saying. The rider did not have the strength to fight the mountain cold and his own injury, and be any use against Turner. Sarah finished tightening the bandage, wrapping it snug against the bony ribs. What she must do now was the only way.

164

She slid down next to the cold, shaking body, tight and drawn up against the warring fever. Red covered them both with blankets. "Missy, I'll wake you before the others." He knew he had said enough; more explanations would embarrass both himself and the girl. He went back to the dun mare and led the tired animal to the picket line for her nosebag of oats. Morning would come soon enough for all of them.

CHAPTER FOURTEEN

Someone was pounding at the door. Hard. And again. Turner rolled over to stick his head under his arm. "Go 'way, git." he muttered. The pounding continued, beginning an echo in his head.

The door opened and a seamed face peered cautiously around the frame. "Turner, the Judge is God-awful angry, wants you up to the main house now, on the run." The face withdrew in anticipation, and just in time, as an empty bottle broke on the door frame at eye height, sending shards up against the closing door.

Turner finally sat up. "Damn him, waking me this way." But then he went over the message and decided to get up to the house. Another bottle was waiting for him, and maybe the Judge had word of the horses. And the girl. Those thoughts got him moving.

A short search produced his boots, with more cursing when his hand found more pieces of glass. He sucked on the small cut and finally opened his eyes wide enough to really see. The boots had been sitting in their lonely glory on the floor surrounded by broken bottles. His hat and jumper occupied their own bunk. There was no sign of anyone else in the bunkhouse, and from the looks of the cots, no one had spent the night there except himself. Turner grinned. Guess he'd thrown a scare into these tame nursemaids. He'd spent the evening figuring out his plans, must of been pretty descriptive to drive out the rannies from their warm hole.

The sun was bright and high, making Turner shield his eyes as he stumbled up the back steps. Mrs. Hutton was there; she was always there, mouth set in disapproval, holding the door for him. Saying nothing, the woman handed him a cup of coffee and motioned for him to follow. They did not go to the library. Turner hesitated briefly at the familiar door, then followed the housekeeper. The Judge was alone at his dining table, papers strewn about him. Hat in hand, two men waited at the opposite end of the table. By the weight of their holsters, the set of their eyes, they were not the Judge's usual cowhands. Judge Breen barely acknowledged Turner's greeting, waved him to stand at one side of the table.

"I want you two men to repeat what you just told me. Turner," the Judge looked over at him, a faint tracing of a scowl on his face, "listen to what these men have to say and then I will expect a full report from you. Gentlemen, proceed." The older of the two stepped forward tentatively, hand lingering casually over his gun butt. Greasy hair combed back over a high forehead, a long narrow face with hooded eyes, and a prominent Adam's apple gave him a suspicious look. His voice was high and light, mocking his fierce appearance.

"One of our riders was up spooking out some wild stuff from the badlands this side of Cottonwood Pass. Saw a file of horses led right up near the pass. Musta been on the old trail from Badger. Said he could make out a woman riding with them. Good looking buncha stuff. 'Nother day or two and they'll be out to the plains near Elkin." The man stopped, looked at the Judge and then Turner. His voice continued to squeak. "Hubbard's horses be his guess, and once out to Elkin ain't no way to get them without some killing; no place to ambush. Killing ain't what you got in

167

mind, right, Judge?"

The man hesitated again, shifting his weight and putting his hand comfortably on his pistol. The other man moved in closer to his partner. His hand too came to rest on his gun butt. "We figured out the best place to hit 'em is just as they come down from Cottonwood. Fellow that saw them knows the trail, knows a spot, real narrow. We can get them horses running, knock out the hands. Got a buyer lined up for them broncs down in New Mexico. We leave now and we'll have no trouble being ready for them coming down out of them mountains."

The two men moved back against the wall, their piece said. There was a brief suggestion of a gloat on the speaker's face. He knew Turner from a long time back, and it looked to him that the man had blown a good job with his drinking and blustering. He hoped to step in and take over. Turner could read Digger's mind. The bastard had this all set up, just waiting to move into his place. *His* place. All he had to do was take Digger's plan and put it into action, make a wild finish of the herd, roll that drifter and Willis out of the picture, and the Judge would be his again. He turned to his boss, a placating smile ready. "Judge, I told you I had these men all set up, don't know what the fussing's about. Digger here knew I would be heading over to Tyson's today. No need for all this horray." He turned to Digger and his companion. "Well, get going. My chestnut needs to be saddled, time to move."

Judge Breen smiled to himself. Turner's attempt to take command was transparent and pathetic. He admired the man's gall, but distrusted the lack of leadership. Turner was drunk while all this planning was going on, and now he would fight to keep control and swear the plan was his. Keep the men fighting among themselves. That way he could guarantee the toughest and fiercest would always be the head man. He gave his approval to the hulking man, returning temporary leadership to him. Now Turner had to prove himself.

The two outlaws left to get the horses. Turner stayed behind. He wanted to get things straightened out with the Judge. "See, Judge, I got all this figured out. In two days them horses will be scattered and sold, and Hubbard's widow will sell that stud to you and be glad. Don't know what those two bums fed you, but that's been my plan all along." Turner's face showed his smug satisfaction. He'd turned this mess around and now had a good idea of what to do.

Judge Breen interrupted the self-congratulations. "Good Lord, man, do you think I believe you, that you know what is going on? You've had a plan each time you've gone up against these people and each time it has failed. Now Hubbard and his horses have gotten almost out of our reach. I do not want Hubbard or his crew shot. If anyone is hurt, it must look like an accident. A landslide or stampede." His voice became sharp, with an undernote of hysteria. "I must and will have that stallion. Destroy the herd, flatten Hubbard and his brood. But get me that horse." He spaced the words carefully. "Do you understand, there will be no further mistakes."

Eyes shut against the light, Turner came out into the sunshine. That damn drifter again. At least the Judge didn't know about him still being alive. Always coming out ahead of him, just pure luck. He glanced across the yard to see Digger and his friend with the chestnut saddled and waiting. The horse's fine coat was dulled, his eyes half-shut, head low. Turner half-thought to bring up a fresher horse; this one had acted poorly on the ride back yesterday. Stumbled a lot. Digger held out the reins, a slick smile on his face. "That Judge is sore at you, says you take too much time, too slow for his liking. Too bad to lose such a cushy job." Digger grinned as he spoke, showing a mouth of chipped and blackened teeth.

Turner grabbed the reins, the chestnut half-rearing from fright. A hard fist landed on the horse's forehead to stun him. Damn anything that did not work his way. Turner's heavy bulk hit the saddle hard, and the horse hunched against the burden. Spurs sunk deep in his ribs drove the horse to a mad run, spinning out of the ranch yard. Digger and his companion walked to their horses, slowly mounted, took their time leaving the ranch. Turner would have to slow down on that chestnut, and they'd catch him easy. The two jogged out to the road, thick with the dust raised by the chestnut's furious strides.

The horse maintained his frantic gallop longer than possible. Only the erratic last few strides gave Turner notice that the horse was going down. He barely had time to free himself from the stirrups before the horse stumbled and flipped over to lie still. Turner rolled away from the tumbling body, and in a moment found enough breath to stand up. The horse was dead, a thin trickle of blood coming from the grinning mouth. Turner looked in disgust at the body, now nothing more than a bag of meat. He stripped his gear and walked over to settle under a tree.

He'd been planning and replanning the rousting of the herd. Unaware of the horse's condition, he had driven it until it had failed him, unable to stand up to his needs. To hell with these fine-blooded animals. Digger and friend would be along soon. They'd give him a lift to find another mount. Turner finally calmed down enough to look around. A dirt track off to the left was a familiar sight. It led to Red Willis's place. Not much, but the horse trader should have something to ride. And Turner knew he wasn't to home. A cruel smile played on his dusty face. They could do some rearranging at Willis's while they "borrowed" a horse.

Poking in his saddlebags, he found the ever-present bottle, cushioned from the fall by a winter jacket. Turner took his usual big drink, wiped his mouth and took another. Nice not to have Jack hanging around always wanting another drink. He felt a whole lot better. Never did like that chestnut jughead, too quick to jump. Another drink eased the anger at having to face Digger and friend. They better make no cracks or he'd crack their heads for them. By the time the bottle was half-gone, his anger had grown. Damn Digger for being so slow. To hell with Willis.

The steady sound of two horses came to him just before the men rode into sight. Turner stood up, waving the bottle and laughing at the look on Digger's face. His companion pulled his mount up short, and stayed behind as Digger rode to face Turner. Leaning on the saddle horn, he looked down at the drunken man and then at the stripped carcass. Took another look at Turner, and then swung his slab-sided roan around, offering his stirrup to Turner, who hauled himself up behind the saddle. Digger spoke in short words to the other man, who rode over and picked up Turner's gear.

"Give us a drink of that. Where we headed?" The two statements ran together and tickled something in Turner's soaked mind.

"Here you go, boys," he threw the empty bottle at the silent man, spooking his sorrel. "We're headed down that way. Horses down there, whiskey too. Let's get going." He pointed the way to Willis's simple ranch.

Digger's roan stumbled under the double burden, but sharp spurs dug into his sides and moved him faster down the weedy path. The pale sorrel followed, side-stepping at the saddle banging along his side. The small ranch came into sight after a silent twenty minutes. Turner slid from the roan before the horse stopped, and slapped it hard on the rump. The horse jerked forward and pitched, almost losing Digger. Turner roared his delight. "Can't ride worth a damn, can you. And you figured you could take over from me, the Judge's man." He roared again. "Let's find me a horse and torch this place. Willis ain't got no right riding against the Judge. Let's teach him some manners."

Digger's first thought was to ride the idiot down, stomp him into the dirt. But the suggestion to burn the small ranch turned him. Turner could wait. Spying two horses behind the barn wandering in a big pasture, Turner yelled at the silent man to rope the bigger bay. The horse moved away from the swinging rope, limping slightly. "Lame, Turner.

171

Won't do you no good." Digger found pleasure in this, Turner might be walking after all.

"Don't matter to me if'n he's off, just need to get to Tyson's, plenty of horses there. Rope him up, you fool." The weedy sorrel took out after the lame bay and the rider swung a wide loop, catching the gelding on the second try. Turner tied the horse to the corral rail and tacked up the restless animal. He wanted to get to the burning.

The door to the small house was latched. A good hard kick broke the wooden catch and the door swung open. Inside, everything was neat, tidy, and primitive. A big black kitchen range dominated the small building. To one side was a bunk; nails hammered in the wall held bits of clothing. A rough table and one chair served as both desk and eating place. Two more stools hung on pegs, evidence that the owner expected some company. But the stove was the focal point to the room. It was Red's pride, his faith that someday he would own a bigger place. Turner's first words were to Digger. "Put your rope round that. You, bring up Digger's horse. We'll drag that thing all over hell. Only be bits of it left around the yard. Get going."

The thin roan gelding strained back against the pull of the rope, but the heavy black stove refused to budge. His rider hauled back hard on the bit, the horse's mouth opening wide against the pain. The horse kept pulling, his haunches almost on the ground in his effort to move the black object. A crack appeared around the base of the stove, a shift of weight, and then another crack. The roan took a step back, still straining. With a heavy metal groan the main body of the stove slid from its base and fell hard on the swept floor. The roan sat down in surprise in the yard. Turner yelled. "We got it now; haul that black bastard outa here."

The roan was yanked around; the spurs sunk in, and the little horse leaped away from the pain, dragging the stove body across the wood floor, soot and dirt clouding from the broken pipe, the heavy weight gouging the carefully planed floor. The doorway wasn't wide enough for the stove to fit through and the roan was stopped hard by the bulk jamming against the frame. Digger started beating the horse with his hat, rowelling his sides in great raking sweeps. The horse plunged sideways, trying to escape. The frame gave way and the stove body came skipping out into the yard to settle heavily in the dust. The roan went to his knees when the weight was released, then lunged to his feet to stand with head hanging and sweat pouring from his matted coat.

Turner gloried in picking up big pieces of the stove piping that remained in the room, throwing them high and wide through the shattered door frame. Bit by bit the remains of the stove landed in the yard, followed by smashed pieces of the crude furniture. Turner stood in the widened doorway. "Bet a good horse could pull this here shack down. You," he pointed to the ever-silent rider. "Bring that bay here, fitting that Red's own horse pull down the rest of his home."

When the three men rode out of the small yard, little was left of Red's buildings. Turner had easily pulled down the house frame, then set fire to the pile of boards. Digger and friend had ransacked the barn, tossing hand-plaited gear and odd bits and ropes in a big pile, then set it on fire. The lone remaining horse fled from the yelling and the fire. He stood wild-eyed and suspicious as the three men rode out. His lonesome whinny brought the bay gelding's head around. A fist slammed against his face and he shied violently. Turner cursed the horse and drove his spurs in deep, lifting the animal into a gallop. They turned abruptly onto the main trail to Tyson's. Turner knew there would be plenty of whiskey there.

When the mountain men of the past had used the faint trail they found between the two passes, an enterprising trader had put up a small hut near the trails' convergence, and had made himself a good life selling whiskey to anyone having something to trade, white or red. His death one winter had gone unnoticed until spring thaw. The trail was no longer used as often; the ranchers moving into the settled area found it too tough on the stock. One man, tired of begging for handouts and weary from trekking over the rocky pass, had taken the time to pound open the barred door. He'd buried the remains of the old man, dead five months from a broken back.

Still in the store section of the shack were some resellable goods: traps, cooking utensils, the odds and ends needed to survive. He figured he saw a life ahead of him, trading and swapping. No one seemed to care that the old trader was dead, nor did they show any interest in taking over the store. A new sign went up. Tyson's Station. And slowly a reputation began to grow. Anything could be found at Tyson's. Anything could be fixed, could be bought or sold. No questions asked. Messages could be left, information passed on. Rooms and meals were available for a day or a week, at a price. Tyson wanted only to survive and to make his profit. The local ranchers began to depend on him for short-time labor, quick repair work, cheap horses. It was a living.

When the station door pushed open hard and slammed against the wall, four heads turned to watch, four hands reached quickly to rest on gun butts. Turner smiled when he saw this reaction. These men were ready for what he had in mind. He pounded on the counter that served as both bar and store. Tyson shuffled slowly from behind a stack of pots and moldy saddle blankets. Of an indeterminate age, the man was totally bald; a dent in the flesh over each eye served as eyebrows. His well-fleshed face held no expression; his washed-out blue eyes barely looked at his customer. He only nodded when Turner demanded a bottle, shuffled to another stack and produced a quart of clear liquid. "Here, three dollars. Glasses over there." Tyson pointed to a stack of glassware near a bucket of water. If you wanted a clean glass, you washed it yourself. Most didn't bother.

Turner grabbed his bottle, took his usual drink, coughed and wiped his mouth, and walked over to the four men still

174

watching. Digger and the silent man waited by the bar. A dark-haired man with a wide, infectious smile laughed at Turner's offer of the bottle. "Trying to charm us with that booze? No thanks for me, that stuff'll split your head. Set, Turner, and let's get to the job. Had enough sitting here for a long time to come."

Brad Dixon could not have been more different from the men around him. He did not have the look of a gun hand. He had smiling eyes, a ready grin, and a joke for anyone; he was too relaxed and easygoing to be dangerous. But his carefree attitude led most people astray. They did not read the minute signs of his trade. Hand close to his gun, eyes rarely still, back always to the wall. He did not want to work hard, and the only other way to get what he wanted was to take it. He liked working for Turner and his Judge. Easy money for easy work.

The other three men had worked with Dixon, but not with Turner. Ron Murphy was barely out of his teens: skinny, vicious, with a violent hatred for anyone successful, anyone better than himself. His gun was his only friend; his face lit up when he drew down on a man to kill him. The older man next to Murphy had an Indian's dark face, a blade nose, black hair and eyes. A half-breed, he had grown up in these mountains as an outcast. He was the one who had spotted the horse herd. His odor was strong enough that the men with him made him sleep outside. He didn't care.

The fourth man also appeared out of place in this company. His neat dress and carefully washed and barbered person presented a picture of effete dandyism. Nails trimmed and polished, tie set just so, Alan Rasmussen had shot several men who had laughed at his appearance, not reading the man at all.

Turner pounded again on the table. "We've waited long enough. That horse herd needs stopping; that drifter needs to be buried. We go out tomorrow morning early light. Drinks on the Judge."

CHAPTER FIFTEEN

Before the silver dawn light, Red Willis slipped from his warm blankets. With care he walked to where he had left Sarah Hubbard, to touch her gently on the shoulder. The young woman rolled over and wiggled from the covers, careful not to awaken the sleeping man beside her. Holly was on his left side, and she had pulled herself close to his back, placing her arm over his right shoulder, too aware of the raw wound on his side. During the early hours the warmth from her body had finally stopped his violent shivering.

The unlikely pair, the easygoing horse trader and the slender, well-mannered girl, stood over the injured man as he slept. His breathing was even and light, no signs of fever or restlessness.

Sarah found it difficult to meet Red's kind eyes as he led her away from the other sleeping forms to the picket line. The horses stirred softly in the early gray light, their breath sending short spikes into the cold air. Red kept his voice low. "He looks better this morning, miss. That good sleep will put him ahead of infection. Today's going to be a long one." He began filling the feed bags and tying them over eager muzzles.

Sarah picked up a bag and filled it, the action clearing her mind. Handing it to Red, she looked at him straight and clear. "He didn't stop shaking for a long while. I thought he would never get warm." She stopped. Anything more would seem an apology.

A hint of sun came through the rock formations, letting slices of light into the dark camp. Paul Hubbard sat up, then stood with effort, his injured leg stiffened from sleeping on the hard ground. Sarah smiled as she watched her father go through his usual morning chore of shaking Jimmy to get him from his blankets. The simple everyday act covered the memories of the night, allowing her to focus on her own routine chores. No fire, so there would be no coffee. Only the remains of the cornbread; more cold bacon and water. She parceled out the meager rations, smiling as her brother gulped the food and hoped for more.

Red was saddling the dun when Holly finally woke. He lay quiet for a moment, testing out what was going on, ready for trouble and uncertain where he was. Camp was breaking up; horses milled about, ears back, resisting the cinch pulled tight against their bellies. But there was no trouble. He stood. A stab of pain reminded him of the wound. It was still there but it no longer throbbed. The bandage was fresh and tight. He felt ill at ease; something was unfinished in his mind. Memories intruded, a hand searching his face, lingering on his neck, touching his shoulders and back. The same hand rested on his hip, pulling a warm and soft body closer to him. If this was a dream, he had a good imagination.

Sarah Hubbard brought a square of cornbread, a thick slice of cold bacon. High color bathed her face; her eyes flickered over his face, unwilling to settle and met his in greeting. Holly reached for the proffered food, and in giving it Sarah stepped back, her fingers jumping when he touched her hand. Maybe those weren't dreams, maybe they were why Sarah blushed when he looked at her. Holly remembered being cold, so cold his hands were tight on the saddle, the shakes going through him and threatening to dump him

177

from the horse. The battle with a rising fever. Then warmth, soft sweet warmth. He jerked his head, flinging away the images. No time for dreams now.

Holly walked to the picket line to meet with Paul Hubbard, struggling to cinch up a resistant black. Hubbard kept his back turned to the man, acknowledging his presence only by a slight turn of his head. Putting his hand to tugging the cinch on the off side, Holly spoke over the horse's back. "Move out soon and we'll be more than halfway by evening. There's a canyon that would be good for the night, shelter for a fire, good graze. I'll stay behind, watch the back trail." The black let out his breath in surprise as Hubbard's knee went into his ribs. Unaccustomed to such treatment, the animal shuffled nervously sideways. Hubbard jerked on the picket line, further confusing the black.

Hubbard glared over the shifting back of the horse at Holly. His words were brief and sharp. "Good, you stay behind, away from the herd and my family. We'll work out the rest tonight, but you stay away." He closed his mouth on the sentence and stalked away, dragging the black with him, and leaving Holly bewildered over the odd, one-sided conversation.

Hubbard was ashamed of his thoughts. Perhaps the drifter didn't know what had been done to him last night. Perhaps all his anger was in vain. But the picture of his daughter snuggled close to this man, a stranger, rattled his sense of family. He'd best get to the business of the horses and leave the tangled thoughts to deal with later.

The grullo thought very briefly of bucking out under his rider, but Red's hat slapping up against his shoulder and a firm hand on the bit changed his direction. Yesterday's trek had taken the edge off, and the horse's mind was more inclined to water than to fighting. Red lined up his string and waited in the warming sun as the others mounted and worked their strings into order. Bishop's dun offered no hint of a fight. Her day had ended late and was starting early. For

Holly, mounting the horse had been tough, even with his renewing sleep. Once again, keeping his arm held tight against his side was the only comfort. The day promised to be a long one.

Once the last horse in the string fell into position, Holly checked over the campsite. Little had been left behind to expose their stay, only depressions dug in the ground by restless horses, scars on the trees that held the rope. This evidence of their night here would quickly disappear. In a week these signs would be worn to oblivion by the winds and rains. Turning his horse back down the trail, Holly felt as if something had been decided and then left behind, something he did not understand. He rode carefully, keeping the mare to a slow walk, listening for sounds that did not fit. He rode a long way back, more than halfway to the main trail. He would catch up later.

At midday, Holly found himself back by the campsite. Sitting loose in the saddle, he tried to work out what was tickling him, nudging his ingrained instinct for survival. The sensation that someone was watching had ridden with him since leaving Hubbard's ranch. He knew they were going around Tyson's Station, and there was a possibility that a rider could come up into these hills from the Station and by chance see them riding over the old trail. He tried to talk himself out of the trip, but in the back of his mind he knew that the security of the Hubbards depended on no one knowing yet they had taken the old trail. It was their edge in the coming battle. He kneed the dun into a slow walk and circled around the back of the camp. The jagged terrain sloped slightly down into a shallow, boulder-strewn meadow. Beyond was another rocky wall, and out beyond that would be the backside of Tyson's.

His mare picked her way carefully across the slick meadow. Grass grew precariously on the thin soil, easy to dislodge and making treacherous footing. The sun beat hard against the two walking across the rough ground. Holly kept his head bent, checking for hoofprints, especially of a shod horse. Looking for anything out of place in the desolate high land. Few animals would come up into this hellish area on their own. A dusting over an unshod print caught his eye. Too old, but it said that horses sometimes did come to the rocky meadow. The dun snorted in displeasure at the tedious gait she was held to by the rider and the fist-sized rocks.

The pair finally reached the far side of the flat land, walking easily onto a ring of good soft grass. Unexpectedly, the dun ducked her head and let out an enormous buck. Holly reined her in hard, but the quick-footed horse had gotten in a good tearing leap before she came back to the rider's control. Ringing in his ears and a now-familiar dampness on his side told Holly that the wound had reopened.

Holding the restless dun still, Holly inspected the graze, and saw an area of trampled grass. Following the signs with his eyes, he went up and across a rock wall, which flattened out at the top and slid away to a sharp incline. Below, he could make out a faint trail zigzagging down into an open meadow. Beyond it must be Tyson's. He checked the small patches of dirt between rock and shale, and finally found the deep imprint of a shod horse carrying weight. Fresh tracks. Someone had ridden up here recently.

Holly swung his left leg over the saddle and slid off the right side of the dun. He stood for a moment, fingers wrapped tight on the horn for support, then squatted for a closer look at the tracks. The horse that had made them was a poor one. Its prints showed a narrow chest and close stride, toeing out in front, the stride short, the shoes old and worn. One front hoof had split the thin metal to leave a distinctive track. Holly tied the mare and followed the tracks. The horse had finally stopped on a rock slab and from the number of droppings had stayed for a good while. He looked out across from where the pony had stood, and he could see well across the meadow. The campsite of last night was visible far to the left. Whoever had stayed here had seen something they

180

wanted to check out further. The tracks returned down the incline with no more wandering, as if the rider had seen what he wanted and was on his way back with his report.

Holly yanked the dun's head up from the high thin grass and stuck his left foot in the stirrup. It took a moment for him to get his breath once he hit the saddle. Damn this thing. Fingers stiff and slow, he fumbled in his saddlebag for a few pieces of broken cornbread and a bit of bacon. A poor lunch, but better than cold water and ferns. It was a long ride back to the herd. But plans had to be changed, and changed fast. He could see a vivid picture of the old trail as he had walked it: a long, narrow rock alley, the perfect place for Turner to put some men and pick off the riders as they brought the horses through. Once inside the alley there was no way to turn back, or to defend themselves from their attackers up on the rim. If the man who waited patiently back at the slab had seen the herd filing along the old trail, then the chances were good that this same man also knew of the vulnerability of the far end of the old trail.

The consequences of riding into that trap spurred Holly. He pushed the dun into a stumbling trot across the scattered rocks. Several times the cat-footed mare went to her knees in the rubble, but came up quickly each time to make her way up through the campsite and onto the trail. There Holly lifted the tired dun into a lope and traveled quickly down the trail, retracing his earlier ride, eager to catch the herd. He could see in his mind exactly what could be done to catch Turner off guard. It would take a long nighttime ride, but with a fresh horse and a bit of sleep he would make it. And this running fight with Turner would finally come to an end.

By the afternoon, the horse herd had settled into a steady job, each horse following the one in front without thought. Paul Hubbard kept his gray at the good pace, and the entire line moved forward in a single beat. The late spring sun had been bright throughout the day, unrelenting in its heat, giving them all a taste of the summer heat to come. They had crossed a deep stream an hour out of camp, where horses and riders had drunk deep of the sweet coldness of the mountain water. Now, a strong wind had come up to cool the sweaty bodies. Once again, the evening would be cold.

Bishop's horse appeared alongside Red's grullo. The dun was sweaty and tired from the fast trip. The two men rode for more than a mile, the horses carefully picking their way over the rocky trail at an easy jog. Red glanced over at his traveling companion. The dark face showed the effects of the day's riding: lines packed with dust, eyes suspiciously bright. With no build-up, as if he could read the sympathy in Red's face and wanted to deflect it, Holly spoke. "Trouble, Red. Someone knows we're up here, where we're headed. There's a good place ahead for an ambush. No way out once we get in the narrow trail. No defense. Be sitting ducks for Turner and his crew."

Holly stopped talking and rode a minute more with no further words. Red kept his silence. Finally Holly finished his thoughts. "Not far from here, 'bout another hour's ride, camp for the night. A canyon, shelter enough for a fire, good grazing. I'm riding ahead, check it out. If it is safe I'll take me a rest. When you ride in, I'll have a hot meal, and a fresh horse, go down to the ambush spot. Figured me a way to take the fight from these boys. And I'm looking forward to seeing the last of Turner." A quick smile came to his face. "Yeah, it would be easier if you came along, but if this don't work, that would leave Hubbard with only Sarah and Jim. Poor odds and you know it. Best stay with them."

Red's protest died with Holly's last words. He knew the man was right, they couldn't leave Hubbard with just his kids. He listened as Holly spoke further. "Pick me out a horse that ain't worth much but has some bottom. Don't want to lose a good mount. Saw you checking over that brown with the boggy hock, he'd do. Just need to get about

182

eight miles further down the track fast." Holly signaled the dun and passed down the line to ride with Hubbard. Sarah heard him coming and felt herself smile in anticipation. Her smile dimmed as he rode past without looking, his face grim under its covering of dust.

Paul turned his head at the sound of the approaching horse. He stared hard at the man who had lain with his daughter last night, and his anger glittered in his eyes. Holly angled his dun away from Hubbard. Whatever had stirred up this man, he didn't want it interfering with the next few hours. He tersely outlined his plans to the man, wanting to move on as fast as possible. Done, he hesitated, wanting to smooth out the anger in the man's face. Then he let it be and pushed the mare away from the line. She resisted leaving the herd, then gave in to her rider's demands and settled into a long lope that carried them away from the others.

The canyon came up suddenly. Distances were different when you weren't on foot. He halted the dun at the mouth and dismounted, tying the mare in a clump of high brush. He stood still, listening to the birds and watching for any startled movement, any signals that something unusual was inside the canyon walls. Small noises, rustling of branches, chattering birds, small rodents moving importantly—all convinced him that the canyon was clean. At the entrance he checked for broken twigs, chipped rock, any sign of man entering the small oasis. Nothing. Finally he walked easily through the mouth, staying to the bushy scrub growing along the high-walled sides. A deer raised its head, alert to his presence. He took more steps and the animal bounded up into the far side. Two more deer followed. He was alone in the quiet canyon.

Holly walked back and untied the dun. Inside again, he loosened the cinch and slipped the bit, then tied a neck rope and staked the horse in knee-deep graze. The dun dropped her head gratefully into the grass and tore large hanging mouthfuls of the lush forage. Holly, too, felt the effect of the long day and the beautiful canyon retreat. Up against the canyon walls soft pines offered shelter and a soft bed. He found a fallen tree with a depression beneath it, covered in needles. A hidden spot, perfect for sleeping. He eased his shoulders into the shallow pit, tipped his hat over his face, and was asleep, secure that the crackling branches or a whinny from the dun would wake him.

The mouth of the canyon was inviting, as Holly had said it would be. Paul Hubbard stopped his gray and sat. No sign of Holly, and no sign of anyone else. He motioned for Jimmy to come up and take his string. He spoke quietly to the boy. "Here, I don't see sign of more than one horse going inside. Must be Holly's. If there's trouble, drop the horses and go back to Red. Take your sister. He'll know what to do." The boy grumbled his displeasure at having to go to someone else in case of trouble. His father caught the muttered resentment and called him on it. "Son, you got us this far into this mess by your loose talk. Hurts, but it's true. We need level heads like Red and Holly. Do what I say." He rode his gray into the canyon, leaving behind his angry son and restless horses.

Eyes down, Hubbard rode checking for prints. Only one set of shoes broke up the smooth path. As he lifted his head to search the open floor, he saw the mouse-colored mare pulling at the grass. She lifted her head and nickered as he rode up, glad for the companionship. There was no sign of Holly, but this was his horse. Paul checked his gray and sat for a bit, then called softly. "Bishop, you here?"

A voice directly behind him startled the gray. "It's clear; nothing but deer inside. A fire will be fine." Holly stepped out from behind a pine, rifle held carelessly in his left hand. He walked stiffly, his thick hair woven with pine needles, his shirt dusty with crushed branches. The man's wide mouth was set, the beard stubble highlighting the gray look to his face. Hubbard could see dots of blood on the right side of his shirt. He started to speak, but another voice came quicker than his.

184

"See you made it. Had a good sleep from the looks of you. Ready to fight the tiger." Red Willis eased himself from his grullo's back and rolled a smoke. A look went between the two men that bypassed Hubbard, a sense of companionship that excluded him. "How about a hot meal now, a longer sleep."

"Sounds fine to these ears."

Willis's wide grin spread to the hard-faced man.

Within a short time the animals were stripped of their gear and turned loose to roll and graze; a fire was going, and Sarah pulled out more bacon and airtights of beans and tomatoes. She had pan bread cooking and a coffeepot working to brew the strong black liquid. The smell of the hot food cheered up the crew, and they busied getting camp ready.

CHAPTER SIXTEEN

Good food revived a man almost as much as a good sleep. And this meal tasted better than his last meal in this small valley, watery rabbit stew. Holly leaned back against a knobby pine and wiped up the last of the bacon fat with the pan bread. Even out here Sarah was a good cook. He willed his thoughts away from her. Tonight he would tackle Turner and his crew, with good odds he wouldn't come through in one piece. Whatever happened, it was time for him to move on. For tonight, and for later. He was to ride down that long alley, to that thin tight break in the wall, then climb up the side, using those carved handholes. From the top he would look down on the ambush spot and be ready to take out the raiders. If his guess was good.

Once on top, on that high flat slab, once he started shooting, he was wide open to the killers. If he didn't get them all in the first few moments, they could regroup and take him. His years had been spent in working horses, running from troubles; not standing to fight, especially at such long odds. Holly refused to dwell further on the coming fight. What he needed now was a good tight bandage and a fast horse. His head jerked up; sleep had almost claimed him, but someone was walking up to his secluded pine.

Sarah Hubbard stood in front of him, her body outlined

by the glow from the distant fire. In her hand was a pan of water and some clean white cloths. Before he could stand, she knelt beside him and put her hand out. He caught her wrist to stop her touch. But the young woman leaned into him and gently kissed him on the mouth. His careful control shattered. Her warmth, the sweet taste of her mouth, destroyed his will. He responded to her urgency with a wildness of his own. His left arm went around her to hold firm to her back. His twisted right hand came up to find a soft breast. Sarah pushed her body into his, demanding more with her mouth. Long-dormant yearnings came loose in both of them. Holly raised himself to his knees and pulled her body to his. Sarah was instantly aware of his hardness; she moved closer, asking with her mouth and hips for more. Both her arms went around his chest to hold him tight to her.

Pain flared through Holly's side, making him gasp for air and move away from the embrace. Sarah realized what had happened when her left hand found wetness in its searching embrace. "No." Holly's voice was low and strong. This was wrong; the woman was good, and she would give herself to him without thought. His mind flashed from a twisted body hanging from a rope, the gentle smile of a tired woman, the eternity of those close four walls, the bright pain of a whip across his back. All reminding him of who and what he was. He sat back against the tree, willing all expression from his face. Sarah settled on her heels, her eyes still holding contact with his, her feelings strong in them.

Holly shook his head vehemently. Words came to his mind. "You can't make me into something I ain't, lady. You see more than there is. Just a thief and a drifter. Not enough for you. God, you're beautiful." He did not know if he had spoken or not.

Sarah reached for his shirt; his hand snaked out to stop her touch. Her voice was calm and serene. "You need attention if you are going to get through tonight." She unbuttoned his shirt and tugged at it, her hands gentle and easy on his flesh. "Please, take off the shirt. I need to clean your side." Holly shrugged off the garment and turned his face away. Light fingers removed the bandage holding the tear together. The edges were raw and inflamed, yellow pus oozing from the infected gash.

Holly glanced quickly at Sarah's face. The firelight enhanced her soft skin and shining eyes. Her face mirrored the concern in her voice. "This is bad; there's some infection. You should be in bed." Her eyes widened at her own words. Holly felt himself redden at the implications. Then her voie returned to the discussion, the tone once more impartial. "Your ribs are inflamed. I need some whiskey to cut the infection. Perhaps my father brought some along." Then she was gone, leaving Holly to rest his head against the tree. She returned before his fevered mind had accepted her being gone, with bottle in hand. The fire had dimmed and the vague shapes of people rolled up in blankets could just be seen. "Holly, a bit of whiskey inside will help you." He took the proffered drink, coughed, and remembered the last time he had a drink and this woman had come into his arms. "My father says Red has the brown saddled and waiting, for you to use him and not worry about him. There are extra shells for the rifle. Everything you need."

A bright flame of agony ran along his side; the sharp smell of whiskey met his nostrils. In a brief moment the pain subsided, and Sarah touched him lightly. Her voice echoed the concern in her eyes. "I'm going to pull the wound apart. Now." Holly bit hard onto his lower lip as her fingers worked at the bright red flesh. His body tensed, lights flashed in back of his eyes, and then all was dark.

Holly struggled to awake. He was alone and the immediate pain had ceased. The tight bandaging felt firm and secure. He rose and stretched tentatively. The wound throbbed slightly, but no longer pulled at his every move. Holly walked away from his secluded pine to the tired brown gelding waiting for him and dug out the old smelly sheepskin. Tonight its warmth would be most welcome. Red Willis stood there, head turned from the firelight, watching beyond the canyon mouth and alert to any movement. Holly eased over to stand next to the quiet puncher. Willis dipped his head in greeting. "A good night for a fast ride. That sliver moon will make the going some easier. Where do you plan to meet up with Turner? Wish I knew the area better. How come you know what's ahead? Thought you'd just drifted through." Red's last question received only a stubborn silence. He knew he'd gone outside the unspoken boundaries with his question. He shifted his weight and took another sip of coffee from the tin cup in his hand. A muted sigh escaped him. "God that tastes good. Never do like the coffee I make myself. Guess you really need a woman for that." Holly tensed at the words, searching for disapproval. Then he relaxed; there was nothing behind Red's words, just an observation. He was too touchy for conversation. It was time to get going, and leave the words for others. He was going to miss this man, came close to being a friend.

No words passed between them. Red handed Holly the tin cup and he took a long swallow. Better than whiskey. Good; strong and hot, to keep a man going. Holly broke the silence. "Tomorrow morning you wait till later to move out. Give me time to get Turner. The trail'll lead you right out onto the plains near that town. Can see it as you come out of the rocks. If you get the horses into the alley and hear shots, drop them and turn back if you can. Don't get in deep unless you feel safe. No way out." The enormity of the evening's work stayed Holly's words. How could he tell Red to ride in first and draw any fire?

Holly moved to leave; Red's hand on his shoulder stopped him. "Friend, don't need to say be careful tomorrow, but it would be nice if you came back. Lotsa folks kinda gotten used to you, want to know what happens. Yeah, and I know what you ain't saying. Use myself as the target. We don't want nothing happening to these here easterners." A big smile lit his homely face, "You made a place for yourself here, best come back and claim it."

The brown gelding moved out easily; only a slight hitch let Holly know that the hind leg wouldn't hold up long to hard use. He gigged the brown to a steady trot and eased himself by standing in the stirrups. The eight miles to the alley would go fast at this gait. Plenty of time to get in the right spot before daybreak. By the height of the moon it was after midnight. He'd be at the bluff by four easy, if they kept up this trot. He reached down and patted the warm dark neck. "Son, you're going to earn your way tonight. Hope you know where to put your feet in this damn rock bed." The brown snorted as if in reply and lengthened his stride.

Finally, Holly eased the brown to a halt. The horse's breath came in labored heaves. One dead horse on this trail was enough. The path had gotten rougher, and they'd just hauled up a long hill covered in fist-sized rocks that almost looked like someone with an evil mind had planted a crop. The gelding had worked hard, picking his way and keeping to a smart trot. By the time they'd reached the crest, the sweat stood hot and thick on his neck, and Holly could feel the hind leg hitching over the rough ground. Poor cuss, by the end of this ride he'd have only three legs. Couldn't be helped, but he hated doing it to a game horse. He slapped the brown with the reins, sending him downhill into his trot again. Another half-hour and the horse could be stripped and turned loose.

His hand rested on Red's pistol, snug in its holster at his side. Too bad Red was right-handed. The crossed holster made a fast draw nigh to impossible. Still, if the fighting got to pistol range, accuracy would be the telling point, not speed. Accuracy and plain guts. Red had easily given up his gun, and Hubbard, too, had been willing to give up his new rifle, a Winchester. With these weapons he could stand off the bunch.

The ground on either side of the trail had slowly begun to

190

rise, starting to form the large funnel that drew the rider into the narrow gorge. Holly slowed the brown to a walk. The horse became nervous as the walls grew closer to the trail. There was still room to turn a horse, but the tight walls leaned in on the traveler. If a rider did not know the trail worked its way through the gorge, it would be easy to believe there was no exit from this side of the canyon either. It was that belief that had sent Holly searching down the thin line that night over a month ago. He eased his weight in the saddle and pushed the reluctant horse deeper into the file. His eyes strained in the early light looking for the crack that would lead to the overhanging bluff. Once again he marveled at the construction. These ancients had been well-versed in fortification.

The abrupt turn in the trail warned him, then a shallow dent in the left wall came to his eye. A few more strides and he could just reach out and touch both sides from the back of the brown. It was here that there was no return. One shot from the bluff above and confusion would jam horse and rider tight into the alley, leaving them easy targets for the marksmen above. But he would be up there before them, above the bluff. And it was up to him to be fast and accurate.

He backed the brown away from the walls and turned him once he had the room. The brown was unwilling to turn around, showing evidence of the hard ride, unable to bear weight on the near hind leg. Holly finally got the horse back to the scrub beginnings of the gorge, then stripped off the gear and dumped it under a bush. If he could, he'd be back for it. Otherwise it could rot with no great loss. A hard slap on the rump sent the brown gelding away down the trail. Holly watched the horse disappear beyond the brush, bobbing on three legs. Now he was back where he had started less than two months ago.

He stood still for a bit, holding the rifle, hunched in his coat from the early morning chill. Walking back down the gorge brought his earlier trip to mind. Boots still were no way to travel, but this trip had been a lot faster and easier. Food and company made the difference. He thought back over the Hubbard family: Amy, her big eyes wide with delight as she sat her old paint; Mrs. Hubbard's concern for him, her care and acceptance of him. He winced when he thought of the boy, still holding anger and resentment. Hoped the kid worked it out. Unconsciously he wiped his hand over his mouth. That youngster carried a good wallop. He'd never stood and taken blows before.

And Sarah. Holly shied away from his feelings about her. It was a family he was fighting for. He'd never had a reason to stay and fight before. He'd always been able to walk away. Never felt he had a stake in anything very important. Sarah had changed all that.

Holly walked down the alley. The moon was gone; a pale line of gray separated the distant plains from the sky. Dawn was on its way, and time for him to be in place. The early glimmer made finding the thin crack leading to the carved footholds easy. He marveled he had found this well-hidden secret on his first flight through the pass. Climbing with rifle in hand was fairly simple. Those ancients had worked this path up the rock side with carrying some sort of weapon in mind.

Reaching the top, Holly squatted down and rested his head between his hands. His side throbbed in heavy rhythm with his breathing. A stronger band of gray showed now beneath the remains of the night sky. If he guessed right, the raiders should be leaving Tyson's now, and would reach the bluff within an hour's ride. The oncoming daylight gave him a better look at his perch. It commanded almost a 360-degree view of the plains and the rock wasteland in back of him.

Toward Tyson's, a small dust cloud let him know his guess was correct. A good-sized group of riders were headed this way. He had no shade up here, but by mid-morning control of the rock pass would be decided, and shade would not be needed. He hadn't bothered to carry a canteen. It would be extra baggage on the climb, although his mouth was dry and a sip of water would ease him some.

Holly shrugged his shoulders to loosen the bandolier of shells. The movement brought a sharp thrust to his side. Damn it, even Sarah's careful treatment and heavy bandages had not kept the wound from breaking open again, leaving his shirt soggy with fresh blood. At the rate he'd been oozing, he would slowly bleed himself dry. A grim thought came to him. Give Turner his way, and he would bleed quick and hard.

After checking around the perimeter, he slowly set his weapons out along the rock floor. Next to his left hand he laid Red's pistol and extra shells—his last-ditch defense if he didn't take out all the riflemen below him first time. He sighted along an imaginary rifle, aiming at and checking each place below that might conceal a marksman. He could reach into almost every spot, except right below him. To his far left it was possible to fire into his perch. He would have to leave that spot unprotected once the battle begun; it would take his attention away from the rim where most of the shooting would occur. From behind the scrub pines and large boulders, there a good shot could get to him if he had to kneel to make his shot. If he didn't get them all first.

CHAPTER SEVENTEEN

In grim silence Tyson produced another horse for Turner. The "borrowed" bay now limped so badly that he refused to take the horse in trade, demanding full payment from the Judge. Slapping his gear on a rangy sorrel, Turner yelled at the breed who was methodically saddling a thin cream mare. "Get going to where we want to be. You boys make sure I get that drifter, don't care what you do with Willis. The girl ought to give us some fun before we bury her and her pa under a rock slide." He whooped loudly, spooking his sorrel, and waved his bottle in a wild circle. "Let's get going, get that herd and that son-of-a-bitching bronc rider."

After the horse settled into a traveling gait, the breed rode up beside Turner, his face impassive in the dawn light. "Good place to start rock slide not far up Cottonwood. Easy to push big rocks, good ambush spot. Easy targets below." Turner caught a whiff of the man and reined his horse to stay behind the cream. Perfect. Shoot them all, then bury them under a pile of rocks. No one could say the Judge had been responsible. The horses would run free, be easy to round up and sell. He took a wild slap at the breed's back, and his hat fanned an empty space. The man's weedy cream sidled away from the restless sorrel, leaving nothing for Turner. The rest rode in silence, each in their own thoughts, looking forward to the battle for differing reasons.

The sorrel's trot was much rougher than the chestnut's. Turner took his annoyance out on the animal beneath him, as the Indian watched the senseless brutality, no expression in his face. This man was a fool to destroy his only transportation. He was a fool, but his boss paid well so he could be tolerated. It was easy to keep his temper, shut his mouth, and take the money. The other three men had their own opinion of the drunkard who led them. Turner had finished a bottle, and the broken remains were left along the trail back to Tyson's. Digger and his forever-silent companion had chosen not to ride out with them this morning. They weren't missed.

Another drink settled the vague uneasiness with the plans. Turner jabbed the sorrel once more with his spurs, and the horse jumped forward to come alongside the breed's scruffy cream. The Indian's wide sullen face gave Turner no idea of what was in his mind. "We better be almost there, you; time for us to be getting that ambush set. Sun's coming up." The breed stopped the mare, and waited while Turner fought the hard-mouthed sorrel to a stand. The others trailed up and stopped right behind them.

The words from the breed were short, the voice deep. "There. Tie the horses. We walk up there." Blunt fingers pointed to a grove of trees and a bare line of a path leading to a sloping, grass-covered area. Above and beyond the treeless bluff rose inpenetrable rocky walls. Below the rim wound the narrow canyon file.

Holly watched the five cross the plains. At first only specks, hidden by their own dust, they became faces, then sounds. It was easy to wait; the hint of sun touching his perch brought some warmth. Colors and patterns crossed the plains, highlighting the mountains to the left and right, deepening some shadows, raising strong yellows, brilliant greens, then losing to the dark tones as the sun's rays reached beyond to the next hidden space.

195

And then the five reappeared at the base of the bluff, on foot, rifles in hand—stopping in the middle of the steep climb to rock back on high riding heels. Only the Indian walked easily. Holly tried to pick out each man, to discover their abilities in the fight to come. A guessing game that could win or lose him his life. A skinny kid, barely a man, held his rifle with an easy grace that showed affection. A dandy, bet he was accurate, good in a street duel, not much for hard fighting. Not a stayer. He'd find out soon enough. The cowboy looked out of place with the rest of the crew. Smiling face, relaxed easy walk. But here for a reason, money. The black-haired Indian was the real menace: quick, sure, at home in these hills. His narrow-chested cream mare could well be the horse who had left those tracks up at the meadow. He was the one leading them now up the difficult trail. If anyone knew how to get to his overlook, it would be this one. The black-haired man was his first shot. And then there was Turner, last in line, waving his ever-present bottle.

The temptation to fire came now, to take a steady bead on Turner and squeeze off the long shot. With Turner down, the rest would leave. It was a gamble he couldn't take. He could use a rifle, was accurate to a point, but no great shooter at a distance. If he missed, they had him. They'd scatter and flush him out. There were five of them, chosen for their talents, their expertise with a rifle. Five paid to kill. Holly shook his head as if to discourage himself from attempting the shot. He was no marksman. His best chance was to let them settle in place, become complacent, then pick them off as best he could, starting with the breed.

Time was close. He watched the men settle into their positions, check their weapons, aim and sight. Then their wait started. He had the edge now. A sardonic grin crossed Holly's face. Turner had another bottle. By the time the herd came close to the canyon the man would be too drunk to be counted. That left four to worry about, better odds. He checked the sun. About now, Hubbard would be moving the herd. Time for him to pick his man and start firing. Each shot must count. The five men were well-spread along the lip of the bluff, the breed closest to him, Turner nearest the path to the horses. From where he lay, shooting these men meant shooting them in the back, a bitter way to die. Then the breed shifted, working closer to the rock overhang, almost out of sight of Holly. That left Holly's first shot a tough one. The breed was the one to take first, and partially hidden by the wall it would be hard to do more than cripple him.

Holly moved his rifle into position, lying flat along the rock slab, the butt of the weapon tight against his left shoulder. His right hand could cradle the rifle, but the fingers were too bent to easily pull the trigger. His twisted right hand steadied the barrel as he sighted on the thick back just below him. He squeezed the unfamiliar weapon and the heavy boom of the rifle rang out in the stillness. The body jerked with the impact, then the man rolled to his right, hidden under the hideaway. Not a fatal shot, and too late for another. Quickly, Holly drew sight on the thin youth, who was rolling to his left, looking up at the unexpected rifle flash.

That shot was dead on target. The kid's bony body slammed back into the ground, a flush of bright blood quickly covering his thin chest. The ragged shirt stained wide with the tear through his lungs. The youth struggled to sit up, pushing with weakened arms at the ground underneath him. His head flopped forward as if trying to look down at his shattered chest. Then the lifeless body toppled back to lie still, the flow of blood easing as his heart stopped.

Holly moved on quickly to the dandy, set along the lower side of the bluff. After the first shot the man had rolled violently away from the flash above him. The second shot gave him a target; Rasmussen raised and sighted, then fired at the unexpected enemy. A bullet rang past Holly's ear; another followed from a different direction, crossing above his shoulders. Holly fired again without sighting at the dandy. Grass in front of the huddled figure erupted as the shot dug into the ground. Making a quick adjustment, Holly sent another round to seek out the rolling outlaw. This one found its target; the top of the man's head blew apart from the impact. His limp body went sideways from the force, thumping in a lazy roll down the incline, blood and brains spilling in ever-slowing circles as the body hit against a large boulder.

The silence shocked Holly. Below him were two dead men, another at least wounded. Turner and the cowboy were left unharmed from his shooting. The cowboy had slipped behind the boulder that now had a mangled body wedged beneath it. From there his rifle spoke, and the bullet winged harmlessly over Holly's head, off into the towering rock pile behind him. Turner had yet to fire. Holly did not know where the breed had gone. And he was the man who would know how to get to Holly.

He waited. Someone else would get impatient and fire, exposing their position. Random shooting would give him something to do but would be a waste. He couldn't see any target within reach. Holly inched his way to the left side of the slab, nearer the edge. Then he hunched sideways, to follow the curve of the rim, hoping to get a glimpse of the injured Indian. If he stayed huddled up against the base of the rock, there would be no way Holly could see him. But if he tried climbing the handholds to reach the top, Holly would hear him and be ready to take his one shot. There was little he could do if the man came up another way, except trust to luck and keep waiting. Nerves on edge, distrustful of luck, Holly lay flat, hugging the slab. This would soon be over. His eyes were pulled to the destroyed bodies below. Two men he had killed, without warning, without challenge. He had never killed before. And he didn't like starting now.

Turner stayed tucked down underneath the edge of the bluff, quite near the restless horses. The sudden shooting had caught him behind the others, taking his last drink. From this angle, he could just make out the top of the shooter's head. The man was working his way around in a circle, checking his position, watching and waiting for one of them to expose themselves to his rifle. Dixon was tight behind his rock, needing only a quick exposure of flesh to put a bullet into. He was good at his profession.

Dixon had watched Turner duck at the start of the shooting, and with his face set in disgust he had turned away from his supposed boss. Dixon could see the Indian, nestled up against the base of the rock overhang. A bright furrow of blood showed across the man's left shoulder and along his forearm, a deep graze from the awkward first shot. The Indian finally acknowledged the wound and bound it with a filthy rag, pulling it tight to prevent more blood loss. Determinedly the breed worked his way along the base, as if he knew where he was going.

Glass shattered, pieces scattering far, sending rainbows of color. The rifle crack followed close on its destruction. Turner cursed too late, and ducked, to wriggle deeper into the thick sod under him. That drifter owed him a lot. That was his last bottle. Dixon laughed at Turner's discomfort, then dismissed the man. He could guess what the breed was working toward. Something around the other side of the sniper's position. Only once did the breed look back, and Dixon tilted his head toward the rock and briefly held up his rifle. The breed nodded his head and waved. So Dixon settled to wait. Rather than anger or fear, he found himself close to admiring the man set up on the rock slab. He'd taken two of them fast, hurt one more, knowing all the time that unless he got all five, his life was short.

Brad Dixon laughed when he saw Turner's bottle disappear. One more underestimation of the man above them and Turner would have a hole in his dumb head. No loss, as long as the Judge paid for the scattered horses and Hubbard's family buried. Dixon turned his attention back to the Indian, who had started up the rock wall and was just visible to the cowboy. Brad figured to start a covering fire just before the breed's head got near the top. An odd thought came to him, normally an unreflective man, that here he was set to take killing shots at a man, been working on it all morning, and he didn't even know the gent's name or his face.

The Indian paused in his climb to look back at Dixon. He released one hand from the wall and pulled out the six-gun stuck in his belt. The shiny metal caught Dixon's eye, and he read the signal. Without bother to take aim, Dixon sent a series of shots across the rock slab to keep the sniper from raising his head and by chance seeing the Indian as he came over the wall. The breed took another cautious climbing step, the gun held tight in his mouth by the trigger guard. Dixon fired again, pinning the drifter down.

The series of shots came close to Holly's face as he tried looking down over the rim. He jerked back, but not before one bullet richocheted off the rock and laced a line across his face, just under the old thin scar. He wiped at the oozing line absently. He'd bet the firing was covering the Indian being close to the rim, ready to rise and shoot. He reckoned the ancients would have made the other access to the high oval diagonally across from his ladder. It was an expensive gamble; winner take all.

In the center of the rock floor, Holly put the rifle up against his shoulder and lined up with where he was betting the Indian would pop up. He would take his cue from the cowboy. When the firing got heavy again, the breed was coming over the top. A deep breath to steady himself, then he'd come up on one knee, lean over the side, and with luck be face to face with the Indian. The move would put him in sight of the cowboy, but he was gambling that the man wouldn't expect him to make such a vulnerable target, and it would take the man a heartbeat to set his sights and shoot. He was counting on surprise and speed, and a bit of luck, to give him the first shot. Once the Indian was down, he could turn on the cowboy. Turner be damned; he hadn't fought yet, so he was nothing to worry about now.

A flurry of shots raked the slab. Holly tensed and drew his

legs underneath him, waiting for the right moment to make his move.

Jimmy Hubbard stayed out of sight and watched Holly's moves. His sister went up to the man, then pushed herself against him, kissed him; held him tight, and would have lain with him. Only the saloon girls did that. Hidden in the shadows, the boy experienced embarrassment, then jealousy. No one should treat his sister like a whore.

Red, too, had seen Sarah go to Holly, but he took it much more kindly. By her concern that first night out, he had known she was taken with the man. Poor timing to leave him thinking of her instead of the fight ahead. Red shook his head. Of course a woman wouldn't see it that way, and an easterner would have no understanding of the danger facing the man. Not much Red could do but wait until the woman left, then speak his piece to Holly before he rode off.

Red stripped his smoke, and buried it in the pine dirt as Holly came out to the brown gelding. They spoke briefly, the words short and terse. Then the drifting cowboy rode out at a strong trot; a gone-away man on a throw-away horse.

Jimmy Hubbard was there, standing right in front of Red, his confusion clear on his soft-edged face. "Mr. Willis, uh, Red, what's going on, how come Bishop's riding out now? Why won't Pa talk to me, tell me the plans? I count too in this."

Red took sympathy on the kid. He was reaching to grow and needed to understand. He quickly outlined what was ahead, what Holly had figured out, and what he was doing right now. "Chances are pretty good he won't get all a them bushwackers before one gets a clean shot at him. Too bad he's alone, but he's the only one what knows the spot, how to get there. We needed one man to go with him, but your pa said he couldn't spare me, and he's right." Red tugged at his ear and shifted his feet. "That poor son of a bitch is heading to a tough finish. Hellfire, it just ain't right to go it alone."

Red tried to point the boy right. He'd fed him all the

signals, now he hoped the boy could read sign. And Jimmy caught the direction. Here was his chance to make up for his talking too much in town, getting them all in this fix. His chance to make his mark as a man. He saddled the other staked horse, the solid bay Holly had ridden from town that first day. As if Red followed his thoughts, a rifle appeared on his saddle, extra shells were shoved into his jacket pocket. "Won't be time to catch up, but you can be mighty close behind. Remember, pull up when you reach the rock walls, go in on foot, listen for the firing. Good luck."

The boy swung into the saddle without touching the stirrups and laced the bay's shoulders with the reins. The horse leaped into a fast gallop, tearing out of the grassy haven onto the old trail heading south. The racing hooves woke Paul Hubbard. He came stiffly up from his roll and walked over to Red, who was still standing and watching where the horse had just disappeared out of the valley. Before Hubbard could ask his questions, Red gave him the answers. "Your son's gone to tidy up his mess. May make it too. He's going to track Bishop to the ledge, then cover him, give him some support from the ground. Could make the difference if Bishop gets out alive. Was the kid's idea, his own, wants to make up for the mess in town. Got a good heart, that boy."

Red stopped his talking, he'd interfered enough. But Hubbard's face broke into a rare smile. "His mother will be after me when she finds out. But these past few days have been hard on Jimmy, hard on all of us for that fact." His hand rested lightly on Red's shoulder. "Thanks for coming with us." They remained silent in the graying dawn, their thoughts with the two riders heading toward battle.

Jimmy lost the trail several times; only the reluctance of the bay to continue let him know he was off track. The rock-strewn hill slowed him; the bay had carried a rider all day, and his tired muscles found the steep incline tough going. The heavy sky showed yellowing stripes as the boy came to the beginning of the gorge. His tired horse side-stepped and snorted at a dark shape on the side of the trail. Jimmy pulled to a halt, dismounted, and searched the dark shadows with a stick, poking to find what spooked his bronc. Holly's rig, dropped carelessly in the brush. There was no sign of his horse.

He tied his own bay securely to a deep-grown pine, and picked the rifle from the scabbard. He had enough shells, pockets full of them. But from what Red had said, it would only take a few well-placed shots to flush out the raiders. He walked cautiously down the sloping trail, stumbling over the random rocks, some as big as sides of beef. What a God-awful trail to ride over in the black night. The rising sun let the boy see what he was working toward: a high narrow canyon, its sheer rock walls almost close enough to touch on both sides while standing in the middle. It was hard to believe a horse and rider could work their way through the twisting, close trail.

He heard a shot. More shots followed rapidly. Jimmy ran along the narrow corridor, then stopped short as another series echoed down past him. Shaking attacked his legs, weakening them. His stomach flopped over as if to be sick. Sweat covered his face, and his hands trembled, their grip slipping on the wet rifle stock. Fear kept the boy rooted to the trail. Ahead of him the drifter was fighting for his own family; he was here to help, and could not move. Jimmy's young frame shook violently, torn with fear and courage.

A shape rose against the bright skyline above Jimmy. A man knelt, rifle to his shoulder. Shots rang out, but the man he could see did not fire them. Then the man sighted and squeezed the trigger in one practiced motion. The firing echoed from almost in back of the boy, up and away from the canyon wall. Jimmy could see a slit in the heavy rock wall to his left. The man above him stood, confident that his shot had hit home. Hands still shaking, Jim raised his rifle and took a line on the man on the bluff rim. He fired. The sound bounced and magnified down the canyon. In a slow dance the man on the bluff put his hands to his middle and hugged himself, took several steps backward, and with an odd, stilted grace fell to the earth.

Rifle shots bounced back and forth to Jimmy's left, the actual shots hard to distinguish from the echo. Then nothing was left but the smell of cordite in the rising heat. He was paralyzed; he had shot at a man, and the man had fallen. He had taken someone's life. The next few moments would let him know if he had been successful in helping Bishop, or had only killed his one man too late. Jim stayed on the rock trail. He could hear a scratching noise, then falling rocks, rustling from the slender break in the wall. A shape came at him: a six-gun waist high, a rifle held loosely.

The boy sighed in relief. It was Bishop who came from the shadows to stand next to his unexpected ally. A smear of blood colored his face; the smelly sheepskin coat was tight around his thin body. Bishop faced the boy, the sounds around them easing as the last of the echoes faded to nothing down the long canyon. Holly spoke first, his voice rusty and uneven. "Boy." He swallowed and tried again. "Jim, you saved my life." The man hesitated, his face pale and worn in the new sunlight. A shiver went through him. "Done yourself and your pa proud. Thanks." The effort he made to speak seemed to take all his energy. Jim looked long at the man, but the drifter seemed unaware of him now, indifferent to his surroundings, a long-away look in his eye.

A hand took the boy's shoulder, its grip like a claw. Bishop spoke urgently, "Horses coming; quick, back in here." The claw pulled him with unexpected strength, drawing him into the chiseled gap. Holly brought up the handgun in his right hand, the rifle still hanging from his left. His eyes were a glowing amber, his body tensed against something unseen. A clay-colored horse walked into view. Its rider's flaming hair was accentuated by streams of sunlight. Jim relaxed as he recognized Red's easy sway in the saddle. But it took Holly longer to see the rider, his hard hand still tight on the boy's shoulder.

Red reined in the grullo and sat easy, his words soft. "How

do, boys, beautiful morning, now ain't it." Jim smiled up at the man, but still Holly remained tense, as if distrusting. Red seemed to tune in to the intensity of the man. "Bad up there, huh? Seems you must of got them all, you being down here with the boy. Take it Jim was a help. We can take our time now with those scum out of the way, get these broncs to the fort easy."

Holly's words ignored all of Red's prattle, the tone harsh and grating. "Need another horse, quick. Turner let his men do the fighting. He got away. I got to get him now." His gaunt, beard-stubbled face had a wolfish cast as if he had tasted blood and wanted more. The events just passed had put an extra leanness on him. Still wrapped in the smelly coat, with the sun coming down strong, he looked out of another, fiercer, time. Red found himself unwilling to deal with this man. It was almost as if the quiet drifter of the past few days had changed into a killer.

He responded slowly, gently, not wanting to light the fuse. "The Hubbards are coming up; they got your dun, saddle too. Found your gear 'side the road. You can take this one if hurry means that much, but they'll be here right quick."

Holly brushed past the grullo, not even glancing at the rider or the young man standing near. He needed a good horse, his dun horse. He would have to run Turner down soon. A tremor took his body; a sharp grimace shadowed his face. He was on a thin edge; time would be his killer. He had to move now. A horse stopped in front of him; he grabbed at the bridle and the copper-colored mare shied at the move. Sarah Hubbard's sweet voice reached through to him for a moment. "Holly, you're all right; oh, thank God." Her hand came down to touch him, but he backed sideways to avoid the contact. The familiar rolling eye of his dun mare came into view, the leather rein held in Sarah's hand.

Holly pulled at the strip of leather and jerked it free from the stunned girl. Words of explanation formed in his mind, built from the need to smooth away the fear in her face. But he had no energy left to waste on words, or time. He mounted the mare and kicked her hard past the chestnut. Sarah slipped in the saddle as the dun shoved her mare against the rock wall. Holly wove his mount around Red and the boy. He saw none of these people. Deep in his mind he could see the heavy shape of the blond-haired man who still rode free, who would still harm these people. With that face ahead of him, Holly whipped the dun into a plunging run down the long corridor. He had to get Turner.

Sarah's brown eyes sought out her brother and Red. "You're both all right. What happened?" She smiled wanly at her brother; he nodded and raised his rifle.

"I used it, Sarah; shot a man, kept him from killing Holly." He could read the pleasure mixed with distress in her face. The brother and sister turned to Red, sitting on his gelding, a smoke taking shape under his quick fingers.

"What's going on, Red? What happened? Where did Holly go?"

The puncher shook his head in response. "Don't rightly know, miss; seems to me the job is done, and now he's got himself a revenge to finish. Best we head back to your father and the horses. You shoulda stayed back with him like we said. Could have been ugly up here. I just plain don't know." Red looked down the narrow gorge. "That man had a devil after him just now." He held out his hand to Jim; the boy took it and swung up to sit in back of the saddle behind Red. The horses backed a few steps, then turned carefully and worked their way back to the waiting herd.

Paul Hubbard watched as his daughter rode toward him, her face heavy in thought. Behind her came Willis and his son. A releasing sigh went through him. The boy was all right. But there was no sign of Bishop. He searched Sarah's face; her eyes were filmed with tears. She rode past her father without speaking. Paul stopped Red and demanded an answer. "Did they get Bishop; what the hell happened back there? Why's Sarah in tears?"

Red went over what he had learned from the boy and could piece together, but could give no answer to the last

206

question. "That damned fool took his dun, went by us with no word and headed fast down the canyon out to Elkin. 'Spect he'll find his killing before the day ends. Don't like it much myself."

Hubbard questioned further. "Was he hurt, Red, did he show any signs of being wounded?"

Red answered slowly as he thought over what he had witnessed. "His face was covered with blood, looked to be a scratch. One thing, kept his coat tight around him, even in the sun. Wouldn't talk, just wanted to go."

Sarah had returned to stand her mare quietly beside her father. The questions remained in her eyes. Jim brought his tired bay up to the circle of riders, while Red continued his summation of what he thought had taken place up on the bluff. "Guess Turner had a good-sized crew, but between Holly and your son here, they got them all, 'cepting Turner. Jim took out the last one." The boy broke into the monologue, "But Red, the man got off a shot just before I shot at him. He stood up only after his first shot, acted as if he got his man." The four were quiet for a bit, each trying to put together what had happened. And what to do now.

Hubbard spoke first. "Red, take Jim and go after Bishop. My guess is Turner will head back to Guffey Creek; he can go around the hills and pick up the trail again beyond Tyson's. I'm betting he'll head for town, won't dare to go back to the Two Crown after failing. Sarah and I will bring the horses. We still have the deadline to meet. Come to the fort as soon as you know something."

Sarah's head came up. "I'm going with Red; I've got to find Holly. Dad, this is important, I . . ." She ran out of words and stopped, struggling to put the words together. She flushed under her father's hard stare, but held her ground. "I've got to help, to be there. We already know he's wounded, and it could be worse."

Paul battled with his pride. At least this time his daughter had picked a good man, a fighter. He nodded his understanding and started to explain to his son. But his boy was

207

ahead of him. "Sure, Sarah, go with Red. Holly needs you. I'll help Pa bring in the horses." The boy smiled a conspirator's grin at his sister.

Red took the lead through the long narrow canyon, keeping his horse to a walk, saving him for the long ride ahead. The girl rode impatiently behind him, aware that the pace was wise, but fighting her sense of hurry. Little was said on the downhill ride. Almost at the end of the canyon they came across the lumpy mound of a dead horse, partially eaten by scavengers. The carcass spooked both horses, and by the torn-up ground around the body, Holly's horse had fought going by the stinking mess. Part of the hindquarters had been taken out, evidence that someone had used the downed animal for food. Sarah shuddered as she edged her mare past the gruesome lump. The thought that someone would be so desperate as to eat their horse turned her. Whoever had done so would have been at the bottom of their luck.

Once out of the canyon, Red did not take the trail to Elkin, but swung his grullo to the left, keeping to a slow jog, searching the ground. The two riders worked their way around the rocky slope that led to the bluff above and the scene of the fight. Tracks finally told them what to do next. Two horses had come racing out of a clump of trees; by the depth of the tracks, one was led and the other carried a heavy rider. Intermingled with these tracks was evidence of another horse, following to one side. Red glanced at Sarah, his grin lifting the heavy mood. "Look here." He pointed to the three sets of tracks. "Bet Holly be on Turner's trail. Keep wide of them tracks. Don't want to blot them out." He gestured at droppings still fairly fresh in the heat. "We ain't that far behind, 'bout an hour. Let's go." They touched their horses and the tired animals responded with a slow lope. Periodically they checked the tracks. They were pointed straight toward Guffey Creek.

CHAPTER EIGHTEEN

He had panicked, simple as that. He hadn't expected anyone to be up above the bluff, hadn't figured on being fired at. He was glad he'd been behind the others, holding back to finish the bottle. The shot that had creased the Indian caught him off guard. He'd dropped to his belly and ducked his head, as if to ward off further shots. Fear had overwhelmed him when the kid's chest had flowered into bright red blood; then the next body, head blown apart, white spurs of shattered bone gleaming, had rolled near him to snug up against the boulder. It was as if each bullet landed in him, paralyzing him, not touching the others. All Turner's rattled energies went into remaining head-down while the firing continued. The brief bits of time when no shots sounded, no bullets flew, were paradise.

One quick look had shown him the breed, perched halfway up the far side of the rock slab that overshadowed their ambush spot. Turner knew that Dixon was behind the boulder near the rim, the one with the torn body wedged under it. Dixon had glanced in his direction, as if expecting orders from the boss. Turner had only burrowed his face deeper into the warm ground beneath him. Two dead, one wounded, and only one man up on the rock had done the damage. More than he could handle.

209

Turner did watch as Dixon rose to his knees and fired. One moment of glory lifted him as he saw the drifter go back under the force of a bullet. Dixon, too, had seen his shot find home, and stood to let the breed know he'd scored. Skylined against the drop of a canyon wall, Dixon had grabbed at his own body and dropped onto the bluff grass. The rifle shot echoed grandly. Dixon had never known someone was down below. Turner panicked again with this new death. He had started down to the horses tied in the grove when more shots came from the rock slab. Shots that could only have come from the drifter's rifle. Turner spun around just in time to see the breed, his last hope, fall in a backward tumble from his precarious position at the top of the slab wall, almost flying for a short time, landing flat on the bluff below, to lie well beyond Dixon's stilled body.

There was an endless time of silence when all the echoes had stopped. Then the lean form of that goddamned man, wrapped in a heavy sheepskin coat, had risen over the lip of the slab, to work his way carefully down the chiseled ladder. Turner left before the man finished working his way down the break.

He took another horse with him, figuring to change mounts when the sorrel quit. He knew it would quit. He had no faith in Tyson's horse, or anything Tyson would do for him. Town was his only hope; those people knew he was still the head honcho. They'd hide him, feed him, take care of him until the drifter rode on. Then he could come out and claim his position again. The Judge was a fool. It would take a threat, a push, the flash of a knife or gun to keep his job as chief among the thieves. Turner drove his spurs deep into the torn yellow sides.

The animal fought valiantly to carry the heavy weight and keep his footing on the plains. The rider gave him no help or encouragement, just sat deep in the stock saddle and kept flailing with his quirt, using his spurs. The tired animal kept the pace for a long time, putting any pursuers far behind. It took the rider a long time for him to realize that the hated drifter had come down off his perch with no thought to Turner, no respect for his power.

The insult was almost enough to get Turner mad. But he had gotten free. And deep in his mind was etched the knowledge that he had run, when others had stayed to fight. In a twisted way it was to his advantage to be ignored, otherwise he would be dead, along with the others now up on that bluff. This way, he could protect the Judge, draw the drifter back into Guffey Creek and finish the fight. A break in the sorrel's stride shifted Turner's attention to his horse. Another lousy broomtail giving out on him. He needed a good horse.

Turner hauled on the spade bit and the horse jerked to a stop. He climbed down from the worn-out bronc and looked at the led horse he had grabbed from the trees in haste. It was Dixon's mount, a deep-chested, stocking-legged buckskin; not fancy, but built for staying. Finally, he had a good one. Stripping the dead man's hull off the restless buckskin, he resaddled with his own fancy rig and let the lathered sorrel go. This horse would get him to town in good time. Then he could plan for when the drifter showed.

Holly kept the dun to a manageable lope. He had to keep an eye on Turner's tracks. The man could head anywhere in his flight. He had figured right when he circled the base of the bluff and found the grove. From there the tracks were simple. The dun mare fought his tight rein. Out on the flats she wanted to stretch out and run. But Holly kept the leathers short. Once again his right arm and hand were pressed tight to his body. Pain lit a fire in him at each stride. His gamble in rising when the cowboy let loose his barrage had paid off. But this time the price had been too high.

Dixon's one shot had caught him just above the first slice from Turner's back shot. This one had gone through him on the diagnonal, coming out just above his left hip. Something felt torn inside; blood rose in his throat and some spilled out his mouth. The thick salty taste made him nauseous. The sheepskin was a good pad, absorbing the blood, held tight by his arm. It only had to last to wherever Turner got off his horse. The play would end there.

The mingled tracks where Turner changed horses out on the plains gave Holly a bad time. His fogged mind stumbled over the confusing message in the shuffled footprints. He finally realized that an extra saddle lay partially hidden in the brush, and that one horse had gone on without a rider. Then Holly let the dun out along the deeper set of prints. This new horse had more speed; the pace was faster, the tracks clearer. He let the mare have her head. The plains were shining in the late morning light. Way off to the right, the town of Elkin floated in a haze. Turner's tracks headed straight back toward Guffey Creek.

He had to pull in the dun. His own breathing came hard on his ears, sounding like a train working up a steep hill. The horse steadied at the walk, as if to give her rider a break. Then the eager mare picked up the gait to an easy lope. Holly's body swayed loosely with the motion, riding by instinct. His mind was shut to everything but keeping to the saddle and finding Turner.

The town of Guffey Creek was quiet in the sun. The horses at Kelleher's shuffled slowly in the warmth, their tails flickering at the spring flies. To Holly's feverish mind, no time had passed from the first day he'd slid off the buckboard tailgate in front of the stable to now, when he was here searching for something. He reined in the dun at the back of the stables, reluctant to show himself on the dusty main street. Turner was here. Tracks of the long-strided horse that carried him led to this back door. Perhaps the enemy was inside, waiting in cold deliberation to shoot when he opened the door.

Holly shook his head to clear the fuzziness. The motion set his body burning, reminding him that he had no time to sit and outguess the man; his blood-soaked shirt and trousers were evidence that not much was left to him. He had to use himself as bait, stand out and defy the man, go through each town business and bully the owner. Make these bought-and-paid-for townsfolk give him Turner. The man had sold his companions with his cowardice; now it was his turn to be betrayed.

With no further thought, Holly rode his snorting horse through the partially open door. His back tensed against the expected bullet, but Turner was not waiting. He didn't have the nerve to stay close to his horse and fight it out with a walking dead man. Holly slid from the dun and hung to the horn, legs threatening to collapse under him. A hand touched his shoulder; Holly hunched his back and reached awkwardly for the unfamiliar handgun. A remembered voice stopped the move. "You don't look so good, sonny, let me put this here horse away. She sure enough looks done in for the day. Too hot to ride so hard in this early heat . . ." The voice wandered on, the words becoming garbled, but the message was clear: George Kelleher was helping him, would take care of him. The garrulous old fool muttered on, finally saying words that Holly could focus on, that gave him direction.

". . . saw that bum Turner heading like hell was after him over to Rand's, but I figure he only went there for a bottle, can't seem to live long without one now, 'spect he'll be headed to Hoffmeyer's, the barber. The old idiot built himself an extry house out back, for his son's family but they didn't stay long, didn't like the town." The voice went on, but Holly could hold on to the important words, telling him to get over to the barber's.

He lifted Hubbard's rifle from the scabbard on his worn saddle. He knew Turner would never let him close enough for a handgun. Just as well; with his busted hand he never did get any accuracy with a short gun. He stuffed some shells in the pocket of the sheepskin, Kelleher's sheepskin. The coat swung open from the uneven weight, and George caught

213

sight of the widening stain. Holly followed his eyes and realized what George was staring at. Wouldn't do to let Turner know how bad he was hit. A piece of string tied the coat shut. The snugness gave him something to lean into, made him feel pulled together. As long as he lasted for the next few minutes, or however long it took.

The barbershop. Hoffmeyer's barbershop. The hint of a rough smile came over the drawn gray face. That barber wouldn't be any too happy to see him again. Been upset enough his first time there; all this blood and shooting would send the man flying in fear. The bright sun closed Holly's eyes in its fierceness. He adjusted to the sharpness of the noontime light as he walked with deliberate steps to the striped pole outside the small, neat shop. The tiny nervous man held the door open, nodded violently as Holly walked inside. "He went out back, tried to make me promise not to say he was here; that man must be stopped, he has no right to hurt so many."

Holly remained inside the cool, dark shop, a part of his mind struggling to accept what the barber was giving him. "Yes, he did stay for a short while in my house, my son's house. They left because they were afraid of these men; they were not used to the shootings, the fights. The lack of the law. Turner, he drove my son away, left me alone. I hope you can stop him. He thought I did not look, was too afraid to look, but I saw. He went out and around to the unfinished sheriff's office. Maybe he will put himself in jail, save us all the trouble." The small man smiled at his feeble joke, then slapped a hard hand on the tin washtub. "A drink, that would do you good, help you. You are too pale; you look too tired to fight such a man. Here." A glass of clear, thick liquid was handed to Holly. Fire burned down his throat, with none of the harshness he was used to. A warm heady feeling came from his torn stomach; a sharp cough brought a foam of blood to his lips, which he wiped on the smelly leather sleeve. Shock flooded the small man's face. "You cannot go

214

after such a man. You are hurt. Please to stay."

The concern in the pinched face surprised Holly. This man was worried about him. Saying nothing, he lifted his rifle and walked in measured steps to the back door. Outside he could see the forlorn and empty house. Hoffmeyer pointed to the right. "See, that is where Turner went. You can see the back door of the jail." Bitterness crept into his voice. "If we all had not been so eager to take the Judge's money, then there would be a man in that building who would help you, could take care of Turner Allward. And the Judge. I am sorry there is only shopkeepers to help you now."

"Wait." Holly stopped at the voice. "Don't go out there. Let me go across to the mercantile. Perhaps Allward got frightened by himself in the jail, and has tried to hide among all the goods. The MacKenzies will tell me if they have seen anything." The small man walked with great dignity across the dusty street, to disappear into the cavernous mercantile building. Holly waited for what felt to be an hour, his head resting on the door jamb, his back lightly touching the solid wall. He was afraid to sit or lie down, afraid he would not be able to get back up in time.

"I was right, Mr. Bishop; he did not have the fortitude to remain in the jail by himself. Mr. MacKenzie said that Allward came into their store not too long ago, threatened them with horrible deaths if they said anything to you, or anyone else, about his whereabouts. I believe the man is running now, and will head back to the stable, too frightened to stay in this town. He must know we no longer support him. He must feel that. You best go back there now, get to the stable ahead of him."

Holly took tentative steps out of the barbershop doorway, around the end of the building, moving very slowly. He could see the stable, still and quiet in the noon sun. Kelleher had left the door open, inviting. The barn appeared calm. But something was wrong. Three horses in the side pen stirred restlessly, unusual in the heat. They trotted around

215

the corral, heads raised, ears pinned flat. Kelleher's presence would not disturb them. They accepted his comings and goings.

Holly grinned to himself. Turner had backed himself into a corner by returning to the livery stable. He could ride out, or he could come out the front and face Holly. But he could not get back to the other buildings in the small town. He had isolated himself in the stable. Holly stepped cautiously as he crossed the white expanse of street to the stable. Kelleher popped out of the front, and in quick motions gestured for Holly to meet him at the far side of the building.

The balding man had taken a long look at the battered man weaving unsteadily in front of him. Instinct had told old George that this was a wild one, and he was still here to prove it. Bloody, shaky, but ready to fight. Only George knew about the damage hidden under that coat. Only he could guess at the effort it took to remain upright, willing to carry the fight. George made his choice. This one man had the courage and savvy to get the Judge and his pack out of the town, give decent folk a chance to live. He waved his arms, encouraging Holly to come to him.

"Turner's inside, thinks he can slide out the back, don't know I bolted the door from the outside. You go in this here side door, one not too many folks pay attention to. Puts you in my office. Turner, that fool, thinks he's well hidden in the last stall. Guess he figures he'll slip out the back once he knows you're inside, then fire away at you and get running again. That big buckskin can carry him a far piece once he gets going."

A solid hand on his right arm led Holly to the side door. Opening it, he slipped through into the warren of paper, bits of bridles, old stirrups, several horsehair chairs, the stuffing dribbling out of many tears. The light-headed sense of drifting, of wandering through a pale, ghostly town left Holly. It was here. Now. He would face Turner and end the nightmare. In the stillness he could hear blood pumping

216

through his body. His pulse throbbed heavy in his wrists, his throat. Beyond that door was Turner, believing himself invisible, secure with his escape route. Waiting.

Holly lifted the latch slowly and carefully with the rifle butt. Then, in a quick move, he jammed the door open and rolled through to hit the packed dirt floor. A burst of engulfing pain tried to overwhelm him, to block out what he had come to finish. He rolled again to the left, up onto his belly, then sighted down the rifle at a hunched figure running for the back door. The man pulled at the latch handle, but the door refused to give. He jerked harder, terror adding to his own enormous strength. Nothing gave. Holly shoved himself to his feet, unwilling to take a shot at a man's back. But Turner refused to face his tormentor; instead he kept pulling and tugging at the door, freedom just outside.

"Turner, stand. Look at what's coming to you." Holly called out to the man. But Turner kept pounding and jerking at the heavy door. "Face me, make a fight of it." Holly's voice broke in a cough, choking him on his own blood. Something clicked in the frantic mind of the coward. He heard the catch of Holly choking, stopped his efforts and stood still, his back wide and inviting to a bullet. If his enemy meant to kill him at any cost, then he would be dead now. Not standing wide open to a back shot. Eyes calmed, Turner set his face and turned to face the man who had become his hunter.

The gamy sheepskin coat had loosened in the rolling fall, the string broken, the front fallen open. Turner saw the damage. His enemy had given him the needed edge. Blood covered Bishop's midsection, fresh bright blood covered darker brownish stains, streaks of blood down his pant leg, blood clinging to the lambswool of the dirty coat. A devil's grin crossed Turner's face. The man in front of him, the man he had been running from, wasn't strong enough to hold a gun, didn't have the guts left to pull the trigger. Turner pointed his six-gun at Holly, took two steps forward, and

217

laughed when he saw Holly's useless effort to raise his rifle, hands shaking in the close of battle.

Turner took two more steps, to come closer to the man who had stood up to him, had fought back, had taken his fists and his bullet, and had come back for more. This black-haired devil, this high-line rider, could have no more fight to him. Turner stopped; the rifle in Holly's left hand came waist high, the twisted right hand steadied the barrel, the shaking, bloodless fingers found the trigger and pulled. Turner's pistol leaped in reaction as the heavy slug tore into his belly at close range, the flare blinding him, the pain killing him. He went down. His bulk shook the manure-covered floor as his body twitched in an ugly revolt against the ragged hole in him. His hands grasped at the straw under him, seeking relief from the enormous pain. One more bucking lurch from his body, and he collapsed with a long sigh and lay silent.

Once they were certain that Turner and Holly had ridden into Guffey Creek, Sarah and Red put spurs to their horses and rode at a fast pace to the back of Kelleher's stable. Breeding told, and the copper chestnut mare reached the barn first, hardly winded from the lengthy run. Sarah sat and waited while Red brought up his mustang. The close high crack of a rifle came from the dark stable, sharing an echo with the lighter blast of a handgun. Sarah flew from her mare, Red right behind her, leaving the horses to stand alone in the ominous quiet. Voices gathered at the front of the barn, moved inside. Sarah could see two figures, one in an inhuman sprawl, life gone from it. The other was wedged up against a post, heavy sheepskin coat holding his thinned-down frame, blood covering his front, more welling from a fresh hole in his upper thigh, to pool on the straw-covered floor.

"Oh God, Holly. No." Sarah reached him and stroked the bearded face, gray in the dim light.

His eyes lifted to seek hers, weary beyond relief. He

218

coughed and the blooded froth hung from his mouth in strings. The words came slowly, unevenly. "You . . . all set . . . Turner won't get to . . . you now." His amber eyes shut and a deep sigh escaped, ending in another bloody cough.

Sarah turned to Red, crouched down with her in front of the drifter. He looked to see the barber standing above him, as townspeople began to crowd through the door. "Quick, get the doc, he's got to help."

Hoffmeyer spoke gently. "He is already to come, Mr. Willis, we sent word, but I think it best we take Mr. Bishop to my house behind the shop; there he can be tended to. Please. To come."

With infinite gentleness, the townspeople laid Holly in the arms of three strong men, who carried him with a tender lightness to the long-abandoned house behind the barbershop. Doctor Simonson was waiting, tools laid out, hands washed. He had been told of the blood-soaked man who would soon be his patient. One man stayed to cover the flattened body that remained, the last of the Judge's power in Guffey Creek.

EPILOGUE

The small town glistened in the August heat. Those few having to attend to business did so very slowly, walking along the single town street.

Holly lay quietly in a wide bed, listening. He coughed lightly and a head poked around the bedroom door; an anxious voice queried, "You're awake, good, can I get you anything? Nice cool water, taste so good on this kind of day, yes?" The pinched face of the town barber came into full view. His hand stretched out toward Holly, holding a tumbler of water, the coolness beading on the side of the glass. One hand went behind Holly's head to help him raise up to sip the water. Even with the help, the slight activity caused a grimace of pain across the invalid's face, a tightening against the burn in his middle.

"That's all right, you are mending now; the doctor says it will be fine soon. I will get him, yes?" The little man left the tumbler on a small table and hurried out of the room. Holly raised his head for a short look around, then lay back in the softness. Even that small movement left him weak, sweating. He scrubbed a hand across his face, surprised to find himself clean shaven. A quick grin followed. Of course he would be clean shaven; the barber was caring for him.

Slowly, bits of the nightmare in the dim stable came back

to him. He knew from the wrapping around his stomach that the wound was not yet healed, and each move brought a twinge of reminding pain. A sensation of falling back, of one leg becoming numb and unwilling to hold him was also a part of that memory.

His twisted hand fumbled under the light covering to reach for his right leg. No bandage, no sign of a wound. He rested a moment, then reached across to his left leg. At the top of his thigh he could feel a puckered knot, barely tender. The hole told him two things: his memory of being shot by Turner and falling was correct, and he had been lying here a long time. Long enough for the thigh wound to heal. Nothing that he could see gave him any sense of time, and the thought of getting up from the soft bed was an impossibility. Just the effort needed to sort out his thoughts and explore his own body had tired him. The barber would be back soon with the doctor. He could sleep until then.

Hoffmeyer stood just back from the doorway, ushering Doc Simonson into the cheerful room. The patient was asleep, his shaggy dark hair spread out across the pillow, his breathing light and regular. The quiet footsteps were enough to wake Holly. He raised his head and watched the approaching doctor. Simonson smiled; it was almost a triumphant smile. "I thought you would make it, been some doubters around here, but I put my money on you. Anyone who could fight with such a big hole in them could keep death and the devil away one more time."

Holly's eyes widened at the strange words, and a question formed in his mind. As if he could read his patient's thoughts, the doctor continued: "Yup, you've been in this bed for near to eight weeks. All tore up inside; did some fancy sewing and a lot of praying. Whole town's been praying and lending a hand. The Hubbard women stayed here until you looked to be gaining, fever mostly gone, could keep some food down. Sarah still comes by every day, stays some few hours. Even Amy's been in, actually caught her

221

reading to you. Said you knew the book, would hear it even if you were unconscious. Bright one, that youngster. Townfolk been taking turns seeing to you, even fixed up this room."

More questions came to Holly, slowly, too slowly, because the effort needed to put them into words was too much. He nodded at the men, eased his head back into the softness of the down pillow and closed his eyes. He was asleep immediately. "He will be fine now, Doctor, will he not?" The nervous, fussing barber edged by the unmoving physician who stood watching his patient. It wasn't really necessary to answer the question. The man's recovery was the answer in itself.

Sarah Hubbard's sweet voice broke Simonson's revery. Even in the heat she looked fresh, lovely, and full of energy. "Mr. Hoffmeyer says that Holly woke up, spoke." Tears filled her eyes. It was her love that had carried the injured man through the bad weeks of infection and high fever. It was for her that he had lived.

"Go sit with him. He needs you now more than ever."

Something firm and gentle took his hand, held it lightly. A sweet, light pressure touched his face, his mouth. Holly's eyes opened to look straight into the warm brown eyes of Sarah Hubbard. A lovely smile came to her face. "You're safe now, we're all waiting for you, home is waiting for you."

Home.

VISIT THE WILD WEST
with Zebra Books

SPIRIT WARRIOR   (1795, $2.50)
by G. Clifton Wisler
The only settler to survive the savage Indian attack was a
little boy. Although raised as a red man, every man was his
enemy when the two worlds clashed—but he vowed no
man would be his equal.

IRON HEART   (1736, $2.25)
by Walt Denver
Orphaned by an Indian raid, Ben vowed he'd never rest
until he'd brought death to the Arapahoes. And it wasn't
long before they came to fear the rider of vengeance they
called . . . *Iron Heart*.

THE DEVIL'S BAND   (1903, $2.25)
by Robert McCaig
For Pinkerton detective Justin Lark, the next assignment
was the most dangerous of his career. To save his beautiful
young client's sisters and brother, he had to face the mean-
est collection of hardcases he had ever seen.

KANSAS BLOOD   (1775, $2.50)
by Jay Mitchell
The Barstow Gang put a bullet in Toby Markham, but they
didn't kill him. And when the Barstow's threatened a
young girl named Lonnie, Toby was finished with running
and ready to start killing.

SAVAGE TRAIL   (1594, $2.25)
by James Persak
Bear Paw seemed like a harmless old Indian—until he stole
the nine-year-old son of a wealthy rancher. In the weeks of
brutal fighting the guns of the White Eyes would clash
with the ancient power of the red man.

*Available wherever paperbacks are sold, or order direct from the
Publisher. Send cover price plus 50¢ per copy for mailing and
handling to Zebra Books, Dept. 1615, 475 Park Avenue South,
New York, N.Y. 10016. Residents of New York, New Jersey and
Pennsylvania must include sales tax. DO NOT SEND CASH.*